BLUE

MURDER

A Tyler and Mills Novel

MARK L. FOWLER

Copyright © 2018 Mark L Fowler

The right of Mark L Fowler to be identified as the Author of this work has been asserted in accordance with the Copyright, Designs and Patents Act 1988.

First published in 2018

All Rights reserved. No part of this publication may be reproduced, copied, stored in a retrieval system, or transmitted, in any form or by any means, without the prior written consent of the copyright holder, nor be otherwise circulated in any form of binding or cover other than that in which it is published and without a similar condition being imposed on the subsequent purchaser.

All the characters in this publication are fictitious, and any resemblance to real persons, living or dead, is purely coincidental.

For Peter Walton – Egg

CHAPTER ONE

Dusk was falling as he made his way onto the canal towpath. A storm had whipped up out of nowhere, delivering a hard rain edged with ice that had all but cleared the streets.

It was Thursday, March 20th, 2003. A date that would soon be etched into the dark history of the city, haunting it for years to come.

A raw, bitter wind was joining forces with the driving, stinging sleet, intermittently blinding him as he traced the course of the canal through the middle of Hanley Park, following the late-winter gloom westwards towards the distant glow of the Norfolk Inn pub. As he passed the old pavilion, the ghostly shapes of the trees appeared to surround him, bending under the fierce weight of the still-gathering storm, the sinister branches giving the impression that they were reaching down to greet him as he passed through Fisherman's Bank. The dim outline of the college buildings in the distance loomed like ghouls.

Spring had lately been knocking on the door, making its yearly promises, but on that March evening the bitterness of winter had returned with a vengeance. The pounding rain had already turned the path into a quagmire, and the strength of the chill wind threatened at any moment to dump the solitary figure into the dark water.

Sight of the low stone bridge ahead brought a momentary sense of relief. It might be an idea to take shelter, he thought. Allow the worst of the storm to blow itself out.

Then something caught his eye; a shape in the distance, a silhouette on the far side of the bridge.

The survival instinct was signaling immediate danger; an inner red light flashing.

He quickly dismissed it. *Just someone else sheltering from the storm. Someone else with reason to be out on such a foul night as this.*

Someone dressed in dark clothing, their face in shadow.

He noted a familiarity in the movement and was about to call out, hesitating in the uncertainty. Not so long ago he had been a student at the college that backed onto the canal side, adjacent to the park. This was not the time or the place for a casual encounter with a stranger.

Whoever it was had already started walking on, disappearing quickly from view.

Reaching the bridge, and already soaked to the skin, he took shelter for a few moments, squinting through the deluge. There was no let up; if anything it was getting worse. All ahead of him was darkness and a cold, driving rain that stung as it hit exposed flesh.

He had somewhere to be.

Someone to see.

Emerging from the cover of the bridge he sensed movement over his shoulder. Turning towards it he recognised the silhouette, coming straight at him, approaching from the left, the canal bank to the right.

As though in slow motion he opened his mouth, first to question, then to scream; understanding too late the purpose of the hand raised high in the air - the hand clutching something and bringing it down, swinging hard and fast, catching him square across the side of the head, sending him keeling towards the black water.

His eyes filling with blood, he staggered, disorientated, hearing the cries of a wounded animal begging for mercy, not recognising the cries as his own; feeling the brutal shove from behind and then nothing at all beneath his feet.

The water was freezing and it wrenched the breath out of him, leaving no way to go but down, flailing helplessly before finally sinking like a stone through the silent, pitiless depths.

Gone.

CHAPTER TWO

"So, where's Johnny?"

Billy Steele was slightly built, and it was well testified amongst the rest of the band that hauling amplifiers and drum kits in and out of gigs was not apt to put him in the best of humour. He had followed George and Rob out of the daytime darkness of the Thirteen club on Trinity Street, and was looking sweaty and harassed in the unexpected surge of late afternoon sunshine.

"He was supposed to be here an hour ago."

"Ease up, mate," said George. "He'll show. He's hardly likely to miss this one."

Billy glared. "Oh, I don't doubt that. He'll turn up once all the hard work's done, like the prima donna he is."

"Perhaps he got held up at work," said Rob.

"*Perhaps,*" said Billy. "Come on, let's finish setting up. *Perhaps* he will get away in time for the sound check!"

The Swamp Seeds had been Johnny's idea from the start, but these days the band were known as *Johnny and the Swamp Seeds*, to clear up any remaining doubt.

Johnny Richards and his best friend, Adam Lane, had learned guitar from Johnny's dad, becoming serious about putting a group together the summer that they left school. That was five years ago.

Johnny was the only remaining member of the original line up. Billy Steele replaced Adam on guitar, while George Atkins on bass and Rob Jones on drums replaced the other fallen members along the way. The band name changed when Adam left, and then things started to happen. *Johnny and the Swamp Seeds* had racked up almost a hundred gigs, and a four-song EP sold steadily in the first few weeks after its release.

The EP had been Johnny's idea, of course. It was something to sell at their gigs. Billy had voiced caution over the project, but the others went along with Johnny, as they generally did, and Billy had eventually acquiesced. The consensus was that the gamble appeared to be paying off handsomely.

And now this. The opportunity of a lifetime.

Friday, March 21st, a showcase gig at the Thirteen club. It had sold out a week early on the back of local press features and radio air play. There were strong rumours that serious members of the music-business machinery were going to be present, with media presence coming in from far and wide. Even the local weather appeared to be responding, the brutal storm of the previous evening giving way to a renewed promise of spring.

Everything was set up. Billy looked again at his watch as Frank Watts, manager of the Thirteen club, approached the stage.

"Everything all right, lads? You appear to be a man short."

"Everything's fine," said Billy, a little too quickly.

Frank Watts' eyes instantly narrowed, flicking his gaze between the three figures on the stage. "I seem to recall," he said, "booking a *four*-piece."

Billy glanced at George and Rob. "We're going to pick Johnny up now," he said.

It was the turn of Frank Watts to check the time. "It's traditional to perform the sound check *before* the audience arrive. Call me old fashioned."

Outside the venue Billy announced that he was going to drive around to Johnny's house while Rob checked out Johnny's work place. George would stay at the club to keep an eye on the equipment, and try to re-assure Frank Watts that everything was fine.

Billy swung his battered Ford Escort out of the car park at the side of the club and out into the Trinity Street traffic jam. It was late-afternoon and the usual queue of impatient peak-time drivers, trying to get out of Hanley, was already stretching out of sight.

Cursing to himself Billy checked his watch for the hundredth time. If Johnny messed this one up, that was the end of it. Lately he had wondered what was going on with Johnny Richards, there always seemed to be something. He was going to have to have it out with him again, once this gig was over. Get things straight, once and for all.

On a good journey, the drive over to Hanford, in the south of the city, ought to take no more than a few minutes. But at this time of the day, with the daily exodus reaching its peak, travellers found themselves in the lap of the gods. "If you screw this up, mate," muttered Billy, as he pulled up at yet another set of temporary traffic lights, "If you fucking-well screw this up ..."

George was sitting on his bass amp, sipping at a Coke, when Frank Watts came over again. "So, what do you know?" said Watts. George took another sip of his drink. "Not much," he said. "Should be a great gig tonight though."

"I'm counting on it," said Watts. There was an edge to his tone, and George looked up. The scowl bore down on him. "If there's a problem, son, I want to know about it, understand?"

George felt his hackles rise. Frank Watts had a reputation; he had never been the easiest person to deal with. But like Rob, George was happy to let Johnny have most of the dealings with him. After all, it was Johnny's band, when all was said and done, and hassle came with the territory. It was the price you had to pay for being the main man.

Frank Watts managed the best venue in town. The only venue in town, if you had any real ambition. His money and connections had set the band on its way. If the *Swamp Seeds,* or any band, for that matter, was ever going to break out of the local circuit, the Thirteen was the place that you had to sell-out and win over. For better or worse, Watts was the guy, and his club attracted the right people, with a direct feed to a waiting world for the lucky ones. Without him on your side, it was hard to see any local band breaking out of the confines of the city.

George tried to look baffled. "Problem?" he said. "There's no problem, of course there isn't. Why should there be a problem?"

Frank Watts looked around, and then leaned forward, his face right in George's. "I'm very pleased to hear that. I've worked my arse off to build this place up. I don't intend on letting some temperamental punks compromise everything I've achieved, understand?"

George took another drink, and fought the urge to look at his watch again.

"If your singer doesn't turn up," said Watts, "I'd like you to pass on a little message from me. Tell him not to bother contacting with any excuses. Johnny Richards won't be playing this club again."

Rob Jones was pulling up outside Skeels Pottery Emporium in the centre of Stoke town, where Johnny had worked for the last few years. It was one of the last pot banks left in the city still managing to export fine bone china around the world.

The security guard in the portakabin at the front of the small factory came out as Rob made his way across the car park. "Can I help you mate?"

"I'm looking for Johnny Richards."

The guard frowned. "Is he expecting you?"

"I doubt it. But if he's here I need to see him."

"I've not seen him all day. I'll ask for you. Wait there."

The guard went back into the cabin and Rob watched through the window as the large man picked up a phone.

Rob joined the band after George tipped him the wink that the drummer was about to jump ship, the two of them working together in the record store in Hanley Arcade. Rob had played drums in a few bands, none of them going anywhere; but he had the feeling that the *Swamp Seeds* really could make it, and George had confessed to having the same feeling. Johnny had the charisma and the voice that set them apart. Of course, it wasn't all plain sailing, they could see that. Billy wasn't happy seeing most of his own songs getting sidelined, with only one of them making the EP. But Johnny called the shots and that's just how it was. A great band was rarely a democracy, and Billy was going to have to learn to live with that fact. Or else move on.

The security guard came back out. "Thought I hadn't seen him, mate."

"He was in this morning though?" said Rob. "He was on an early finish. Noon, I think he said."

"He's not been in all day."

"Has he rang in sick?"

"Doesn't sound like it. He just didn't turn up, as far as I know. He'd better have a good reason, that's all I can say. Are you his mate? If so, I'd have a word in his ear. There's plenty of people wouldn't mind working here. Tough times we're living in, just in case you hadn't heard."

Rob Jones walked back across the car park, praying that Billy was having better luck.

Billy Steele pulled up outside the small terraced house in Hanford where Johnny lived with his mother. He liked Mo Richards, she was always welcoming, and not bad looking, for a friend's mother. She had to be turned forty, but she was one of the kindest people he had ever met. Johnny didn't know how lucky he was.

He knocked on the front door and a few seconds later Mo Richards greeted him with a characteristically warm smile. "Billy! How are you doing? Come on in."

Ignoring the invitation, Billy said, "Is Johnny in?"

"Not yet. He should be, though. Any time, I think. Cup of tea while you wait?" When Billy didn't answer, Mo Richards said, "Is something the matter?"

"We've got a gig. We're playing tonight and Johnny hasn't shown up yet."

"Of course, tonight! The big one!"

"He was supposed to knock off work at midday and help set up."

"I've not seen him for a couple of days. I assumed he was staying at Janine's. Have you spoken to her?"

Billy shook his head. "What about his equipment?"

A smile erupted on Mo Richards' face. "I don't think he's had any complaints from Janine, as far as I know. But that's not the sort of thing you talk to your mother about, is it?"

Billy could feel a blush forming. He looked away, trying to compose himself. When he looked again at Mo Richards her smile had been replaced with a look of concern. "Hang on a sec," she said.

Leaving him at the door, she disappeared into the house, returning a few moments later. "His guitar and stuff's not here. But if he stayed at Janine's - let me give her a call. Come in."

Billy waited in the living room while Mo Richards made the phone call.

"Strange," she said, putting the handset down. "Janine's not seen him since this morning. He left for work as usual, apparently. She's due at the club later. Was going to see Johnny there. His stuff's at her flat." Mo Richards looked at Billy, and brightened. "Unless he went over to his dad's. That'll be it! Or maybe he's been delayed at work. I'll give them a call now."

But Rob had driven back from Skeels Pottery Emporium and was already pulling up outside the Richards' house.

"He's not shown up?" said Mo Richards. "What's going on?" She looked at the two young men, but all she got back was a reflection of her own mystification. "I don't understand," she said. "Johnny wouldn't miss a gig, not one as important as this." She made another call, and ended it, shaking her head. "His dad hasn't seen him either."

"We'd better get back to Hanley," said Billy.

"I'll come with you," said Mo Richards, grabbing her coat. "Maybe he's there."

"Without his guitar?" said Billy.

At the Thirteen club, a few hours later, Frank Watts was taking to the stage. With his hands gripped around the microphone, as though around the slim neck of a certain singer he could name, Watts announced that, due to unforeseen circumstances, and with profound apologies to everyone who had *taken the trouble to turn up* ... the gig was cancelled.

CHAPTER THREE

DCI Jim Tyler sat on the northbound train back from London, watching the Staffordshire countryside blur past the window. Two rest days had been wasted on his old stomping ground, and with nothing to show for his time but the stoking up of bad memories.

Some clever type had once said that you could never step into the same river twice, and Jim Tyler couldn't fault them. Everything had moved on, except the deep emptiness inside him; the rage that wouldn't die and the thirst that was never further than one bad hour away.

In the seats opposite, as the carriage sped back towards this self-imposed exile in the City of Stoke on Trent, sat a young man and woman. Young to DCI Tyler, at least, the way he was feeling these days. Forty five and depleted; on the journey downhill to nowhere. A different generation already to the one that sat before him.

He watched the couple, observing their easiness together, and the adoring looks that they gave one another. The deft touches filled with promises. Remembering it all like it was yesterday. They each had an unopened can of lager in front of them and he couldn't help but admire their restraint.

Thinking of Kim; the love of his life, once upon a time. Back in London. But not in the London that existed now; a place that had become filled with ghosts and dark visions. A previous life lost to him, gone forever. Married with three children now, Kim had moved on, while Tyler sat in sackcloth and ashes.

He watched the young couple opposite kiss and he wished he could feel nothing but happiness for them. But it was out somewhere beyond his reach.

The kiss ended as the voice over the speaker announced that the next stop was Stoke. He watched the woman pick up her can of Carling at last. It opened with a bang, the lager spilling out down the side of the can. Tyler licked his lips without realising what he was doing; transfixed by the scene unfolding in front of him. The woman and the man were laughing, the woman slurping at the spillage in a manner that seemed ... provocative.

Are they mocking me? Mocking what I have become?

His heart was beating at his rib cage and threatening to burst through at any second. He wanted to taste all that was in front of him and leave his mark on the scene.

Aware that the man was now watching him, Tyler stood up and collected his belongings. As he walked away from the happy loving couple, down through the carriage, he could hear their laughter behind him and the explosion of the second can opening.

He stopped walking. The rage, the thirst, had moved almost beyond the limits of endurance. The train was slowing.

Without looking back, and as though awakening from a dream, Jim Tyler began walking again, out of the carriage and onto the empty platform.

CHAPTER FOUR

DS Mills was sitting at his desk in the CID office when the call came through. A group of cyclists had reported a grim finding early on Saturday morning; the body of a young man floating in the Cauldon Canal, behind the college, little more than a couple of miles from where Danny Mills was sitting now, on the second floor of Hanley Police Station on Cedar Lane.

The DS got up from his desk and walked over to the window, looking across the city towards Shelton, the trees in the distance indicating the near edge of Hanley Park. A little way beyond those trees, close to the southern bank of the canal, was where the body had been discovered.

The death of somebody's son.

Mills had two kids of his own. Whoever this young man was, there were doubtless loved ones who would be left to cope now in the dreadful aftermath.

The previous evening a call had come in reporting a missing person, a local singer by the name of Johnny Richards, aged twenty one. The call had come from the young man's mother, Mrs Maureen Richards. Her son hadn't been home for a couple of days. He hadn't shown up for his shift at work, hadn't been seen by his girlfriend and had failed to turn up for a gig in Hanley town centre.

As Mills gazed across the city, he wondered how he and his wife would cope if they ever found themselves in a situation like that. How did anybody cope?

His training and experience as a detective sergeant in a busy city had taught him not to leap to conclusions. Still, it was hard not to put two and two together. Difficult not to find, in spite of himself, that he was already trying to frame the words that might very soon have to be said to Mrs Richards.

Sometimes Danny Mills hated his job, bringing him, as it frequently did, face to face with the dark realities of a savage and brutal world. How many times had he wondered if he wouldn't be happier trading it all in for a hotdog and hamburger stand. On match days he could park his little van outside the Britannia Stadium, home of his beloved Stoke City, and combine all of his interests. Fast food and football and a few pints to round off the day. Wasn't that enough for anyone?

Try selling that one to the missus. Two young children to support and a crippling mortgage to sustain his family's dream of country living.

Mills shook his head and muttered to himself. He moaned about his job, his lot in life as he suspected most of the population did from time to time. But was life so bad, really? He was blessed with a family that he loved with every bone in his body, and a city he was proud to call home.

Even if he no longer lived in the city, in the heartlands where he was born and raised, at least he got to work its streets and serve its people. Day in and day out. There were worse ways of putting food on the table and keeping a roof over the heads of his loved ones. Compared with the poor souls waiting to hear the news about a missing son found dead in the dirty water of the Cauldon Canal ...

Some days he felt well and truly privileged. Some days, most days, he still believed that he could make a difference. That he could bring justice to the streets, the towns, the villages of Stoke on Trent.

The Scene Of Crime Officers had been dispatched to scour every centimetre of the crime scene, kitted out in their white suits to search for clues that might lead to the who and even explain the why of this latest act of barbarity. Let them do their work, thought Mills. Confirming, amongst other things, exactly which condemned souls were standing beneath the falling shadow, waiting to have their lives ripped apart.

Mrs Richards?

He wondered what she looked like. What her life had been like up until now. Whether, on receiving the news of what had happened to her son, she would scream and rage, or else retreat silently into an unimaginable private hell. Experience had taught him that people reacted differently, and there was never any way of predicting the reaction.

DS Mills was still lost in his reverie when DCI Tyler walked into the CID office and clocked him gazing out of the window.

"You won't catch many that way, Danny," said Tyler, throwing his jacket across the nearest chair. "I believe that we have a body."

Mills turned and nodded.

He hadn't found it easy working with Jim Tyler, at least not to begin with. The senior detective had arrived from London a few months earlier, blowing in a fresh wind that few at Cedar Lane Police Station had been prepared for. But how quickly that wind had become a refreshing, cleansing salve. More than a working relationship and nothing less than friendship had augured a revolution in Danny Mills. Work and even life itself would never be quite the same again, and he had a lot to thank the DCI for.

"Thoughts?" said Tyler.

"I'm trying to keep an open mind until we have some facts."

"Excellent answer, DS Mills. You've got the job."

"Thank you, sir. Much obliged."

"But that doesn't come with a bonus for sarcasm."

"Of course not, *sir*."

Tyler laughed. "Is this how we keep ourselves sane? While people out there are killing each other, maiming each other, ripping each other off, or to pieces? You are right, of course. We need the facts. But I've been looking at the missing person file and I find myself asking: who would want to kill a good-looking, talented young guy like Johnny Richards?"

"That might be what they pay our wages to find out."

"It might be. Or else something very similar. I see that you've spent a chunk of your hard-earned wages on a fine new hairdo." Tyler eyed his colleague's recently refreshed crew-cut. Mills had surpassed himself this time. It had been taken almost down to the scalp.

"Must keep up appearances, sir."

"So I see. Hoping for some good weather, or are you celebrating the clocks going forward for summer?"

Mills glanced out of the window. "Doesn't know whether it's a flag or a balloon out there. Rain one minute, sunshine the next. The wife's insisting on Spain this year."

"And you don't approve?"

"On top of the mortgage? I don't know what's wrong with North Wales, personally."

"Fond of the place, are you?"

"Been going since I was a lad."

"Wales versus Spain. And who will win?"

"Are you joking, sir? When she gets an idea in her head she's keen as mustard. She always wins. I thought that was what marriage was all about. That's why we live out in the sticks instead of where I belong, here in the city."

Mills stopped abruptly and coughed unnecessarily. "Anyway, you were saying ..."

Tyler smiled and picked up his jacket. "Come on."

The detectives made the short drive to Shelton, to see for themselves where this latest tragedy had struck and what it looked like. They found what Tyler thought to be a place manufactured for pain and sorrow.

He had long held the view that canals were natural destinations for murder and suicide. There was something unbearably lonely about such places, the dense water appearing full of secrets. A lonely place to die.

Yet was there a good place? In a warm bed, perhaps, with clean sheets and a woman who cared enough to call it love. And a good scotch to ease down the medicine - *no, don't even go there.* Jim Tyler sucked in the air. *I will run this off later, put in the miles around this city until I'm too weary to care for the balm of alcohol, or the allure of annihilation.*

Shaking off the sharp edge of his malaise, he glanced back towards the canal bridge. Could anyone ever walk under there without feeling spooked? Canals were bad enough, but something about the bridges gave him the creeps.

Mills was likewise taking in the scene, the white uniforms of the Scene Of Crime Officers still busying around the canal side. The meticulous gathering of anything that might reasonably constitute evidence, every blade of grass, every stone and bramble inspected and anything of possible significance bagged up and labelled, to be taken away for closer scrutiny under laboratory conditions.

At the same time, his mind conjured up a sequence of events that might have taken place, leading to this abomination. What kind of person would do this, and *why?* The usual suspects lined up inside the mind of Danny Mills: money, an argument over a woman ...

"Solved it?"

Mills turned to look at DCI Tyler, who now bore a world-weary grin.

"I wish. Seen enough for now, sir?"

The SOCOs did their work whilst everybody else waited, and little by little the facts, such as they were, emerged. The young man found face down in the water had died the day before Johnny Richards had been reported missing. The day prior to the scheduled, showcase gig at the Thirteen club. The gig that, for all the hype and trumpets had, in the end, never come to pass.

The victim was a male in his early twenties. He had sustained head injuries consistent with a violent physical assault, but had entered the water with the remains of his life still clinging on. The cold, dirty water of the Cauldon Canal had done the rest, taking what was left.

The victim had entered the water close to the low stone bridge, his corpse drifting a few metres to the west, becoming tangled up in the thick undergrowth that grew down from the narrow path, obscuring the body from view. The jacket that the young man had been wearing on the foul night of his death had given the brambles plenty to take hold of, and its dark colour had served as perfect camouflage. Perhaps the waves of passing narrow boats had caused the thick and tenacious brambles to finally let their silent prisoner float free, and in the early light the team of cyclists had spotted something sinister in the dark shape that bobbed gently against the canal side.

In any event, he had been in the water for the best part of thirty six hours. Though the dead man had been violently attacked before drowning, he didn't appear to have been the victim of a robbery. His wallet, containing banknotes, was found in his trouser pocket, and an expensive wrist-watch was still attached to his arm. But his wallet contained nothing that could verify his identity.

Mo Richards had been asked to formally identify the body of her son. She stood bravely, silently, while the sheet was lifted. As the corpse was revealed, she gasped and looked questioningly at the officers; looking at them as though there had been some mistake.

"This isn't my son," said Mo Richards. "This isn't Johnny."

CHAPTER FIVE

Adam Lane lived in the village of Penkhull, in the heart of Stoke on Trent. He lived with his mother and father but had spent most evenings of late with his girlfriend, Daisy Finch, in a small flat on the outskirts of Hanley. On what turned out to be the last evening of his life, Adam left the flat, taking the short walk down to the canal. According to Daisy, he had been heading towards the Norfolk Inn to meet his friend Ian Taylor.

Taylor, it seemed, was not known for his reliability, and hadn't turned up at the pub. Instead, he stayed in with his girlfriend, watching a horror movie on DVD, having apparently forgotten all about the arrangement to meet Adam for a drink. Ian Taylor had therefore not been at the Norfolk Inn when Adam failed to arrive. Daisy assumed Adam stayed at his friend's, or else returned to his parents' house as he sometimes did. Adam's parents meanwhile assumed that their son was staying with Daisy.

Nobody had been aware that Adam Lane was missing.

When Mo Richards viewed the corpse of the twenty-one-year-old man, tears rolled down her cheeks. She looked up at the officers in attendance, as though they had arranged an elaborate, sick joke at her expense.

"Adam," she said. "Oh, dear God."

Daisy Finch hadn't been well enough to be interviewed. She was still in a state of shock and was receiving medical support, including sedation, after being informed that her boyfriend, Adam Lane, had been found dead in the Cauldon Canal.

She managed to inform officers that Adam left her flat on Thursday evening to meet Ian Taylor for a drink, and that she had left the flat at the same time. Meeting work friends for an evening out in Hanley. Her friends vouched for her. They all met in a pub around the corner from the flat at 6.45pm, and then went into town.

As the news overtook her, Daisy Finch had broken down into hysterics, and any further questioning became impossible.

Ian Taylor and his girlfriend lived in a small flat in Etruria, bordering Shelton. Initial impressions, as far as Mills was concerned, suggested that the couple were too many sheets to the wind to have coherently planned to murder anybody. Mills wondered what it would have taken to rile either of them to anything approaching the energy required for a crime of passion. Or much else, for that matter.

He also wondered if the aroma caused by the plethora of joss sticks filling Taylor's living room, was intended to disguise other smells that officers of the law might not take kindly to, at least in the formal execution of their duties.

Taylor had met Adam Lane at college. They had kept in touch, going for a few drinks together when they had the chance.

"I thought we were meeting up at the weekend. Or it could have been the Friday," Taylor told the detectives. "Are you sure I was supposed to have been meeting him on Thursday?" he said, scratching his head as though to re-inforce his bemusement.

"That is our understanding," said Mills. *We weren't in a position to ask Adam Lane directly*, he thought. In keeping with procedure these days, he kept the sarcasm to himself.

Taylor thought for a couple of minutes. Mills and Tyler waited, doing their best to display what patience they could muster. Then Taylor said, "Who told you it was supposed to have been Thursday?"

Mills groaned inwardly and Taylor's girlfriend smiled politely at the detectives. It was hard to ascertain whether she was tacitly apologising for her boyfriend's dimness, or whether she was afflicted with the same condition. Ignoring Taylor's question regarding who had suggested that he should have been meeting Adam on the Thursday, Mills asked what Taylor had studied at college.

"Social sciences," said Taylor.

"How interesting," lied Mills, glancing at the clock on the wall.

"It got me a job working with the homeless."

God help them, thought Mills.

"Do you know Johnny Richards?" asked Tyler.

Taylor looked confused by the sudden change in direction. "He was at college. He knocked about with Adam. I didn't have a lot to do with him. His band's doing really well, I believe."

"Did Adam mention Johnny?" asked Tyler.

Taylor shook his head. "I hadn't seen Adam for a few weeks. With him at uni, exams coming up, and me at work. You know, I'm sure we were supposed to be meeting at the weekend."

Tyler pressed on. "Did Adam and Johnny knock around together?"

"They used to," said Taylor. "They were good mates. Adam was in the same band but then he left."

"What happened?" asked Mills.

Taylor shrugged. "Dunno, Adam never talked about it. I think he got bored with it."

"Did he fall out with Johnny Richards?" asked Mills.

"If he did, he never said anything to me about it."

The detectives called it a day. In the unlikely event that Taylor or his girlfriend recalled anything further, could they please contact the police as a matter of urgency.

Tyler and Mills sat together in the CID office looking over the statements. Then they looked at each other. "Go on," said Tyler. "Say it."

Mills sat back, one hand resting on the bulging belly that he had promised his wife would be coming off before their holidays. "Okay, then. Adam Lane, twenty one years old, the same age as our man of mystery, Johnny Richards. They were at school together, and the two of them were the original, founder-members of the *Swamp Seeds*. Adam was replaced in the band by Billy Steele, who was at school with both of them. The band changed their name to *Johnny and the Swamp Seeds—*"

Tyler held up a hand. "I'm going to have to stop you there. You see, I thought that you were about to reveal to me something that I didn't already know." He edged forward and lowered his voice. "I'm going to confide something now. I once, as a very young man, came across a biography of *The Rolling Stones*. It was given to me by a friend who meant well. I never read it. I don't regret that." Tyler leaned back, nodded and touched his lips in a gesture of confidentiality.

"I think," said Mills, "that the death of Adam Lane, and Johnny Richards going missing, might be related."

"I see. The point emerges. But in what way are the cases related? Do you imagine that Richards killed Lane and went into hiding?"

"It's a possibility."

"Motive?"

"Too early to say."

Tyler noted that Danny Mills' hand hadn't stopped stroking at the dome of his belly. "Am I keeping you from the canteen, or the chemist?"

Mills sat forward and removed his hand from its caress. "Are we going to see Mrs Richards?"

"I see no reason why not. Maybe she can help shape your theory."

"It's hardly a theory. I've worked with you long enough. I've learned to keep an open mind. But I'm only human. Sometimes you can't help putting two and two together."

"As long as we don't come up with five." Tyler stood up, six foot of toned muscle and beguiling green eyes that sparkled beneath a shock of raven hair. "Perhaps you should start coming on my fun runs. Get you in shape for the beach."

"I'd sooner be fat."

"You want to be Oliver Hardy to my Stan Laurel. Come on, let's work up a sweat."

Mrs Richards made a round of hot drinks and sat down with the detectives in the well-furnished living room of her terraced house in Hanford. There were photographs of her son dotted around the room, almost to the exclusion of anybody else. Mills asked which was the most recent, and how recent.

Mrs Richards pointed to the portrait on the shelf above the TV. "That one was taken a few months ago. Johnny hasn't changed much since, at least not to look at him."

The photograph revealed a good-looking young man, with a mop of black hair and intense blue eyes that came close to smouldering. He appeared to be wearing a biker's jacket and the overall effect was, thought Mills, nothing if not rock and roll.

"Your son hasn't changed physically," said Tyler, "but in other ways?"

The woman sighed and took a sip of her coffee. She looked tired and drained, thought Mills, though that was hardly surprising: your son goes missing and another young man is found murdered a few miles away; hardly conducive to getting a good eight hours.

"Johnny," she said. "Where do I begin?"

The detectives waited for her to decide on a starting place, both of them sipping at their drinks while they watched Mrs Richards carefully. At last she said, "I think he's been putting too much into this band. He's been living on his nerves for weeks now, months even. It used to be fun for him, a bit of a dream, you know how it is. Johnny used to have a laugh. But just lately it's all become very serious, very full on. He doesn't seem to have a laugh like he used to. You're lucky if you see a smile from one week to the next."

"So what changed?" asked Mills.

"I wish I knew. Sometimes I wonder if he wants it all too much."

"Mrs Richards?" said Tyler.

Her attention had appeared to drift and she looked up from her drink, slightly startled, as though she had momentarily forgotten that two police officers were with her. As though she had been merely thinking aloud to an empty room.

"I mean," she said, "it's like all the pleasure went out of it. I mean to say, what's the point if you're not even enjoying it? Success at all costs?" She shook her head. "Nothing's worth making yourself bad for. He's always lived on his nerves to some extent, has Johnny. He's a bit like his father in some respects. In fact I think he's getting more like him, to be honest."

"His father doesn't live with you?" said Mills.

"We separated a couple of years ago. John, my ex-husband, that is - Johnny's the spitting image of his father, by the way ... no, I won't bad-mouth him. We had some good times, me and John, and he was a good father to Johnny. I suppose in his own way he still is. Useless, bone idle, but he loves his son and there's never been any question about that. It's just the way things go I suppose."

"Does Johnny see his father often?" asked Mills.

"Quite often, yes. He only lives a few miles away. Up Ash Bank. Werrington." A sad smile of remembrance appeared to cross her face. "He taught Johnny to play guitar. That's where it all came from. His father was music mad, always has been, as long as I've known him. He taught Adam, too. We used to live next door to Adam and his family when we lived up in Penkhull, before we split up. He was almost like a second son, was Adam. And he and Johnny were like brothers."

Mo Richards appeared to drift back into a world of memory. Mills was about to speak when she said, "He was a lovely lad, was Adam. And so clever. He sailed into university, by all accounts. But there was no airs and graces with him. He had time for everybody. He could have been anything he wanted. His poor parents, I don't know how they'll cope."

She looked at the detectives. "I don't know what this has to do with Johnny. What do you want me to tell you?"

"Anything that might lead us to your son," said Mills. "Anything that you think might be relevant."

"I don't know what to think," she said. "But I know what a lot of people must be thinking."

"What's that, Mrs Richards?" asked Mills.

"Well, isn't it obvious?" There was an edge to her voice now. "Johnny goes missing, just as his band are about to play the biggest gig of their lives, and then Adam is found dead. Everybody's going to think that Johnny had something to do with it. I mean to say, why else would Johnny miss an opportunity like that? It's what he's been working for, dreaming about for as long as I can remember."

She stopped, as though something had struck her. "Listen, I don't want to give the wrong idea, you know."

"About what?" asked Mills.

"When I said that my son had changed these last few months, I'm not saying that he's become crazy, or that I think, you know, he would be capable of, well, you know what I'm saying. I don't know why they fell out."

"Johnny and Adam fell out? When was that?" asked Mills.

"It was sometime last year, I think. Johnny didn't say anything, but Adam stopped coming around and Johnny hadn't mentioned him for ages. Then one day I asked about him, and Johnny said he'd left the band. Just like that."

Mrs Richards took a gulp of her drink. "Oh, God, I'm tying a noose around my son's neck. No, I don't for one second think that my son killed Adam."

"Did your son say why they had fallen out?"

"No, he didn't. He said Adam had left the band but he didn't want to talk about it, and it seemed to me that they must have fallen out. But that doesn't make my son a killer, if that's what you're thinking. Johnny couldn't kill anyone for any reason, he isn't that kind. If anything, Adam would be the one with a grudge."

"Why would Adam hold a grudge?" asked Tyler.

She looked at DS Mills, as though questioning whether his colleague was for real. "Isn't it obvious?"

she said. "Johnny's band is doing really well. He would have no reason to harm Adam. I mean, Adam might feel that he missed out, because he left or they replaced him or whatever. But Johnny wouldn't have any reason to ..."

The words petered out and Mo Richards gulped at the remains of her coffee.

"And you have no idea why Adam was *replaced*?" said Tyler.

"Johnny didn't talk about it. He could be very private. He was most of the time in fact. It might be a bit strong saying they fell out. Maybe it was more that they drifted apart. I don't know what happened, or if anything did."

She went to take another gulp of her drink, but realising that her cup was empty she looked uncomfortably at the detectives. "No, I'm not aware that there was any falling out. If there was, Johnny never told me about it. Maybe his dad could tell you more." She lifted up her cup and again looked surprised at finding it empty. "God, I don't know what I'm saying. My son wouldn't kill anyone."

"Mrs Richards," said Mills, "no-one is accusing your son of anything. We're trying to establish—"

"You are though. Adam's dead and Johnny's gone missing and you think ..." She started to fill up, her voice cracking. "My son could be dead too. You should be out there looking for him."

Mills asked if she would like another drink making. Sobbing, Mo Richards said, "I don't know who would do this. I want to know Johnny's alright. I want to know where my son is."

CHAPTER SIX

Pulling up outside a neat semi-detached house in Penkhull, the two officers got out of the car and looked with equal foreboding at the property marked Seventy Six. They conducted their own private rituals in the moments between ringing the doorbell and being invited inside the newly cursed house of death.

Mr Lane answered the door in silence, ushering the officers through the hallway. They entered a small lounge, freshly hoovered and polished. Mrs Lane was sitting by the window, looking out, seemingly oblivious to her visitors.

The woman glanced briefly at the detectives as Mills offered his greeting, and then her gaze returned to the window. Or through it. It was difficult to tell. She could be celebrating her ninetieth birthday, thought Mills, though she was closer to forty. Her eyes betrayed the knowledge that the years to follow could never offer anything to celebrate again.

Mr Lane invited the officers to take a seat, indicating a brown leather couch that dominated the room. Mills took it all in: a matching two-seater and an armchair, the latter occupied by the grieving mother. A family of three, with a house and its furnishings arranged and intended to accommodate *three*.

One of them missing. One of them would always be missing.

Mills watched Mr Lane unfold a camping chair and take his place amid the gloomy, tense silence.

Tyler introduced himself and Mills, and passed on his deepest sympathies. Mr Lane nodded and ventured the approximation of a smile, while Mrs Lane continued to look far into the distance.

After attending to the formalities, Tyler asked his questions. He asked them carefully and sensitively and Mr Lane answered as though he was sitting a test. It was, observed Mills, as if the poor man imagined that getting all of the answers correct might bring his son back.

In the course of the slow, methodical process, the detectives learned that Adam was well-loved and with his whole life ahead of him. That he was a bright, intelligent, talented young man and that he was not in any trouble and never had been. Adam had been preparing for his final exams at a local university and was expected to gain a First in Sociology.

There was no-one who might wish to do him harm, at least no-one that Mr Lane could bring to mind. He might have been in the wrong place at the wrong time. A random attack, a robbery, who knows? Sheer bad luck and nothing more than that.

And then the facade broke down. As Mr Lane's voice spluttered to a halt, Mrs Lane, turning from the window, uttered her first words since the arrival of the detectives into her home.

"Johnny Richards is responsible for the death of my son."

The woman's face was hard to look into: eyes sunken, cheeks hollow; though she was sitting upright, in an attitude of dignity, she might as well have been lashed to the torture table.

Had the grey in her hair been apparent before this nightmare had stolen in, stealing her world, and dismantling everything that had once been called a life? Mills wondered how people could bear such things as this. How life could possibly go on, and who might want such a life. He watched Mr Lane rise from his chair, offering to make drinks.

Mills sensed what was coming. The man needed to be in motion, and he had to hold on to something. But the words would spill out before this visit was done.

Over hot drinks untouched by all four present in the room, Mrs Lane spoke again. In a measured voice that threatened to break down at every breath, she told the gathering all that she knew about Johnny Richards.

They knew the Richards family because they had been neighbours for many years, up until the time when the family split up. Johnny and Adam had been close friends. The friendship continued after Johnny moved to Hanford with his mother, though Johnny had begun to change.

Mrs Lane, speaking in quiet, measured tones, described Johnny as a dreamer, unreliable and immature. She suggested that he became even more "self-obsessed" after his parents had gone their separate ways. That he used Adam, wanting his company when it suited, dismissing their friendship when that was more convenient. "There was another side to Johnny Richards, and his parents splitting up seemed to bring it out of him," said Mrs Lane. "He was hanging around with some unsavoury characters too. I didn't want Adam getting involved with any of that."

Mrs Lane described how things had changed again when Johnny met Daisy Finch. How it seemed to have a positive effect on him, at least in the short term. "He seemed to grow up a bit. Sometimes a young man needs a woman, to keep him on track. But it didn't last. *She* came along. And they were a pair together."

"She?" asked Mills.

"*Janine.* Once he clapped eyes on her that was that. Johnny dropped Daisy like a stone. Nearly broke the poor girl's heart it did. Adam was the saving of that poor girl. But it works both ways, I know that. Daisy repaid our son a thousand times, showing him the truth about Johnny Richards."

"And what was the truth about Johnny Richards?" asked Tyler.

"Daisy spent enough time with him to see what he was. And she saw the dark side of him, and helped steer our son away."

"Dark side?" said Tyler.

"He'd always been in his own little world. *Johnny's World*, we used to call it. So you could never rely on him. He wasn't listening half the time. I never met anyone so caught up in himself, in his own thoughts. Utterly self-centered, he was. Selfish as they come. But he got away with it, because he always had that *charm* about him. Ha, charm! But he never fooled me with it. I always knew that he would put himself above everything else, like he always has done."

"And that's what you mean by his dark side?" said Tyler.

Mrs Lane grunted. "Like I said, he started falling in with the wrong crowd. Adam always had more about him, kept his wits about him. He knew that some of those people were bad news. But Johnny was so easily led."

"What people are you talking about, Mrs Lane?" asked Tyler.

"Oh, I don't know any names. But I saw him changing and I wondered if he was taking drugs. And later on Daisy confirmed that he had fallen in with druggies and it was Daisy who cleaned him up a bit."

The detectives waited to see if Mrs Lane might say more. When she began to gaze distractedly out of the window once again, Tyler said, "In what ways did taking drugs affect Johnny?"

The woman turned back to look at the detective. "Well, drugs make people moody, don't they? Everybody knows they are bad news. I would have thought that a police officer would know things like that. I was worried that Adam might get drawn in, but I needn't have been. Adam was always far too sensible to get caught up in any of that rubbish."

"So, are you saying, Mrs Lane, that taking drugs was making Johnny more moody? And this affected his relationship with your son - and with his girlfriend?"

Tyler waited for an answer, but Mrs Lane appeared to have lost the thread of whatever point she was making. "Adam was beginning to see the truth about his so-called friend, and Janine could see that and she did the rest."

"What do you mean?" asked Tyler.

"She poisoned his mind against Adam. She saw him as a threat."

"What kind of threat?"

"I mean threat to Johnny's success, as leader of the band and all that. And so that was that. But good riddance, I say. Adam was best out of it, away from him and away from Janine Finch too."

"Johnny threw Adam out of the band?" asked Tyler.

"Either that or he made it impossible for Adam to stay. Whatever, it amounted to the same thing. But I don't think Adam lost any sleep over it. I think he knew well enough what was going on."

"Why would Johnny want to harm your son, Mrs Lane?"

She shook her head. "I'll bet she put him up to it. Janine."

"For what reason?"

"Because she's poison, that's why."

"But Johnny's band was doing well. Why would he, or Janine, wish to jeopardise that?"

"Don't you see?" said Mrs Lane. "To hurt her sister. To get at Daisy."

Tyler glanced at Mills. It was time to leave.

As the officers stood up, Mr Lane said, "My wife has a lot of time for Daisy. She believes Daisy was good for our son. But I wish Adam had never met her."

It had taken a while for Mr Lane to open up, but his words were quickly gathering momentum, threatening the outpouring that Mills had anticipated.

"I didn't trust her. I never did. But you can't go around telling your twenty one-year-old son your feelings about his choice of girlfriends, can you?"

"Can you explain -" started Tyler, but Mr Lane cut in. "I think she was as poisonous as her sister. I think she was bitter because Johnny Richards dumped her for Janine. And I think she used Adam to get back at both of them. Those two bitches were using Adam and Johnny to fight out their own war. They didn't care who got hurt. That's what I think, for what it's worth."

Mrs Lane was crying quietly in the corner, but her husband hadn't finished. "I don't say that Johnny Richards was an angel. But neither do I see him as the drug-fuelled monster that my wife seems bent on conjuring up.

"I believe that Daisy Finch made up a lot of things about him because she wanted to hurt him. She wanted to hit back. She was every bit as twisted as her sister. The two of them, between them, turned Johnny Richards sour. And it's because of them that our son is dead."

CHAPTER SEVEN

DS Mills turned off through Bucknall before beginning the steady climb up Ash Bank. "So, pick the bones out of that lot."

"I'd rather not, if it's all the same," said Tyler.

"You're probably right. It's hard to know what to think. Grief can do funny things to people. Makes them come up with all sorts of notions."

"Did you get that from your grandmother?" asked Tyler.

"Yes," said Mills, not missing a beat. "How did you know that? On my father's side, of course. My maternal grandmother talked only about football. She indoctrinated me, making me the man I am today."

They arrived in the village of Werrington. John Richards answered the door to a small terraced property that had clearly seen happier days. Richards was wearing a tracksuit, and Tyler felt a pang of guilt that he still hadn't been out running. It was over two weeks now. The longest he had gone since replacing a thirst for what could be found in a bottle, with a steady habit of thirty-plus miles a week around the roads and lanes of Stoke on Trent.

But the thirst had been creeping back, and the anger with it.

Making a mental note to put on his running clothes and go out later, he followed the pale, thin man through to a chaotic living room that smelt strongly of tobacco. He wondered when the dirty grey tracksuit had last been worn for any sporting activities, or if it ever had been. An acoustic guitar stood in pride of place next to a filthy armchair that might once have been cream.

Mr Richards asked the officers if they would like a drink, and Tyler pictured the top coming off a bottle, with a tumbler of whisky standing at its side to keep it company on the way down. *Definitely a run later*, he decided. "Tea please," he said, quickly enough to draw a quizzical glance from DS Mills.

The officers took seats on the sofa opposite the armchair while Richards disappeared into the kitchen. Mills looked at the guitar. "Ever played?" he asked.

"I had a piano lesson once," said Tyler. "The teacher told me never to come back."

"We can't be good at everything," said Mills. "My daughter's started having guitar lessons. She's really coming on. But I'm like you, tone deaf."

"Who said I was tone deaf?"

"Well, I assumed—"

"Bad habit. I've told you since I'm sick of telling you."

Mills recoiled, at the same time trying to weigh up the DCI's tone. "I didn't mean to—"

"The truth of the matter is that the idiot tasked with teaching me, thought that hitting the back of your hands with a ruler every time you played a wrong note was the best way to encourage talent. I told him where to stuff his ruler and his piano and he didn't take my advice too kindly.

"There. Now you have it."

Richards came back into the living room and handed hot drinks to the officers. He sat down opposite them in his armchair. "Mind if I smoke?"

The man rolled his own cigarettes, and he appeared well practiced. Mills observed that the man was clearly Johnny's father. There was grey in the long, straggled hair, and deep lines cut into his features. But when you looked into his eyes, the same blueness shone in the father as it did in the son.

When Richards had lit up he said, "No news about Johnny?"

"When did you last see your son, Mr Richards?" asked Tyler.

"A couple of days before the gig at the Thirteen. He called here."

"How did he seem?"

"He was excited, naturally he was. He put me on the guest list. I was there when they announced the gig was cancelled."

"Did there appear to be anything wrong, when you last saw your son?"

"Nothing that I was aware of. Like I say, he was full of it. He thought this was the break he'd been working for. He couldn't wait to show them what he was made of."

Richards took a heavy pull on his cigarette. "It doesn't make sense. Something must have happened. He wouldn't have missed that gig for anything."

"I believe," said Tyler, "that Johnny had been good friends with Adam Lane."

"And you think ...?" The man took another heavy pull before crushing the remains of the cigarette in the ashtray balanced on the arm of his chair.

"We don't think anything at this stage," said Tyler. "We're trying to establish facts, that's all."

"Johnny and Adam were best mates. They were mates since they were kids. I knew Adam, I taught him a bit." Richards glanced at the guitar. "He was a decent player."

"He was an original member of Johnny's band."

"That's right."

"Do you know why Adam left the band?"

Richards laughed. "You think that's what this is about?"

"Like I said, Mr Richards. We're trying to establish—"

"I know what you're doing. But there's no dirt to dig as far as Johnny and Adam are concerned. Bands split up all the time. Adam was a good player, but he wasn't as serious about it as Johnny. He was away at university. He'd got other things on. Johnny needed commitment. I think that's fair enough."

"They hadn't fallen out, then?" asked Tyler.

"You're trying to make something out of this, I see what you're up to. You're like the press. It was nothing to do with falling out, it was about commitment, pure and simple."

"Adam was replaced by Billy Steele," said Tyler.

"Been doing your homework?" Richards nodded. "That's right, though. The three of them were at school. They were all into music. Billy was as keen as Johnny. He deserved the gig. He wasn't as good as

Adam, to be fair, but he wasn't bad and he was working on it."

John Richards started laughing as he rolled another smoke. "How could he have been as good as Adam, eh? He hadn't had me teaching him."

He lit up and drew heavily on the tobacco. "No, joking aside, Adam wasn't as committed to the band as Johnny wanted. And that's just how it was. You can't argue with that. The band was everything to Johnny. He wanted to make a real go of it."

"And so Adam left and Billy joined," said Tyler.

"That's all there is to it. It's a shame because Adam really could play. It was a waste. Billy hasn't that level of natural ability, in my opinion, but he was committed. That's the difference. Billy can write a decent tune, too, same as Johnny. They were good, I tell you. They were very good. But too many cooks. I think there would have been trouble somewhere down the line."

"What do you mean by that, exactly?" asked Tyler.

"I don't know what I mean. I talk like I know about the world, and I sicken myself sometimes. If I knew anything I might have a better life than this."

"Mr Richards," said Tyler, "what do you think has happened to your son?"

The man appeared to be about to say something, but then thought better of it.

"If there's anything you can think of, anything at all that might help us to find your son," said Mills. "Even if it might seem insignificant."

"He wouldn't have missed that gig. Nothing could have made him miss it."

Standing up to leave, Tyler said, "If something occurs, you can contact me on this number." He handed him a card, and Richards took it, his hand trembling. Unable to meet the looks of the detectives.

Outside on the street Tyler and Mills stood for a moment in the mild sunshine before getting into the unmarked car. "I think the cannabis fumes in there have actually done me some good," said Tyler. "I believe they've taken the edge off my twenty-first century angst, at least for the moment. I don't suppose it will last though."

"Sir?"

"Don't mind me, Danny. I'm rambling. I'm in need of ... something."

Mills frowned. "Do you reckon Daisy Finch is up to receiving a visit yet?"

"I hear she's getting there. In the meantime, I believe it's time to meet the band. Interesting remark from Mr Richards, don't you think? About the possibility of trouble ahead. Too many cooks. Or in this case, too many songwriters. Let's start with Billy Steele, shall we?"

CHAPTER EIGHT

Billy Steele worked in the Reality cafe at Trentham Gardens, a mile up the road from where Johnny Richards lived with his mother. He was renting a flat in Longton, Danny Mills' old stomping ground before his wife got the notion for living in the middle of nowhere and moving them out lock, stock and barrel to pastures new. Mills relished any opportunity to return to Longton.

Steele's shift at the cafe was due to finish soon and so it made sense, argued Mills, to head back to the station, clear some of the paperwork, and be in Longton to greet the worker as he returned from a hard day in the coffee and cake trade. But Tyler had other ideas.

"When I arrived here," he said from the passenger seat of the unmarked police car that Mills was steering along the A34, "they told me that Alton Towers and Trentham Gardens were the jewels in the crown of this fair city."

Mills laughed. "You shouldn't believe everything you hear."

"I don't."

Mills took his eyes off the road ahead for a second, glancing at his colleague. Working with Jim Tyler had been a steep learning curve. The DCI had arrived in Stoke on Trent under a cloud. Rumours that he had lost it back in London and struck a fellow officer had done the rounds, though the details remained obscure. He rarely talked about his past, but parts of it, echoes, had leaked out here and there. Gaining an insight into his life, thought Mills, was like putting together a ten-thousand piece jigsaw puzzle.

All the same, he had grown fond of the DCI. He wasn't the type of senior officer that Mills had ever come across before. He was a total enigma, in fact. At times formal procedure seemed anathema to him. The man was a maverick, a loner, a complex individual.

Over the months Mills had seen Tyler settle to his newly adopted city, and his new post. He had observed a strange, haunted man, but a man complete with fierce integrity and an unbridled thirst for real justice nonetheless. A man displaced by circumstance, who couldn't give a damn for playing by the rules, or for the politics and statistics of a flabby bureaucracy.

He had watched something flowering, unfolding. A force taking shape. Tyler had his demons, there was little doubt about that; but most days he appeared to be dealing with them. Finding his place again in the world. Yet still the unmistakable signs were there: a man with an old desire for the bottle, though never acknowledged, never voiced; and likewise, a deep-rooted anger and contempt for authority. A man holding the darkness at bay through hard work and physical exercise. Jim Tyler wasn't exactly one for wearing his heart on his sleeve.

Stopping at the traffic lights, Mills glanced again at his passenger. *You look troubled. Thinking over the case? Difficult to tell.*

These last weeks an agitation, an old and sour brooding, had resurfaced in the DCI. Mills had kept his thoughts to himself, hoping that it was nothing but a passing shadow from which Tyler would once again emerge. He had kept both eyes open, keenly watching, but the shadow hadn't passed. If anything it had thickened, and appeared to be following Jim Tyler with increasing intensity, clinging to the man's coat-tails.

"I take it," said Mills, recalling mention of Alton Towers and Trentham Gardens, "that it's time to cross at least one of our 'premier tourist attractions' off your bucket list?"

"As a rule I don't do bucket lists or tourist attractions."

"You surprise me."

In spite of himself, Tyler laughed. "You ray of sunshine! I have a job to do. I want to see Billy Steele. He happens to work at Trentham Gardens."

"And luckily that's where we're headed," said Mills as they moved on through the lights.

"I'm pleased to hear that."

"Is there ... anything that you would like to talk about, Jim?"

"As a matter of fact, yes, there is."

Mills indicated right at the roundabout and entered the Trentham Estate.

"I want," said Tyler, "to ask you what you think about the estranged Mr and Mrs Richards."

"That's not what I—"

"I know. But that's why we're here, what we're paid to do. And that is what we are going to spend the next few minutes talking about."

Mills parked up. He thought for a minute, and then he answered the DCI's question. "They're both protecting their son."

"You don't miss a lot."

"I try my best," said Mills. He smiled but Tyler didn't reciprocate.

Stepping out of the car, Mills was about to say something when Tyler cut him short. "Let's focus our attention on the job in hand, shall we? It's enough—or it should be."

The Reality cafe stood across the car park from the main garden centre. Tables and chairs had been placed outside to catch the early adherents to the arrival of spring. But despite the sun's brave attempts at approximating an end to winter, it was fooling no-one, and none of the tables outside were taken. Tyler chose one and sat down, dispatching Mills inside.

Through the large window Tyler watched a skinny youth serving the tables. A mess of lank mousy hair looked more suited to a life of rock and roll than waiting on tables, he thought. *But would that thought ever have entered my head if I hadn't known a little more about Billy Steele than I can actually see before me?*

He had learned many times not to leap to premature conclusions. Even tried to turn that wisdom into a philosophy of life. It was a human instinct to extrapolate much from very little, and as a survival mechanism it had its roots and purpose. But when it came to police work it could be disastrous.

In an effort of will, he cleared his mind of everything but the facts as he understood them. A technique long-practiced and stoically observed. And then he waited.

Mills emerged from the cafe. "He's about to knock off. I've ordered us a couple of cappuccinos. I hope that's agreeable."

"First impressions?"

"He's as nervous as they come."

"Understandably so?"

"It's generally a bit on the awkward side when a plain-clothes CID officer arrives at your place of work and asks to speak with you."

Tyler looked at Mills for a few moments, trying to weigh something up. "Are you speaking wise words to me, Danny, or expressing attitude?"

"I thought you would have known me better than that by now."

"Just as I thought. Let it go—and that's a direct order, understand?"

"Consider it done, sir. But he's still soiling himself."

"Nice for the customers," said Tyler. "I'm glad we chose a table out in the fresh air."

The drinks arrived, courtesy of Steele himself. "Two cappuccinos?" he said, placing the drinks on the small table.

Tyler noted that the young man's face was flushed and sweaty. The shift didn't look that busy and there was certainly no heat in the sun. As the second drink was placed down, a little of the coffee spilled onto the saucer. "I'm sorry about that, sir. I'll get you a napkin."

Steele had tried to avoid eye contact, but now he looked directly at DCI Tyler. For a moment Tyler didn't say anything, holding the young man's look. Then, "Okay, thank you."

As though a spell had been broken, Billy Steele shot back inside the cafe, returning with a wad of napkins thick enough to have saved the Titanic. "I'll be done in ten minutes," he said, after again apologising for the spillage.

CHAPTER NINE

Mills settled the bill, and the three of them walked to the unmarked police car, where Steele was invited to sit in the back. Tyler joined him, while Mills took his place in the front seat.

Tyler addressed the nervous young man. "I'm hoping this won't take very long. I want to ask you a few questions. If you would prefer, we can do this at the police station. But in any event, this is an informal interview. Do you understand?"

Steele nodded. "Here is okay," he said.

"Good. I believe that you are in a band with Johnny Richards."

"That's right."

"When was the last time that you saw him?"

"Thursday evening. We had a rehearsal the night before a gig we were supposed to be playing."

"What time was the rehearsal, and where?"

"We practiced in Stoke. Liverpool Road studios, seven thirty until ten."

"Was everybody prompt?" Tyler asked Steele.

"We always start on time. It costs us."

"So nobody turned up late?"

"No, we were all on time. We went in at half seven and started setting up, then we kicked in around eight."

"Did anything strike you as unusual?" asked Tyler.

"Like what?"

"Like *anything*."

"We practiced for a couple of hours and everybody was up for it."

"How did Johnny seem?"

"He was okay. He was fine."

Tyler caught a note of hesitation. "Are you sure about that, Billy?"

"Actually, he was acting a bit strange. He has been for a while, to be honest."

"In what way strange?"

"It was since we brought the record out. We recorded an EP and it started getting airplay. I think it was going to his head."

"And that was affecting his behaviour in what way?"

"He was more uptight. No, that's not what I mean."

"Take your time," said Mills from the front seat.

"Well, like, being uptight, I could understand that. The pressure, I mean. Like, you start to get the idea that you might be getting somewhere, and you don't want to blow it. I think it was affecting all of us, to some extent."

"But there was something else," said Tyler. "In Johnny's case?"

"It's hard to explain."

"Try your best."

Billy Steele couldn't seem to nail what it was that he was trying to express regarding the changes he had observed in Johnny Richards. The word 'erratic' came out at one point, though without any corroboration; 'prima donna' soon followed, and Tyler took it up. "I believe that ego issues are not an uncommon phenomenon in bands."

"We'd always got along fine, though."

"Arguments over musical differences?" asked Tyler, his tongue circling the inner flesh of his cheek, his eyes retaining a fierce curiosity.

Steele looked at DCI Tyler and a light came on inside the detective. "Go on," said Tyler. "If you have something to say."

"Johnny was the singer, of course. And when I joined, most of the material was his. But I'd written a lot of stuff and Johnny seemed to have ..."

"Seemed to have?" prompted Tyler.

"He'd dried up a bit, to be honest. He was happy to hear what I was coming up with. I'd been working hard on my singing, too, and I took over the vocals on some of my own material."

"And Johnny was happy with that arrangement?"

"At first he liked the contrasts in our voices, and in our songs. Well, he did for a while, anyway. He seemed excited about the future. But when we were recording the EP, I think that's when it changed. He wanted everything his own way. I thought we would go 50/50, two songs each. But he ended up with three and I got just one. And he made changes to that, too."

"And whose voice are we hearing on the radio, Billy?"

Tyler's eyes instinctively narrowed. Watching and listening carefully, he saw and heard the tension pulling beneath the surface.

"He sang on all four. When they started playing one of Johnny's songs on the radio it was like he'd won. Like he'd proved something."

"I see," said Tyler. "And how did that alter things for the rest of you?"

"He was getting hard to be around at times, getting on a star-trip. He started writing again, all of this new material he wanted us to learn. Some of it wasn't that good, and he was getting impatient that we weren't learning it fast enough. Or that we weren't 'doing it justice', as he put it."

"Where did Johnny go after the last band practice?" asked Tyler.

"He said he was going over to see Janine. That's his girlfriend."

"Had Johnny known Janine long?"

"A while."

"What was she like?"

"She could be a pain."

"In what way?" asked Tyler.

"She started turning up at band practice. Putting her oar in. Up until then, it had only been the band at rehearsals. We used to joke that it was getting to be like John and Yoko - you know, the rumours about the Beatles. None of the band liked Janine being there, but you couldn't tell Johnny. I think it was all part of the rock-star trip he was on."

"Go on," said Tyler.

"I think Janine was, like, trying to push him. To make sure he was top dog."

An image of Lady Macbeth swept through DCI Tyler's mind without any invitation. "Was Janine at your last rehearsal?" he asked.

"No. It was the first one she'd missed for a while."

"What about Adam Lane?" said Tyler.

He swallowed hard. "I don't understand."

"I want you to tell me about Adam. You were at school together, I believe. Take your time, Billy. I want to know everything you can tell me."

Tyler took a few deep, silent breaths. Sometimes the order of the day was patience. The trouble being, he didn't much feel like being patient. Steele looked terrified, and that was reasonable enough. The singer in your band goes missing and a mutual friend is found dead, and now two police officers arrive at the cafe where you work and start asking questions.

Mills was right, there was good reason to be more than a little nervous. Even if you didn't have anything to hide. Fair comment. *So why am I looking into this young man's eyes and having to focus on my own breathing in order to give him time to tell his story?*

Breathing in ... breathing out. Deep breaths, deep, deep breaths. Tyler wanted a drink. He wanted to run through the streets until he was too exhausted to do anything but sleep. But more than anything, he wanted to make a fist and punch somebody, hard, and to go on punching them until the feelings inside him subsided. There was something that he didn't like about Billy Steele, and at the same time something that he did. But none of those conflicting feelings came with reasons and neither did they arise from the facts.

What, then?

"... Johnny and Adam used to hang around a lot, back at school. Johnny's dad taught them stuff on the guitar. They'd talked about forming a band since as far back as I can remember."

He told the detectives how Johnny was obsessed with music and never seemed interested in anything else. How Adam would sometimes wind Johnny up about it. "Adam wasn't as obsessed as Johnny, I mean about music. He was more into girls. He had a lot of interests."

After school ended, the three of them had attended college in Shelton, and Billy recalled how Johnny and Adam had a try-out with a college-based band one evening. They were looking for a second guitarist, and one who could also provide backing vocals. "They told Johnny he couldn't sing and that his guitar playing wasn't much better. They liked Adam's guitar playing and told him he could work on his singing.

"Johnny took it hard. We didn't see him at college for days, and when he did turn up he was a lot quieter, kind of withdrawn. Even Adam stopped his wind-ups. I think he could tell that Johnny wasn't his usual self.

"Adam attended a few sessions with the band, then dropped out. I think he left because Johnny was knocked back by the whole thing. Johnny was saying that he was concentrating on writing songs. One of them suggested they finally get around to forming their own band and done with—they'd been threatening to do it for years."

Mills asked Billy why he had not been involved in the band at that point.

"They didn't need three guitars. And I wasn't very confident back then. I played, but only in private; usually with the sound down, acoustic, like. I concentrated on writing songs, but I never let anybody hear them. I doubted I could ever be as good as Adam, as a guitarist, and I thought my strength might lie in song writing."

Mills was digging into the exact chronology of who played what and who joined when, and Tyler was beginning to wonder whether the detective sergeant was thinking of compiling a biography of the band. "If you can recall," said Tyler, his voice loaded with restrained frustration, "about half an hour ago I asked you to tell me about Adam Lane. I'd like to narrow that request down to what reasons anybody might have for killing him."

"I have no idea."

"Did Adam and Johnny fall out?"

Billy looked uncertain.

"After all, Adam left the band, didn't he?" pressed Tyler.

"I don't think they fell out particularly. I think it was that Adam wasn't showing the commitment Johnny wanted. Like I said, Johnny could be heavy, quite obsessive, and Adam wanted a laugh. He got serious about a girl though and I think he let Johnny down a few times, but I'm not sure."

Tyler pondered for a moment. "Johnny demanded total commitment to the band and Adam couldn't provide it, so he was replaced?"

"Something like that."

"You mentioned that Adam got serious about a girlfriend?"

"Yes. Daisy. Daisy Finch."

"Finch," said Tyler.

"Sister of Janine, Johnny's girlfriend."

"But Johnny had also been with Daisy, isn't that right?"

"That's right. Then Johnny met Janine and Daisy ended up with Adam."

"How cozy," said Tyler.

"Not really. The sisters didn't get on, as far as I know."

"Because Johnny had dumped Daisy for Janine, you mean?"

"I don't know about that. I don't know the details."

Tyler glanced at Mills. "Have you any idea, Billy, who might have wanted to kill Adam?"

Billy shook his head.

"Would Johnny Richards have any reason?"

"Johnny had been acting a bit strange, like I said. But I've never known him be violent. I can't imagine him killing anybody."

"Was he in any trouble? What about enemies?"

"I don't think he was in trouble, and I can't think of any enemies, particularly. He wound people up, it's how he was. He could be irritating and he liked getting his own way but I don't know why anybody would want to kill him."

"You think Johnny may be dead, then?" asked Tyler.

Steele suddenly looked flustered. "I ... don't know."

"We will leave it there for now," said Tyler. "Of course, we might need to talk to you again. And if anything occurs, please don't hesitate to get in touch straight away."

He handed Billy his card and watched him scurry across the car park towards an old grey Escort.

"We need to go back in time, Danny."

"Sir?"

"Five years to be precise. That old school bell is ringing again."

CHAPTER TEN

As Mills drove back along the A34, Tyler appeared lost in thought. Mills had learned not to intrude on the brooding silences, despite the fact that they were growing longer and more intense with each passing day.

He recalled last year's visits to River Trent High School. It had been the first case he had worked with Jim Tyler. The media had referred to it as the *Red Is The Colour* case. The headteacher at River Trent High, Miss Hayburn, proved herself more than helpful during the investigation, clearly impressing Tyler in more ways than one. They had even gone out for a few meals together, once the case had been closed. But he hadn't mentioned her for months now, and Mills wasn't aware that the DCI was seeing anybody else.

You need a good woman, thought Mills. *You need somebody.*

They headed towards the village of Penkhull, where Tyler lived on Penkhull Terrace, just below the main square; a spot that appeared to hold some appeal for the DCI, affording him views out across the city. Mills had visited the small terraced house a few times and always had the feeling that the place had a tentative quality, as though Tyler still hadn't decided to call it home, despite his seeming infatuation with the view from the front window.

On the far side of the square, Trent Lane wound its way down the hill, and close to the bottom of the lane was River Trent High. Mills pulled in through the school gates and parked up. He was getting out of the car when the senior detective asked him to wait.

Watching Tyler disappear through the front entrance, Mills couldn't help wondering ...

Miss Hayburn was at her desk when Tyler entered the office. He noted her look of surprise and how quickly it was replaced with an attitude of professionalism. "Good afternoon, DCI Tyler. How can I help you today?"

"May I?" he said, pointing at the vacant chair that faced her from across the desk.

"I take it that you are here on business."

He took a seat. "I'm looking for some background information on a number of your ex-students."

"That appears to be a habit of yours. Would this be connected to the case that you were investigating last year, by any chance?"

"No," he said. "This is a different case altogether. It is completely unrelated." He detected a slight raising of the eyebrows, but otherwise the headteacher retained an unwavering, somewhat neutral expression.

Noting the pile of paperwork on the headteacher's desk, he compared it with the mountain of files occupying his own. It was a wonder that public servants ever achieved anything. Statistics ruled the world, it seemed. Quotas and the collection of endless data.

His mind whirled on the question: Should I say something unrelated to the present enquiry? Clear the atmosphere that Miss Hayburn is doing her best to pretend doesn't exist? She did it well, though, he had to give her that. It was a master class in the art of concealing a certain chilled, clinical detachment within a contextual wrapping of commendable hospitality. Despite the absence of tea and biscuits.

He couldn't do it.

"I'm interested in three young men who left here five years ago. Johnny Richards, Adam Lane and Billy Steele. I believe they were in the same class."

"What kind of information are you looking for?"

"Anything that might prove ... useful."

"You couldn't be more specific?"

"Not at this stage."

"Detective Chief Inspector Tyler, I'm a busy woman running a busy school—"

"We are at an early stage in our investigations. I'm not ruling anything out and I'm not entirely certain what it is that I'm looking for. A young man who attended this school five years ago is dead. It was not a very pleasant death. His classmate is still missing. I'm fishing and I have to start by casting my line in somewhere."

He felt her scrutiny; her silent curiosity.

"I would like to talk to any of your staff who taught those young men. Their form teacher in their final year, perhaps. Also, if I could have the names of any of the other students from that class."

Miss Hayburn thought for a moment. "One dead, one missing. But you mentioned *three* young men."

"So I did."

The silence grew between them, but neither looked away.

"I can organise that for you," she said at last. "It shouldn't be a problem. Is there anything else?"

One of the things that had first struck him about Miss Hayburn, when he had met her in that same office last year, on a similar mission concerning a very different case, had been her warmth. He didn't feel it now.

"There is something else, actually," he said. "I should like to apologise for my behaviour. I treated you disgracefully. I am ashamed of myself."

She blinked, and for the first time sat back slightly from her desk. After a moment she said, "DCI Tyler, we both have demanding jobs, and work to be getting on with I'm sure. I will organise the information you have requested, and I will endeavour to assist you in any way that I can, in the course of your enquiries. But there is nothing else that we need to discuss."

He looked at her with sudden, intense longing ... and bitter regret.

"Thank you," he said. "I appreciate that."

The students had finished for the day and Ralph Linsell was sitting alone at his desk, in an empty classroom, marking work when the detectives announced their presence. Linsell, while soberly dressed in the professional trappings of jacket and tie, had something of an informal attitude that teetered on the edge of jaunty. A friendly type, easy to warm to, observed Mills. He wondered why the style back in his own day had to contrast so severely. Why back then austerity and a distinct lack of good humour had been the order of the day.

Miserable bastards.

The teacher remembered the three boys vividly, and his face lit up as he recalled them. Then the jauntiness faded. He has clearly read the papers and watched the news, thought Mills. His concern clear enough.

"Johnny Richards was a nice kid, though I have to say that he had his head stuck way up in the clouds. He might be sitting looking straight at you, giving the impression that he was listening to what you had to say, but half the time it was like there was nobody home. A dreamer was Johnny, an out and out dreamer. Like many creative types, I suppose. Certainly not the easiest child to teach."

Linsell knew that Johnny's father had played in bands and that Johnny had ambitions in music.

"It's all he ever talked about. It was the only time he fully came to life. He was an extremely likeable young man, and I think it's reasonable to say that he didn't have a bad bone in him. But it couldn't half be frustrating being his teacher." Linsell remembered Adam Lane as a close friend of Johnny's. "They would hang around together, and more often than not they were talking about music. They had to be if Johnny was involved. Johnny rarely talked about anything else."

"Two of a kind then?" asked Mills.

"Not really. Adam had, I would say, a lot more about him. He was music mad, the same as Johnny, that's fair to say. But he took an interest in the rest of the world too. He was extremely bright, and I think that he was sometimes rather amused by Johnny's single-mindedness."

"What about Billy Steele?" asked Mills.

Linsell frowned. "Has something happened to Billy?"

"Why do you ask that?" said Mills.

"Well," said Linsell," it's just that I know about Adam from the news, of course. And I understand that Johnny is still missing."

"We are not aware that anything has happened to Billy," said Tyler, cutting in impatiently. "If you could answer the questions, please."

Mills glanced at Tyler and then back at Linsell. The teacher was looking intrigued, but quickly picked up the threads. "Billy was, oh, I don't know—a bit of a misfit, an outsider. First reserve, you might say. What I mean is, in some ways he was the same as Johnny, except that Johnny had a natural charm about him, and so people tended to like him. He was lost in his own world a lot of the time, of course, but it was just, well, so hard not to like the guy. He could always make people laugh, could Johnny Richards. He loved the attention. Anything to be centre-stage. What you would call a natural performer, I suppose."

"But they didn't like Billy?" said Tyler.

Linsell thought before answering. Mills saw the impatience growing on Tyler's face. At last Linsell answered, and as he did so Mills watched the DCI lean forward.

"Billy was an interesting case. He lived at The Meadows, just across the road from here. He was in care. I don't know whether that had anything to do with it, but he always seemed to be on the outside of things and at the same time trying desperately to get in."

"Explain that," said Tyler.

"He didn't ever quite fit. He tried too hard, I would say. And that put people off. He could be very intense. I mean to say, so could Johnny Richards, though not quite in the same way. He was generally on the side-lines, was Billy. When he got the chance to move inside whatever was going on, it was like he didn't quite know how to handle it."

Mills watched as Tyler's eyes appeared to burn into the teacher. Linsell was beginning to look a little perturbed at the ferocity of the scrutiny that the DCI was lavishing upon him.

"You okay, sir?"

The DCI shot Mills a scathing look but held his tongue, returning his gaze to the teacher, demanding that he continue.

"I'm not sure there's much more I can tell you," said Linsell.

"Then I would like you to sum up the three of them," said Tyler.

Ralph Linsell looked to DS Mills, then back to Tyler. "I would say that above all Johnny was a dreamer. A music-obsessed dreamer. Naive but not stupid. Full of dreams though not arrogant or in any way boastful. He definitely had what you might call 'star-quality.' I could imagine him succeeding, as long as he was around the right people."

"And were Billy Steele and Adam Lane the right people?" asked Tyler.

"Billy was, what's the word—needful, perhaps? He had Johnny's intensity, but not his easiness and kind of weird charm. Billy seemed to run after Johnny and Adam, like he wanted their friendship. Like he, well, *needed* it. I'm not sure that it was always reciprocated. Billy was one of those who had to work at things. Nothing came easy."

"Imagine you were Johnny," said Tyler. "Who would you want in your band, Adam or Billy?"

Ralph Linsell laughed. "I'm not sure that I'm enough of an authority on music to answer that."

"All things being equal," said Tyler. "I'm not talking about the finer points of musicianship here."

Linsell gave the DCI an odd look, and glanced again at Mills, whose expression appeared to suggest that the teacher ought to humour the senior detective.

"I would say that Adam was a hugely talented young man. Creative and intelligent. I would say that Billy would be a loyal servant with a lot to offer. I remember Billy loving his music too, but he struck me as someone who was always struggling to come up to the mark. Trying to impress the other two—earn his membership into the club, you might say."

"Did they ever fall out, that you can recall?" asked Tyler.

"Not that I'm aware of. I don't recall any fallings out. You're not suggesting ..."

"Suggesting what, Mr Linsell?"

The teacher shrugged, his eyes darting between the two detectives. "I don't know. I mean, with Johnny Richards missing, and Adam Lane ..."

Tyler leaned forward, menacingly.
"Suggesting what, exactly?"

After thanking Ralph Linsell for his time, the detectives made their way back along the corridor.

"Bit harsh?" said Mills as they approached reception.

"If you mean what I think you mean," said Tyler, "then I have to disagree. I'm doing my job. That's all there is to it."

They walked in silence towards the office.

Miss Hayburn had gathered the requested information, leaving it in the care of the school secretaries. Tyler opened the sealed envelope and quickly studied the contents.

It contained a list of other class members from 1998, along with a few teachers, including the current head of music studies, Mrs Statham. Much to DCI Tyler's frustration Statham had left for the day.

Outside on the car park Mills suggested that one of the shift workers could do the rounds. He didn't imagine that there was much likelihood of anything significant emerging, and Tyler agreed.

"Still, in the absence of a break in the case, we do the leg work, put in the hours and hope that something adds up. So: what have we learned today?"

"Less than we'd hoped?" said Mills.

"I'm not so sure about that."

"I must have missed something."

"People change, but sometimes there are seeds. Clues as to what might happen further down the line. What might *develop*."

"Sir?"

"Johnny wanted to be king, but Adam was really on the throne all along, just not wearing the crown. Did you study Shakespeare?"

Mills looked blank.

"I'm thinking about Lady Macbeth."

"I'm not following, sir."

"And Billy ... the loyal servant?"

"What are you saying?"

"You're right, Danny. Not much. I've learned today though that I'm a bloody fool."

They headed north through the city to visit the first of two sisters.

CHAPTER ELEVEN

Daisy Finch lived in one of the blocks of flats overlooking Hanley Park. It was handy for accessing the Potteries Centre, in the middle of Hanley, where she worked at the *Curiosity Art Store*.

She had been on sick leave since hearing the news of her boyfriend's brutal murder. "I'm still under the doctor," she told the detectives as she invited them into the refined chaos of her small flat. "I still can't believe it. He only went out for a drink."

Daisy Finch was a softly spoken, slightly built young woman with a distinctly new-age taste in clothing and adornments. Mills wondered if he had ever seen so much clutter in such a confined space, or such a mish-mash of styles. And yet, oddly, the overall effect appeared almost contrived. As though there was an order to the random chaos, if you could untangle the logic.

This woman, he thought, has been doing a lot of grieving and very little sleeping these past days. She looked hollowed out. Amidst the more obvious signs of grief, he also perceived anger in those dark eyes.

Tyler had been about to raise the subject of Adam Lane when, unprompted, Daisy Finch launched into an account of her previous relationship with Richards.

"... He was cute, I suppose. And I fell for it. I had a thing for him, a big thing at the time, I admit it.

He was intense, driven, but kind of laid back and chilled at the same time, if you know what I mean. I was going steady with Johnny until last year. That's when my lovely sister moved in for the kill."

She rambled on for a few minutes about her doomed affair with Richards, before the words finally ran out. Looking down into her lap she appeared to fall into a sorrowful daze.

Tyler glanced at Mills and a silent understanding passed between the two detectives. This woman's boyfriend had died a violent death, a lonely and horrific death, and yet she had hardly mentioned him. All her talk so far had been only of Johnny Richards. Could be it's the medication she's on, thought Mills, trying to give her the benefit of the doubt.

Tyler coughed, and slowly the wheels began to turn again.

"I knew it was a mistake as soon as Janine laid eyes on him."

"Him?" asked Mills.

"Johnny."

"Of course," said Mills. "*Johnny*."

"I could see that she fancied him something rotten. I knew there was going to be trouble. Janine's like that, she always has been. If I ever had something, she wanted it, just because it's mine. But it was more than that. I could tell that she really wanted him."

She began sobbing, and again the detectives traded glances. Was this woman grieving for Adam Lane, or for the loss of her ex-boyfriend, Johnny Richards, to her sister Janine?

"Miss Finch," said Tyler, "I would appreciate it if you could tell us a little about Adam."

Blotting at her eyes with a tissue, she nodded. "I'm sorry."

"It's alright," said Mills. "Take your time." He could sense the DCI's impatience growing again like a fire at his side. In the heat of it Daisy Finch composed herself and went on. "Adam was twice what Johnny was," she said, wiping at her face intermittently with the sodden tissue. "Adam had real talent, he wasn't some poser like Johnny. Johnny didn't want Adam around anymore because he didn't want him stealing all the thunder. That's how superficial Johnny Richards was ..."

The anger in those dark eyes was in perfect harmony with the softly spoken savagery that appeared to underpin everything that she was saying.

She looked up and smiled. It was a lovely smile, thought Mills. He could see how it could easily break a young man's heart, or even the heart of a man not quite so young. If he didn't already have the blessing of the most gorgeous woman in the world to call his wife, and the mother of his two fine children ... Mills snapped out of his brief reverie in time to catch Daisy Finch say, "I haven't offered you a drink. Tea, coffee? I've got some wine open."

The DCI declined on behalf of both of them. "Do you have any idea why somebody would want to kill Adam?" he asked her.

"They killed the wrong one," she said, the smile evaporating into another fall of tears. "They should have killed Johnny."

"They?" said Tyler.

The crying stopped abruptly, and she looked up at the senior detective. "I don't know who would want to kill him," she said, "and I've no idea what's happened to Johnny. But he had it coming and Adam didn't, and that's all I know and all I care to know."

"Had it coming?" said Tyler. "Could you please explain what you mean by that?"

"Oh, I can explain, alright. He wanted it all his own way. He had to be the centre of everything. Always on his terms, everything, always about him. Like no-one else existed. It was always *Welcome to Johnny's world.* I tell you, that sister of mine didn't know what she was taking on, neither of them did."

"Are you saying," said Mills, "that there were people who would want to harm, or even kill, Johnny Richards?"

She laughed. "Are you kidding? There was a queue! He let people down, he messed them about, and he had it coming. That still doesn't mean I know what's happened to him, or what it has to do with Adam. But I tell you something for nothing: go and speak to my sister. Go and talk to Janine." She practically spat the name out. "There's not much that poisonous bitch doesn't get to know about. Johnny could be a pain in the arse long before he met my sister, but he got a lot worse once that *thing* got her claws in."

"You said that on the night he was killed, Adam had arranged to meet his friend Ian Taylor for a drink in the Norfolk Inn," said Tyler. "Did Adam tell you that was the arrangement?"

She blew her nose, but the already saturated tissue couldn't take this latest assault, and she looked in disgust at the mess in her hands. Mills searched around for a tissue, and failing to find one took out the handkerchief from his pocket, handing it to her. It was a long-standing tradition for Mills, keeping a fresh handkerchief. His mother had always insisted on it, and though his wife had long tried to convert him to disposable alternatives, he had made one of his few stands in a largely subservient domestic existence. Danny Mills had a drawer full of them at home and Daisy Finch was welcome to keep one from his considerable collection.

"Thank you," she said, blowing hard and wiping her fingers. "Sorry about that."

Tyler restated the question, his impatience startling both Finch and Mills.

"Adam said he was meeting Ian for a drink. They met up from time to time. I don't know what Adam saw in him, but they were in the same class at college. Adam thought he was a bit of a laugh though I couldn't see it myself."

The sourness was undisguised, and Mills wondered how many people in this life she had time for.

"Adam left your flat at what time exactly?" said Tyler.

"It was around half six, or just after that. I think he was supposed to be meeting in the pub around sevenish. I went out at the same time to meet the girls from work."

She had met with three work colleagues in the Dewdrop Arms at 6.45pm. They had stayed out late.

"Taylor seemed to think that the arrangement was for another night."

"That doesn't surprise me. He was probably stoned."

"Ian Taylor took drugs?"

"I suppose I shouldn't be saying things like that to you. I don't even know if he's still on the weed, but him and his girlfriend used to be. You probably couldn't tell the difference either way, the pair of them were so gormless. Total dipshits."

Tyler asked how credible she thought it was that Taylor had got the arrangement wrong.

"Like I say, him and his girlfriend did quite a bit of spliffing, if you know what I mean. So it doesn't surprise me that much. They were harmless, I suppose, and Adam found them good company. It takes all sorts."

"Did Adam do drugs?"

"Occasionally. Nothing heavy. He was a student, what do you expect? It's par for the course. Spliffs, mainly, a few mushrooms, that kind of thing. He didn't have a problem, or anything like that."

"And Johnny?"

"He liked a spliff. At one time he would give anything a try. I didn't like it myself. My parents were always stoned and it put me off."

"And your sister?" asked Tyler.

"To be fair, she didn't have a lot of time for drugs, for the same reason. So if Johnny stayed with her maybe he took it steady, at least when he was around her - which was most of the time, as far as I understand."

"Are you are suggesting it is not unlikely that Taylor got the arrangement wrong?"

"I think it's *very* likely. And it wouldn't be the first time."

"This happened before?"

"Once or twice, yes. Taylor was the sort who would let people down. I can't be doing with people like that, but you couldn't tell Adam. Like I say, he seemed to like the stupid prat's company, for some reason."

The tears were coming down again, spilling out of her in angry torrents. A question passed silently between the detectives.

Tyler asked if she would like a cup of tea making, and Mills made his way through to the kitchen, the DCI secretly wishing him the best of luck. It would take a detective to find the tea bags in a place like this, he thought, hoping that DS Mills would be up to the mission. He had every faith, though. When it came to refreshments, his sergeant had the nose and instincts of a bloodhound.

While Mills did his best in the kitchen, Tyler listened as Finch poured out some more of her tale.

" ... Once Johnny saw Janine had the hots for him - in about ten seconds of meeting her, and with me there, for fuck's-sake! - he was like a rat up a drain pipe.

"... Johnny just dropped me, like that, and that was the end of it with me and Janine. I've never had anything to do with her since. I hear about her from others, though, from time to time. And I know that she hasn't changed one little bit. Getting worse, if anything. I heard the band can't even get on and practice anymore without that bitch sticking her nose in.

"... And that's how I got to know Adam. They'd started up the band and I would go and watch them and have a drink with them afterwards. That's when Johnny started to change. He always liked attention, but as soon as the band got going properly, getting a few punters in, it was like a switch. Straight away it was like he had to be at the centre of everything, controlling everything, getting paranoid about everything. Only little things at first, but it was there, and I could see it.

"... Adam was always dead chilled. I think he found some of Johnny's paranoia amusing, at least he did to begin with. They were having fun and it was kind of diluted, almost cute. At that time Johnny was *so* cute. But it was changing.

"... Once Johnny fell in with Janine, everything went up through the gears. I sort of copped off with Adam on the rebound. I think he felt sorry for me at first, and I wasn't sure anything would come of it, or that it was the right thing. I always thought the likes of Adam were too clever for the likes of me. But then we started to hit it off and I think in the end he really loved me ..."

Her eyes were filling again and the anger towards Johnny Richards seemed to fall away, replaced by a raw grief that quickly filled the room. Tyler wondered how the search for tea bags was going, and whether reinforcements might have to be deployed to assist the struggling DS.

Then Mills emerged miraculously with a tray of refreshments. "Sorry for the delay," he said. "I popped out for some fresh milk. I got some tea bags and biscuits while I was there."

"That bitch sister of mine," said Finch, apparently oblivious to Mills' entrance, "she finished them off, one way or another. They blamed me, of course. They said that Adam wasn't committed to the band anymore because all he cared about was his new girlfriend. But it wasn't like that. Adam could see how Johnny was changing and it would only have been a matter of time."

"Matter of time?" said Tyler.

"Before Adam moved on. But Janine pushed it, she wouldn't let up."

While Mills served up the tea and biscuits, Tyler asked Finch to explain in more detail what she meant. She appeared to relish the opportunity. "Adam would tell me how Janine started attending rehearsals, and getting in the way. She was always sticking her oar in, that fat arse of hers never knew any boundaries. Always suggesting things as though she knew what she was talking about.

"Adam tried to tell Johnny that it wasn't helpful, Janine being there all the time. At first he listened and she stopped turning up. But then she started again, and when Adam tried to say anything, Johnny would lose it."

"Lose it?" asked Mills, crunching hard on a chocolate biscuit, as though announcing that the buffet was now officially open.

"He was getting less tolerant. He wanted it all on his own terms and he wanted Adam to do as he was told. Just like Janine used to be with me: everything on her terms. They were made for each other, I tell you."

"Did he ever become violent?" asked Tyler.

"That wasn't his style. If someone had raised their voice back at him, he would have run home to Mummy."

"You don't imagine that he would have been capable of murder, then?"

"Who knows what anybody is really capable of, at the end of the day. I don't know, I can't say, can I? I only know that he wasn't violent towards me, or to anybody else that I know of. I never heard any different from anyone, in fairness."

Her expression tightened. "I don't know who would do such a thing. I'm not pointing any fingers, but I wouldn't trust those two as far as I could throw them. *Him* and my sister. I just think it's a bit of a coincidence, that's all."

"Coincidence?"

"Adam's killed and *he* goes missing. Too convenient, that's all I'm saying."

Tyler observed for a few moments as anger and grief appeared to fight the battle for Daisy Finch. When it seemed that she didn't have anything else to add, he nodded to Mills and stood up to leave.

"Johnny wanted all the glory," said Finch, "and *she* wanted him to have all the glory so that she could be seen as the fucking queen. I'm not just saying this, but Adam was the one with the genuine talent, and Johnny knew it. He was scared of it, and my sister fed all the crap that was already inside him and she broke them apart."

Finch stood up. "Like I said, she's the one you need to be talking to. If anybody knows anything about what happened to Johnny Richards, she does.

I'd put my life on it. And she might even know more than that."

"Are you suggesting," said Tyler, "that your sister knows who killed Adam? Or that she might have had a hand in his death?"

"I'm not saying anything. I'm not accusing her of anything because I don't know and I can't prove it. But I think you should go and talk to her, and you can pass on my best fucking wishes while you're there."

Outside the flats Mills said, "So, what do you make of all that, then?"

"What do *you* make of it?" replied Tyler.

"I'm curious."

"About anything in particular? No, allow me: you're thinking that an intelligent young man like Adam Lane must have had a reason to allow a gormless druggie like Taylor to keep letting him down."

"Well, the thought did occur."

"And then you thought, wouldn't it be convenient for Lane to have an excuse like Ian Taylor and his girlfriend whenever he wanted to go out and ... see someone else?"

"Something along those lines."

"Worth bearing in mind, no doubt. Anything else?"

"Well," said Mills. "Be interesting to know who that someone else might be."

"Sarcasm becomes you. But there's no place for it on the force."

"That's a pity, sir."

"If Adam Lane left the flat around six thirty, or soon after, Johnny Richards would have struggled to kill him and get to rehearsal for seven thirty. Though it's not out of the question. Check with the Liverpool Road studios that all of the band were on time, if that's possible."

"Will do."

"What do you make of Daisy Finch?"

"I don't know what to make of her. She seems to still hold a candle for Richards, but at the same time wants to see him pay for ditching her. This Janine sounds like a bit of a character, wouldn't you say?"

Jim Tyler walked on, and it wasn't until the two of them were in the car that he answered the question. "In my experience, there are generally two sides to a story. So, let's see what the other side has to say, shall we?"

Mills was about to drive off when Tyler said, "Oh, by the way, I forgot to mention: good work with those biscuits. You don't take any prisoners."

CHAPTER TWELVE

Mills drove north to Tunstall and parked outside the flats on Summerbank Road. He'd not visited that part of the city in quite a while, but still had fond memories of frequenting a couple of the pubs on the high street. He'd known a few friends up that way, young coppers who'd done alright for themselves. Carefree days, according to memory. Days before responsibilities and country living had eaten into what was left at the end of each month.

Mills wondered that the flats hadn't yet met with the bulldozers, and the thought brought with it an instant pang of guilt. After all, he had a job, and a good one; a family he loved dearly, a loving wife and two children and a house with a garden and still enough left over to get him to the Brittania Stadium to watch his beloved Stoke City play whenever his shifts allowed.

He vowed to count his blessings on a more regular basis. At the same time he wondered how many times he had made that same vow, and what made it so damned difficult to carry out.

Catching sight of the morose, downcast features of Jim Tyler as the two of them got out of the vehicle, he doubled his vow. Then he said a silent prayer for the happiness and well-being of his colleague.

Janine Finch looked almost nothing like her sister. Perhaps, to the trained eye, there was a vague similarity residing in the high cheek bones and in the strong curve of the mouth. For Danny Mills, the jury was out. Janine was bigger, in some way harder, and the new-age whimsy that struggled but just about held sway in her sister was replaced here with an uncompromising skin-head chic.

The seeming chaos of her sister's flat was replicated, though missing was the roller-coaster of emotional outpouring, along with the superficial polish. Here the chaos seemed somehow more genuine, thought Mills. More *chaotic.*

Janine Finch took a seat and invited the two officers to do the same. Mills took care of the formalities, outlining why they were there before asking her to tell them anything she could about the death of Adam Lane and the disappearance of Johnny Richards.

She spoke in a calm, measured voice, betraying an absence of fear, anger or grief that was in itself, thought Mills, rather disturbing. Throughout she maintained eye contact with both detectives, steady and in control, clearly giving thought to every sentence that she uttered. She hadn't attended the last band rehearsal because she had been working. She worked at the Thirteen club and there had been a gig on that night. That's why the band had used the Liverpool Road studios. More often than not these days they practiced in the rehearsal room at the club. She returned home late and both she and Johnny were tired. Johnny had been rehearsing with the band, making final preparations for the gig at the Thirteen.

He was working at the factory the following morning and she heard him leave the flat early, and once it became clear that he was missing of course the thought that something might have happened to him had kicked in.

Tyler didn't appear convinced. Her aura of calmness seemed to contradict any suggestion of fear of anything, and the DCI made the walls of the flat contract by saying exactly that.

Without raising her voice, or batting an eye, she looked straight at Tyler, filling the air instantly with menace. Mills was dearly wishing for another packet of biscuits to demolish and a mug of tea to wash them down with.

Tyler didn't budge. The two of them looked like caged tigers. Then Finch sat back and the walls expanded back to their original, meagre dimensions. "Would you prefer it," she said, "if I ran around like a headless chicken? What would that achieve? Do you imagine that would help you find Johnny?"

"Do you know of anyone who might wish to harm Johnny?" asked Tyler.

"How long have you got?"

"As long as you need."

"Okay, then let me tell you: there are a lot of people out there wishing Johnny harm."

"Why do you imagine that?" asked Tyler.

"I don't imagine anything. It's how it is. Jealousy, envy, call it what you like."

"Why would people be envious?"

"Are you kidding? Johnny has everything. He has the world at his feet. Who wouldn't be envious of that?"

"Everything?" said Tyler.

"Johnny is a star. Don't you listen to the radio, or read the papers?"

"Seldom, it's true."

"He's the biggest thing that will ever happen to this city. Johnny's waiting to be recognised by an entire planet. He's a genius, but more than that, so much more."

"More than a genius?"

"A genius with charisma, style, and vision. Even Johnny Depp must look in the mirror some days and wish he looked more like my Johnny."

"Mr Depp is familiar with *your Johnny*, Miss Finch?"

Mills looked on, feeling the bristling heat.

"Johnny, *my* Johnny, is made for the big time. He's on his way, and every no-hoper in this city wants to see him fail and most of them would stop at nothing to make that happen."

"Could you give me any names, Ms Finch?"

"Daisy."

Tyler frowned.

Janine Finch smiled, and the resemblance to her sister filled up the small room, both detectives catching it. "You've met my sister?" she said, as though acknowledging that the extent of their likeness had been recognised.

The DCI confirmed that they had already spoken to Daisy.

"What did she have to say?"

"I'm more interested," said Tyler, "in what you have to say."

"I get it."

"What do you get?"

"Well, Daisy has no doubt laid a lot of things at my door."

The detectives waited while Finch eyed both of them carefully. "The truth is, my sister is the reason they fell out. She broke them apart because she wanted Adam calling the shots. And that was never going to happen. He couldn't have cared less, but my sister still wanted him to be top dog. Because that way she gets one over on me.

"With Daisy—it's all about Daisy, and it always has been, as far back as you like. She grinds you down. And so, in the end, he pandered to her, like everyone always does. Johnny had a lucky escape. I saved him from that bitch, but Adam wasn't so fortunate. Her stupid games were the end of Adam and Johnny."

"Are your parents still around?" asked Tyler.

"What have they got to do with anything? Couple of smack heads, we don't owe them shit! We were passed around from pillar to post. You're thinking that makes us damaged goods, but you'd only be *half* right."

"Do you think," said Tyler, "that Adam and Johnny had a fight, and Adam—"

"Got killed and Johnny did a runner?" She shook her head. "He would never hurt a fly. You can look as hard as you like, speak to everyone who ever knew him, and you won't find a single example of that. People tried to hurt my Johnny, alright, but he let his talent do the talking. He expressed himself through his music, he had no time for fighting."

"Do you have any thoughts on who might have been responsible for the death of Adam Lane?"

"I haven't a clue. But you can cross Johnny off your list."

"When Adam left the band," said Mills, "was it by mutual consent?"

The woman's features narrowed into a hard grin that Mills found grotesque. A grin laced with malice, dripping with concealed poison. He felt a shiver trace his spine.

"Adam wasn't stupid. He just got stupid over my sister, like they all do, for some reason. Johnny liked Adam being in the band because Adam was a decent guitar player. But it was Daisy poking her face in and wanting him taking over. I don't know why they listen to her, but that's men for you. If it wasn't for my sister, Adam would still be in the band."

"But then Billy Steele wouldn't," said Tyler.

"And that's another story."

"Please tell me about it," said Tyler.

"There's not much to tell. Billy had been hanging around for years hoping to get a sniff of the action. When Adam left he was in like a shot."

"You don't approve?"

"Adam was basically a guy who met the wrong woman, and listened to the crap she came out with. Billy didn't need a woman to do that, he had enough crap of his own. He wanted to take over from the start. I could see it, plain as day. He bided his time, but he didn't fool me. I kept warning Johnny."

"Warning him?"

"Billy was never interested in Johnny's music, you could tell that. But he knew Johnny was a front man with the charisma to make it. Billy wanted all his own songs on that EP. Johnny was even thinking of allowing him two songs just so he'd shut the fuck up. I told him that if he did that, Billy would keep wanting more until in the end it was Billy's band. He's an ego-maniac, and he wants everything his own way."

"Do you think that Billy would harm Johnny if he didn't get his own way?" asked Tyler.

"Do I think that he's done something to Johnny? In a word, yes, I do. I think he's dangerous."

"You know him well?"

"I've seen what he's like around Johnny. I recognise when someone's got a chip on his shoulder. He was twisted from the beginning."

"In what way?"

"It's like he was resentful of everyone and everything. Like the world owed him something."

"Perhaps it did," said Tyler. He watched the seething anger building in her, and wondered how much it would take for him to light the fuse and watch her explode. "You're aware of Billy Steele's background?"

"Do you mean, do I know he was in care? That's got nothing to do with anything. We had a rough time with our shit parents, but you can't keep making excuses all your life. It's not an ace card."

She looked about to say something more, but then paused. As though she had recognised the game and pulled out at the last moment. The hint of a smile brushed her lips, but didn't linger. "I'm not a psychiatrist," she said. "But from what I've seen of him, I'm telling you this: he would stop at nothing to get what he wants. For my money, he hates having to listen to Johnny's voice coming out of the radio. It should be him ... but it isn't. They are playing one of my man's songs and not that piece of crap that he came up with."

"Are you suggesting that he killed Johnny?"

"I wouldn't put it past him."

"Because he wanted more of his songs on the EP and because one of Johnny's songs is getting the air play?"

"You can mock me, *Inspector*. But you don't know Billy. You don't know what he's capable of."

"And what about Adam?"

"How do you mean?"

"Do you think that may have killed Adam too?"

"Are you taking the piss?"

"I'm asking you a question."

The room fell silent. The three occupants looked at each other, waiting to see who would make the next move. At last Finch broke the deadlock. "In the end that's all it comes down to, isn't it?"

"What's that?" asked Tyler.

"You don't really care what's happened to Johnny, nobody does. All anybody cares about is who killed Adam Lane."

In the car, heading back to Hanley Police Station, Tyler said, "So that concludes the business of the Finch sisters for one day. Now we have heard from both sides, what do we make of it all?"

"I'm glad my son is too young to take an interest," said Mills.

Tyler issued a dark, sardonic laugh. "At school they made us read Shakespeare. Macbeth. I remember being scared of Lady Macbeth, I still am."

"They thought we were all too stupid for Shakespeare," said Mills. "When we were done with the colouring books they pointed us at the factory gates."

Tyler looked at Mills, and all the edge, the raging gloom, was swept away by a generous, compassionate smile.

"Sir?" said Mills, unnerved by the sudden transformation.

"What we have here," said Tyler, "is two for the price of one."

"Is that a quote from Mr Shakespeare?" said Mills.

CHAPTER THIRTEEN

The next morning Tyler made the journey to River Trent High school alone, while Mills organised shift workers to contact as many classmates as they could find. Pathology were completing their report and Mills was hopeful that he would have something to show the DCI imminently.

Making himself a drink back at Cedar Lane Mills found himself thinking again about his troubled colleague. The man was a cross between an iceberg and a volcano, hot and cold, hidden depths and often on the cusp of an eruption. He'd never met, let alone worked, with anyone quite like him before. Maybe there wasn't room for two such encounters in a single lifetime.

Is the crisis looming or passing?

It was hard to tell. No two days were the same in his company. He was like the weather of late, changing by the hour and impossible to predict.

They had all been under pressure lately, Mills was aware of that, and Jim Tyler was only human. The further up the chain the worse the pressure got, that was the general rule. Across the city the work was relentless and the staffing situation verging on pathetic. Everybody was stressed most of the time, nothing unusual there, and it was doubtful that it would be getting better anytime soon.

Still, the DCI was a complex individual. He carried a lot of baggage and Mills wished that he would share some of it out once in a while. You had to choose your moment carefully, though, when you crossed that line and attempted to enter the forbidden zone. Most of the man was marked 'private' and it took a brave soul to venture there.

Mills finished his drink and pressed on.

Tyler made his way into River Trent High. The Head of Music, Mrs Statham, had a free period that morning and she had agreed to have a chat with the detective.

The music classroom contained a few notable clues as to its purpose: an upright piano, a couple of acoustic guitars, a few items of percussion, a stereo system. Mrs Statham was sitting behind a desk marking homework when Tyler took a seat opposite.

"Discovered any young Mozarts?" he asked her.

The woman, looking to be in her late thirties, beamed a warm smile across the desk.

"A glut of aspiring Gallaghers, perhaps. But I will keep a close eye and let you know."

Tyler wondered whether he might have developed more of an ear for music in the company of a teacher like Mrs Statham. The dragons he recalled from his youth had all seemed to want to make the subject as dull as ditch water, with a smack across any 'tone-deaf' ears as the only encouragement. Boys at his school hadn't dared show too much interest in the formal study of music for fear of reprisals on the playground for being gay. Happy days.

Despite her warmth, Mrs Statham was clearly a busy woman, and her manner suggested that she would prefer to get straight down to business. Tyler was happy to oblige, beginning by asking for recollections of three of her keenest students from five years ago. The teacher seemed to be more astute than her colleague, Mr Linsell, he thought. A sharper eye and an undimmed memory for detail.

"I don't think I ever encountered three keener musicians than Adam, Johnny and Billy. They didn't give a damn about the curriculum, of course. But they lived and breathed music."

Johnny had been the dreamer, Adam displaying considerable natural talent, while Billy worked harder than anybody else she had ever encountered in her entire teaching career. "Billy had to work to keep up. He was never a natural, like Adam. But he was very competitive. In his own way."

"How do you mean?"

"He liked to keep that part hidden, for some reason. Fear of failure, possibly, I don't know. It was there, though. I recognised it early on.

"Adam, on the other hand, didn't seem to need to be competitive. That young man could get a tune out of a pair of old socks! He was so gifted, and it always seemed effortless with him. I thought Adam might do very well one day, though I was never certain which direction his talent might take."

Tyler asked her to elaborate and Mrs Statham thought for a moment.

"Take Johnny," she said. "Head in the clouds, dreaming of becoming a rock and roll star. Learning from his father how to play guitar, listening to music obsessively and talking about it to the exclusion of just about everything else. Perhaps not quite the talent that he imagined himself to have been born with, but with a certain charisma that I always thought might carry him somewhere.

"Adam, on the other hand, shone at everything he did, and it was no big deal to him. He picked things up so quickly, and the only thing he lacked was that rather odd charisma that Johnny had. I know that they played in a band together, after leaving school, and I wondered if they weren't a perfect fit. Complementing each other's strengths. But where Johnny was single-minded to the point of being, well, obsessive - a one-trick pony, you could say - Adam seemed to me to be a young man who might, well, keep his options open."

"And Billy?" asked Tyler.

"Billy was always on the outside, struggling to get in. I keep my ear fairly close to the ground, and I heard that he had replaced Adam in the band. I bought a copy of the record they brought out, and I actually think it's very good."

"I wonder why Adam might have left the band," said Tyler. He watched Mrs Statham as she tried to articulate what was going through her mind.

"When I first heard that he had left, my first impression was that it was simply a matter of life taking over. I knew that he had gone to university. And you know how it is, after a few years of playing local gigs and not particularly getting anywhere - I could imagine it being fun to Adam, but not the be all and end all.

"Johnny could be so uncompromising. I sometimes wondered if that might one day be his undoing. I could see them falling out, though it's always easy to be wise after the event." She smiled again, and Tyler felt the warm empathy that the woman generated. "Or maybe it was the usual, you know, 'artistic differences'. Isn't that what musicians usually say when egos begin to clash?"

"I'm sure that I wouldn't know," said Tyler.

"I wondered how Billy would get on, trying to live up to Adam. A tough act to follow, I imagine. But then it occurred that there's generally only room for one leader, and neither Adam nor Johnny were the type to let anybody else take over. I took quite an interest when the record came out, and noticed that most of the compositions were Johnny's. I thought to myself: Johnny Richards has got just what he needs."

"Meaning?"

"Meaning someone who would work his fingers to the bone, but not get in the way of Johnny's ego. I can't imagine Adam would have remained in a band changing its name to *Johnny and the Swamp Seeds*, for instance." She shook her head and laughed. "I mean to say!"

"You think Billy's the type to take a back seat, do as he's told?"

Mrs Statham's fingers drummed lightly on the desk. "No," she said finally. "Not when I heard the record, funnily enough." She appeared to agonise. "You do ask difficult questions."

"I apologise," said Tyler. "It's a bad habit of mine."

"I think Billy had a lot of ambition, as I have suggested. The one song credited to him, *Blue Murder,* is the best of the lot, in my opinion. But to my mind you can hear that Johnny's heart isn't in it. A slightly better arrangement and a more passionate vocal performance from Johnny and I could see that song being a hit. It's so good. Billy has developed his craft as a songwriter, and I'm rather impressed."

"But?"

"I'm reading between the lines - or should that be listening between the notes - and I may be a long way out of line."

"Go on," said Tyler.

"The song that's getting the airplay isn't bad, it's reasonably well put together, with a good arrangement and I would have to say a decent vocal. Johnny's voice has actually matured quite a bit, I think he must have put in a lot of effort - but you hear a lot of stuff like it, and I don't think it's all that special. Billy's song is rather special, in my opinion; I think he's really got something. But it's like the band, or at least Johnny, threw it away."

"Why do you imagine Johnny would do that, Mrs Statham?"

"Another good question. I really don't know. I think that song has so much potential, and to me it smacks rather of letting Billy have his token contribution, but being careful not to give him too much of a platform. When I hear that record, well, I hear trouble brewing.

"But, again, that's me being wise after the event. Reading too much into things. I mean, what do I know, really?" Tyler waited for her to say more.

"After all, bands can be notorious, didn't you know? Crucibles of creative angst and clashing egos." She laughed.

"Do you think," said Tyler, "that any of this might be relevant to what happened to Adam Lane, or to the disappearance of Johnny Richards?"

"Now that *is* a question," said the teacher. "If you've come here today to ask me if I think, five years or so ago, that I saw the seeds of future murder, my answer would be categorically 'no.'

"Five years ago I saw three young men who loved music. Two great friends and one outsider, possibly. From what I saw then, I don't for one moment imagine that Billy or Johnny killed Adam or that Billy had reason to hurt Johnny. But five years is a long time. Anything might have happened, I suppose. And if Billy wants a bigger slice of the pie, he could form his own band and find a better singer than Johnny Richards.

"There's a lot of talent out there. No, I don't look back and see a killer amongst them. I'm sorry to disappoint you."

"I see," said Tyler, trying not to look disappointed. "And there was me thinking that you were about to wind up the entire case."

"Sorry."

"But you must have your own ideas on what happened."

"Maybe. But that's all they are, ideas. You don't want to hear a music teacher's speculations, I'm sure you must be far too busy for that."

"I would," said Tyler, "very much value your thoughts, even if they are what you call 'speculations.' What you have told me is very insightful. I would be grateful to hear anything you have to say."

Mrs Statham looked flattered. "Okay, for what it's worth, I would imagine that there will have been a lot of tension in that band, given the people involved. But on the basis of the individuals as I knew them, nothing suggests that any of them might be capable of killing anybody. But people change, and circumstances arise."

"You're saying that music alone is insufficient motive for murder?"

"Oh, I don't know about that. I can think of a few acts I wouldn't mind killing off myself. Fame and fortune can be powerful motivators. I think people kill for power, greed, revenge, or maybe to hide something. Or because they are in the grip of something, or somebody. Because they want something, badly. You see, in my spare time I also read detective novels."

"It shows," said Tyler.

"I'm not certain how to take that remark."

"Take it as a compliment. You have been most helpful," he said, standing up and shaking the teacher's hand.

"Really? Well, I wish you luck. I hope you find Johnny and whoever killed Adam. Whatever's happened, it's a tragedy all round."

Tyler made his way through the corridors, a phrase echoing ... *because they are in the grip of something, or somebody* ... and he couldn't help but conjure the images of Daisy and Janine Finch.

Passing the headteacher's office he thought about knocking. *Why? To apologise again and beg for a second chance? To run something past her that I can't quite bring in to focus myself?*

Heading out into the fresh air he was surprised to find Miss Hayburn hurrying towards the building. Tyler stopped in his tracks, almost glued to the spot. The two of them traded nods and polite smiles, and after she had asked him if he had found his visit helpful, he asked if she might spare him five minutes of her time.

Eyeing him carefully, and then checking her watch, she asked him to call back in ten minutes.

Returning to his car Tyler rang DS Mills. There ought to be something back from Pathology by now.

As it turned out there was, though it didn't tell them much that they didn't already know. Mills had been about to ring. It amounted to this:

Adam Lane had been struck on the head, a single blow from a blunt object. The head trauma had been substantial but the young man had drowned. There were no DNA traces from the assailant, no evidence suggesting that there had been a struggle prior to the blow that had led to Lane's death in the water.

The time of death was likely consistent with the statement from Daisy Finch: that Adam Lane had left her flat just after 6.30pm, making his way directly to the canal side to meet a friend, Lane meeting his assailant instead, ultimately resulting in his death. If the assailant had been Richards, or any other member of the band, it would have been a tight schedule, as all had been present and correct at the Liverpool Road studios in Stoke by 7.30pm at the latest. They had all signed in promptly.

Not impossible, but nevertheless tight.

As for Janine Finch, she had arrived at the Thirteen club in Hanley at 6pm and had not left until late.

Tyler told Danny Mills that he would be coming back to the station in a few minutes. Ending the call, he felt the weight suddenly descending. He was in the playground again, a boy punching another boy so hard in the face that the recipient went down and stayed down. He had seen this bully for a thousand days, and taken more than a few kicks of his own. It had chipped away but it had never gone anywhere. But this latest brutality had fired a sense of outrage that the young Jim Tyler had not stopped to question.

Without hesitation, breaking free of the shock of what he had witnessed, he ran at the bully, fists flailing, connecting with a couple of good ones even as a squadron of grown-ups finally appeared out of nowhere, swarming over the scene and dragging him away.

Back in the 1970s the police were rarely involved, unless an incident had proven fatal. The recipient of the bully's unprovoked attack had sustained superficial bruising, as it turned out, the blow catching him off balance but failing to inflict any real damage. There was no thank you for the hero Jim Tyler that day, just a sworn enemy for the rest of his school days, and his card marked by the entire teaching staff.

Give a dog a bad name.

The school dealt with the matter in its own way, and Tyler got the worst of it, with more following down the line. The school would not tolerate the actions of a self-appointed hero. An increasingly angry and belligerent one. All those years ago he had been dragged, unceremoniously, to the headteacher's office, to take the consequences of his actions in customary fashion, the ritual of the day. And now, three decades on, he made the journey under his own steam.

He knocked on the door and Miss Hayburn called him in.

Tyler sat across from her, dimly aware that she was asking if he was alright. Some drinks arrived and as he clutched the mug of tea she asked him again.

Has the ice thawed? he wondered. Her eyes looked filled with something that he recognised from another lifetime.

"The teaching staff here," he said, "are nothing short of brilliant."

"Well, thank you," said Miss Hayburn, looking somewhat surprised and at the same time concerned. "We do our best."

He took a sip of hot tea, and as the warmth touched his lips he felt the first trickle of tears gently bathing his cheeks. For the third time she asked if he was alright. Her words appeared to bring him round, as though smelling salts had been gently placed beneath his nostrils.

"Do you think," she said, "that you may need to talk to someone?"

He looked at her, and in that moment of hesitation heard her say, "Professionally, I mean."

CHAPTER FOURTEEN

Tyler had requested that Rob Jones, George Atkins and Billy Steele come in for a chat, and Mills confirmed that all three were waiting downstairs. The two detectives were about to go down when Tyler's office phone rang. Chief Superintendent Berkins wanted a word.

Now.

"I can take one of the team down with me, if that would help, sir," said Mills. Tyler shook his head. "It will be something and nothing. Give me five minutes."

Berkins invited Tyler to take a seat, and then he came straight to the point. "In a nutshell, Jim, I'm concerned for your well-being."

"You really shouldn't be," said Tyler. "I will start back on the cod liver oil if you insist."

Berkins didn't smile. "You are a good officer, Jim. But lately, well, I wonder if some of your *issues* have re-surfaced." When Tyler passed up the unspoken invitation to answer the unasked question, Berkins filled the silence. "I'm recommending that you see one of our staff counsellors."

"Recommending?"

"Okay, I'm insisting on it. An appointment has been made for first thing tomorrow morning. I expect you to attend, understood?"

As the detectives headed down towards the interview rooms, Mills asked if everything was alright. Tyler looked hard at DS Mills. "It seems that people have my best interests at heart."

"I'm very pleased to hear that, sir."

"Are you one of them, Danny?"

"I don't know what you mean."

"You haven't been chatting to our CS Berkins, then?"

"I haven't, personally. But I'm not surprised that others might have. It's not a conspiracy against you, Jim. You are deeply respected around here."

"That wasn't always the case."

"It is now!"

Tyler looked startled at the strength of feeling expressed by his colleague, and somewhat surprised. He smiled at Mills. "I do appreciate your concern."

"Don't mention it. Are you booked in?"

"Word travels fast around these parts."

"Berkins wants to get his money's worth out of the contract with this new counselling agency. It's the cheapest way to deal with the stress levels."

"I'm merely an economic statistic?"

"Better than taking it personally."

"Thank you for that, Danny."

"All part of the service. And anyway, I'm told that she's a bit of a looker."

Tyler and Mills spent a largely fruitless hour talking with George Atkins and Rob Jones, bassist and drummer respectively. Neither seemed able to pour any new light on the situation. They had joined the band around the same time and seemed equally oblivious to any politics involved; wanting to play music and excited that the band was taking off appeared to sum them both up fairly comprehensively. Neither had noticed anything unusual or odd about Johnny or Billy at the band's last rehearsal. Both confirmed that the session got underway promptly, with everyone arriving keen and eager and in time for a 7.30pm start. They had all been buzzing and there had been a great atmosphere, with everybody looking forward to the gig the following evening. There had been nothing to arouse anybody's suspicions.

Towards the end of the interview with Rob Jones, Mills asked about tensions between the other band members, including Adam Lane.

"I didn't really get to know Adam," said Jones. "He was a good player, better than Billy, to be honest. I don't really know why he left. Maybe it was his uni work, but I'm not sure about that.

"I wouldn't say that Johnny and Billy always hit it off, though. I think Billy was expecting to get more of his songs in the set. Maybe that was the problem. But Johnny wanted to be the main songwriter and he generally has the final say."

"Johnny was always the main man?"

"He certainly was after Adam left. I always thought he had something, you know, like charisma, or whatever. A terrific voice, too, though some of the material didn't really suit him. He was still finding his niche, honing his style, whatever you want to call it. It was definitely coming."

Tyler asked the drummer about Johnny's girlfriend attending band rehearsals.

"It was usually a bit tense when Janine came along," said Jones. "I think she was protective of Johnny's position. It was a bit weird, really, like she thought Billy was a threat or something."

"Who wrote the hit?" asked Mills.

"You mean *All Colours Are Blue*? Johnny, I think. We already had it before Adam left, so it definitely wasn't one of Billy's."

The bass player, George Atkins, told a similar tale. When Mills asked him about Billy, he said, "He wanted to get more of his own songs in, but the harder he pressed for that the more dictatorial Johnny was getting. And later on his girlfriend was always around. It was like she was making sure that Billy didn't take over."

Mills asked Atkins who wrote *All Colours Are Blue*.

"It wasn't Billy. I reckon it was one of Johnny's. Adam had written a few, not many, but I'm not sure. I think Billy was getting a rough deal, to be honest."

"Can you explain that?" said Tyler.

"Me and Rob thought some of Billy's stuff was good. Better than Johnny's, actually. His song on the EP was a cracker. *Blue Murder*. We all liked it, but I don't think Johnny did it any favours."

"You didn't think *All Colours* was so great then?" asked Mills.

"It's a decent song, I'm not saying it isn't. It's perfect for Johnny. That's the point, I reckon."

"What do you mean by that?" asked Tyler.

"Well," said Atkins, "I think it suited Johnny's voice, and it seemed to mean something to him, you could tell. He really put his heart and soul into it. It's the vocal that makes it. Johnny is at his absolute best on that song. Funny thing, though."

"What's funny?" asked Tyler.

"After Adam left we dropped the song for a while."

"Did Johnny say why that was?"

"Not really. When Rob and I asked about it, Johnny got uptight. He said it needed a bit of working on, and that he might come back to it. But with Billy and Johnny constantly trying to outdo each other, we always had plenty of new stuff to try out. Then one day Johnny put the song back in the set, but it was the same version we'd always done, more or less."

George Atkins shrugged his shoulders, apparently at a loss as to what had caused Johnny's change of heart over the song.

Mills asked both musicians in turn about contracts, but neither seemed to have an inkling. They were happy to have a recording under their belts, and one that was getting airplay. They had been swept along in the excitement of being in a band that was building up a following and gaining some interest, and everything else seemed secondary.

After the interviews had been concluded, the detectives walked up to the CID office.

"What do you make of it?" asked Mills.

"I'm curious about that song," said Tyler. "Adam Lane leaves the band and *All Colours* is dropped, and then later restored as Johnny Richard's finest hour. But I can hear Berkins pulling the bones out of my neck for quibbling over who wrote a bloody pop song!"

"You don't think either of those two killed Lane and abducted or killed Richards?" asked Mills.

"Do you?"

"I think we have a couple of serial killers there, sir. It's as clear as the moustache on Berkins' face. I think they might have been hired by the council to keep the city's natural talent under control and I don't suppose they'll stop until they've wiped out the entire music industry."

"For any particular purpose?"

"Because they can, sir. *Because they can.*"

"I see. Detective Sergeant Mills?"

"Sir?"

"Your diabolical Potteries sense of humour may be all that's keeping me going."

"We do our best, sir. Sometimes against the odds."

CHAPTER FIFTEEN

Mills observed that where George Atkins and Rob Jones had appeared borderline bored in the interviews, Billy Steele had been like the proverbial cat on hot bricks. Mills asked him about contracts and songwriting credits and Steele was clearly beating around the bush. Noting that his senior colleague was getting sick of it and looking about ready to say so, he tactfully tried to move things on. But when Billy Steele continued to paw the questions around, Tyler finally erupted.

"A man is dead and another missing. I don't have the time or, frankly, the patience to listen to any more of your ..." Tyler rose to his feet. "I'm going to put a series of questions to you and you are going to answer them fast and straight, do you understand me?"

The answers came pouring out like blood from an open wound. He had fallen out with Johnny over which songs went on the EP. He wanted two and only got one, and Johnny changed the title of that. Johnny wanted all the titles to have 'Blue' in them and so *Dangerous Times* became *Blue Murder.*

He wanted Johnny to re-record the vocal on the song but he refused. *All Colours Are Blue* was written by Johnny, as far as he knew. He didn't know about any contracts, and he was unaware that any deal had been secured with a record company. "Who paid for the recording time?" asked Tyler.

Steele's eyes were darting between the detectives. Tyler repeated the question.

"We clubbed in," he stammered.

"You funded it yourselves, the four of you?"

Steele didn't answer.

"Billy? You could only get one song on the EP, and that one not performed to your satisfaction. But you were still willing to stump up the cash?"

"There was a change of plan."

"Let's hear about it then," said Tyler.

Another outpouring followed. "A couple of days before we were due to start recording, we played a gig in town."

"The Thirteen club?" asked Mills.

"No, but Frank Watts was there. He came up to us afterwards and asked about recording us. Watts offered to fund a proper, professional recording. He said there was a condition, though."

"What condition?" said Mills.

"We had to include the song we finished the set with. It was *All Colours*. Johnny agreed right off, without asking any of us, and Watts offered us a gig at the club to showcase and promote the recording."

"Very generous of him," said Tyler.

Steele was again looking from one detective to the other.

"What is it, Billy?" asked Mills, leaning forward. "You can tell us."

Billy Steele bit his lip and then appeared to make a decision. "We went out that night to celebrate and Johnny got drunk. Johnny said that the irony was brilliant."

"Irony?" said Mills.

"That Adam had written the song and given it to him. Given it to Johnny."

"Why would he do that?" asked Tyler.

"He said that Adam thought he - Johnny - was depressed and that's what inspired the song. Adam wrote it for him. But after they fell out and Adam left, Johnny stopped singing it because he was pissed off. I didn't know whether to believe him. He was very drunk, and I wondered if he was making it up. He never mentioned any of that stuff again."

"Did he say what they fell out over?" asked Mills.

Steele shook his head.

"Why did Johnny start singing that song again?"

"I don't know. It meant something to him, you could tell the way he sang it. Everyone in the band agreed with that. He was different when he was singing it, like he really came to life. It was from the heart and it's the best thing Johnny's ever done."

"*Was* Johnny depressed, would you say?" asked Mills.

"He acted weird sometimes, but I don't know about depressed."

"Was he doing any drugs that you know of?"

"He might have been. I never saw him taking anything, personally. He knew the rest of us weren't into any of that."

Tyler appeared to be thinking out loud when he said, "Some fans seem to believe that the song is a suicide note. But if it was, then it was a suicide note written by Adam for Johnny. Though that fact isn't common knowledge. Do you believe that Johnny might have taken his own life?"

Steele couldn't look at Tyler as the detective bore down on him.

"Did you kill Johnny? Did you kill Adam?"

Billy Steele was staring at the desk that stood between him and the detectives, and he looked to be on the verge of tears. In a gentler voice, Mills asked him the same questions.

"I didn't kill anybody," he said, the tears trickling down his face.

"Do you know who did, Billy?"

"I don't know anything."

When he stopped crying they let him go.

CHAPTER SIXTEEN

Out of the silence Tyler's voice sounded like a gong. "It's blitz time, Danny. We're going full-on public on Richards."

Mills was driving the unmarked car, and he glanced across at his passenger. Tyler continued to look straight ahead, seemingly beyond the highway.

"We re-issue the request for information from anyone who may have been in the vicinity around the time when Adam Lane was killed, and we ask for anything on Richards. I want anyone who is hiding anything regarding his whereabouts to be in no doubt that he is wanted in connection with the death of Adam Lane. We don't say it in so many words, not quite. But we leave nobody in any doubt."

"You think Richards is still alive and kicking, then?"

"I haven't a clue, frankly. There's no credible motive that we're aware of for anyone to kill Richards, or for Richards to kill Adam Lane, for that matter. If Richards is dead, it's a stretch believing that the two deaths are coincidental. Which leaves a double-murder committed by the same person or persons, though clearly not at the same time, or even on the same day.

"*But why?*

"And if Richards is alive ..."

Another tetchy silence descended. Mills did his best to fill it.

"According to our three musketeers, Richards was still alive at 10pm on the evening Lane was killed. And according to Janine Finch he returned to her flat following the rehearsal, spent the night there and apparently left as normal for work the following day. Making Janine Finch the last person to see him alive. That's apart from his killer, of course, unless Janine Finch killed him."

Mills seemed to be warming to the game. Many an evening of late he had sat in the house watching detective mysteries on the TV with his wife after the kids had gone to bed. The absence of a decent pub in the area where he was now living, that and the absence of money in his pockets these days, had combined to reduce him to the simpler pleasures of life. *Like early nights*. Though there hadn't been many of those, of late, to help sweeten the pill.

Getting a grip on himself, Mills focused back on the case at hand. "But how can we speculate on possible motives for a double murder, when we don't know Richards is dead? We're driving around the city, filling our days, but we don't know a thing, not really."

Mills drove on, his mind whirling. First stop Ash Bank, Werrington, and then on to Hanford. Mr and Mrs Richards, estranged parents of the missing singer. Both fearing the worst - that Johnny was dead? Neither having any idea who might want to hurt their son or hurt Adam Lane.

Or else covering up? Hiding their son? Mills couldn't help wondering what they might be fearing the most: that their son was dead, or that he was a killer? And if they really were covering for him, was that because they knew or because they merely feared?

Mr Richards sat in his customary chair, rolling his customary cigarette as he once again faced the detectives. Tyler raised the subject of the Finch sisters.

Richards lit the smoke in his hand and shook his head. He'd met them at his son's gigs but that was about it. They seemed "nice enough," he thought, shrugging as he said it. He knew Adam had been "seeing Johnny's first one, what's her name, Daisy?" but he hadn't heard Johnny suggesting that was a problem. He thought Johnny seemed "happy enough with the other one, Janine." Re-lighting his hand-rolled cig, he said, "Adam was a bit of a one for the girls. He could be a bit clingy around women."

"Is that why Adam and your son fell out?" said Tyler. "Over Daisy Finch?"

"Shouldn't think so," said Richards. "You know what it's like at that age. It's all fun, then you move on, don't you. Like I say, Johnny seemed happy enough with his latest girlfriend, and Adam was still with Daisy. So they must still have been enjoying themselves."

"So, why do you *imagine* they fell out?" said Tyler.

"I don't know that they did."

Tyler took a breath. "Okay, so why do you think Adam left the band?"

"Lack of commitment, like I already told you. Had other fish to fry, uni and all that, I don't know. Maybe he cared more about his love-life than rock and roll."

Richards made his last remark with a sneer of bitterness, Mills thought. As though Adam Lane had committed the gravest sin imaginable, putting a woman ahead of music. Ahead of Johnny's band.

"Are you hiding your son?" said Tyler suddenly, causing Mills to blanch.

"What?" said Richards. "Are you out of your mind?"

"I'm asking a question."

"And you're bang out of order. I'm going to put a complaint in. My son might be dead, for all anyone knows, and you come here accusing—"

"Who would kill your son, Mr Richards? And why?"

"That's your job to find out."

A few miles across town, Mo Richards told the detectives that she wouldn't be surprised if girlfriends hadn't featured in the rift between Adam and Johnny. "But like I said to you before, Johnny didn't have any grudge against Adam. Adam left the band and now they're doing well. Johnny's happy with Janine, and I understand Adam was happy with Daisy. So I don't know about any jealousy. But with Daisy going with both of them, well, you never know, do you?"

Tyler asked her to elaborate.

"Well, it all gets a bit complicated sometimes, doesn't it. Daisy seemed a nice girl, I got on well with her. But I believe the two sisters don't exactly see eye to eye. That's what I've heard, anyway. Maybe Daisy poisoned Adam towards Johnny because Johnny went off with her sister, I could see how that might happen."

"How do you know that the two sisters don't get on?" asked Tyler.

"Things Johnny mentioned. But he didn't talk much about that part of his life, not really. He could be quite shy, and very sensitive, could Johnny. I haven't seen as much of Janine as I did Daisy. Johnny seems to spend most of his time over at her place, and she hardly comes here at all. I think that's just how she is. As long as Johnny's happy with her, that's the main thing, though, isn't it?"

"What do you think about the other members of the band?" asked Tyler.

"They seem okay. Nice lads. I'm glad Billy's in the band."

"Why's that?"

"Oh, I don't know. I suppose that I'm quite fond of Billy. I think he's had a tough time and he's so keen. He deserves a chance."

On the drive back to the station Tyler re-iterated to Mills his intention to step up the request for information from the public, and his determination to set the wheels in motion. "It is a depressing fact - and one that isn't lost on Chief Superintendent Berkins - that at this precise moment in time we have, to coin a phrase, precisely *Jack Shit*. We are officially treading water and we need a break. At the risk of sounding melodramatic ... we need Johnny Richards, dead or alive."

CHAPTER SEVENTEEN

Jim Tyler knocked on the door at the stroke of 8.30am. A presentable young woman greeted him with a gushing smile and the offer of a seat at a small table for two. She introduced herself as Theresa, and all the time she was talking Tyler couldn't help but agree that the rumours were indeed correct: she was a looker.

He had always imagined staff counsellors to be humourless and unattractive, for some reason - not that he had given the subject a great deal of thought. For some the opportunity to tell their story, their life and its attendant difficulties to a stranger clearly had its appeal. There was an industry out there banking on it, after all. But if Berkins hadn't demanded it, wild horses could not have brought Jim Tyler to that small room, no matter how good looking its other occupant happened to be.

Still, sitting in close proximity to a cheerful and kind young woman who only wanted to help an officer in distress ... couldn't he at least be civil? Couldn't he, if not for his own sake, then for hers, for Berkins, for the sake of appearances - could he not, for once, simply play the game?

It took seven minutes from entrance to exit.

Seven minutes from the first rays of warmth from that radiant greeting, to him storming out of the room.

What had upset the DCI so much, he couldn't even have said. It was somewhere out beyond him and he didn't for another second wish to dwell on it.

Tyler made the short journey through Hanley alone and on foot, the walk through the streets clearing his mind, allowing him to wrestle his thoughts back to the case at hand, and closing off all other distractions.

Trinity Street he found to be singularly unremarkable, with its ramshackle collection of shops, many closed down, and available office space at 'competitive rates'. But one place did stand out. It stood out like a beacon.

Number 13.

On a large sign proclaiming THE THIRTEEN CLUB the attendant art work portrayed an assortment of guitars, drums and saxophones, with an illustration of a thin figure that might have been Johnny Richards himself clutching a microphone.

Beneath 'THE THIRTEEN CLUB', in smaller lettering read the words:

Lucky For Some

Tyler entered the club and found the owner and manager, Frank Watts, busy with paperwork in a small office down in the basement. Watts was a short, slightly chubby guy, with a short-sleeved, white collared shirt tucked into a pair of grey flannel trousers. His tie reflected the art work that decked the sign hanging outside his club. Corporate integrity, thought Tyler. Business man first, music lover second. Watts reminded him of photographs he had seen of Al Capone.

Shaking his head, and shaking out the speculative thoughts with them, Tyler walked into the office with every intention of maintaining an open mind.

Watts invited the DCI to take a seat in the cramped office space. There appeared to be an inordinate amount of papers and files, considering the relative size of the place, and Tyler had no doubt that the club was one of many plates that the man was currently spinning.

Neither man seemed inclined to idle chatter, and the conversation focused quickly onto the missing singer. "They don't let me down twice," said Watts. "Nobody gets away with that. That gig was a sell-out; there were a lot of disappointed people, I can tell you. A lot of important people, too. I have a reputation to maintain and that kind of fiasco can do a lot of damage."

Tyler asked Watts if he had any information about the possible whereabouts of Johnny Richards, or what he imagined might have happened to him. Watts allowed a slight, sardonic smile to play around his mouth, while his eyes, small, like everything else about him apart from his flamboyant tie and generous girth, shone hard and unforgiving.

"Ask yourself this," he said. "A singer in a band gets the chance to play a showcase gig at the most prestigious, connected club in this city. Now, I don't know how much you know about the entertainment industry in general, or about the music scene in particular ..."

Watts paused, giving Tyler the opportunity to answer the implied question. But Tyler sat mute and waited for Watts to make his point. After a moment Watts went on. "Well, anyway. You might not imagine that a gig at a modest-sized club on Trinity Street is any big deal, but let me tell you this. You'd be surprised how many bands have broken through following a showcase gig upstairs."

Watts paused again, and still Tyler waited for the man to say whatever he was getting around to saying.

"Johnny Richards threw away the opportunity of a lifetime. Why would he do that?"

"Are you going to tell me?" said Tyler.

"Let's look at the options," said Watts. "Abducted by aliens? Perhaps he was taken ill? But then you have to ask why he didn't contact anyone and tell them. Or maybe he ran scared?" Watts shook his head. "I don't think Johnny Richards is the type to come down with stage-fright. He wanted that gig, by all accounts, so why didn't he show?"

Tyler sighed heavily and checked his watch with a theatrical flourish.

"Am I boring you, Inspector?"

"I wouldn't quite say that. But if you have anything to tell me, now would be the time."

"Let me spell it out to you. You may not be aware, but since our mystery singer went missing, sales of the band's EP have started going through the roof. Good advertising, I'd say."

"You're suggesting a publicity coup?"

"I'm not suggesting anything. I'm telling you what I know."

Tyler frowned. "You are implying, Mr Watts, that Johnny Richards has gone missing to encourage interest in his music, resulting in favourable sales of his product."

A grin was subtly emerging from out of the corners of Watts' mouth, and it wasn't long until the rest of his face was joining in the party. Tyler could feel the blood pumping inside him. He wanted to make a fist and introduce it to the middle of that grinning facade. Watts reminded him of someone who once slid out from under a rock and didn't belong in the daylight.

"Are you playing games with me, Mr Watts? Can I remind you that wasting police time is a serious business."

Watts shook his head, but the grin was still fastened to it. "I'm trying to help you with your enquiries. I'm a very busy man giving up his valuable time. I think you could show a bit more courtesy."

DCI Tyler made the fist and Watts saw it.

"I see," said Watts. "It is true, then. The police haven't entirely given up on their favoured methods of extracting information. Nothing changes."

Tyler felt the mists clearing to be replaced by something else; an overwhelming curiosity that consumed all anger and spat it out again. In a considered, calm voice, he said, "You don't believe, Mr Watts, that anything might have happened to Johnny Richards? Say, for instance, Richards gets a lesson on behalf of all of those disappointed people, yourself included? A serious lesson, one that went a little too far?"

Watts tipped his head back and let out a long and humourless laugh. "Are you seriously suggesting that I arranged to have Johnny Richards killed? For not turning up for a gig! What kind of books do you detectives read when you go to bed, Inspector? Fairy stories?"

Tyler stood outside the club thinking. Berkins had agreed to the statement being released, and there would be a media onslaught beginning any time now. If the publicity surrounding the case so far had encouraged sales of the record then God knows what was to follow.

But what else could they do? They needed information, and fast.

He rang Mills. "I've been talking to Frank Watts at the Thirteen club."

"Nice for you, sir."

"He's suggesting that our missing man is trying to make a name for himself and pump up sales by doing a disappearing act."

"He's not serious?"

"Hard to say. I'm not sure what game he's playing. Perhaps he enjoys winding up police officers, or bears a grudge for some reason. I want you to run a check, Danny. See if he has any previous."

"Will do."

"I can't see why he'd want to wind us up, though, if he has anything to hide. Doesn't make sense, same as everything else in this case. Did you track down previous band members?"

"I did, but nothing to report."

"Left of their own volition?"

"One went off to uni. Bristol."

"Poor soul."

"One was about to become a father and was selling his equipment off to buy a pram."

"Did they have much to say?"

"Not really. Johnny could be moody, Adam seemed to be losing interest, and the band weren't getting anywhere. Johnny Richards was getting on people's nerves."

"Any specifics?"

"Wanting everything his own way. And his girlfriend was starting to poke her nose in."

"Janine Finch up to her usual tricks?"

"That's the one."

"Would you say that any of them are concerned for Johnny Richards?"

"That's the thing," said Mills. "It's like the current lot, Atkins, Jones and Steele. They are obviously disappointed about missing their big opportunity, but they don't seem concerned about Richards. Sounds like he could be pretty unreliable and, to be honest, quite an unlikeable character. But even so."

"You don't get the feeling any of them are hiding anything?"

"Not at all. Everyone seems very open. Steele's cagey, of course, but then he seems frightened of his own shadow. Are you suggesting—"

"I don't know what I'm suggesting." Tyler thought for a moment.

"What is it, sir?"

"I'm not sure," said Tyler. "There's something not adding up. There's something about Watts, something he isn't telling us. Or that he is telling us. I once saw a film about a record company who killed their own stars so that they could sell even more of their records. I think you would call it a satire."

"You don't think Frank Watts saw the same film, do you, sir?"

"One of these days, DS Mills, your sarcasm is going to get you into serious bother."

"Funnily enough, that's precisely what my parents and teachers used to tell me."

"That's what parents and teachers tell every child, isn't it? The thing is, though. In that film, the stars were all on the way down. The record company was interested in re-packaging what they had already sold and grinding what they still could out of the market with a few obscure tracks and previously unseen photos."

"Sounds interesting. Is it on DVD?"

"The point is, Sergeant Mills, Richards is supposedly still on the way up. And why would Watts even mention any attempts to play the market if there was anything to it? Why go there? I asked him if he'd arranged a lesson for Richards, on behalf of all the people he has let down - you know, Richards being unreliable and all that."

"You asked him that, sir? What did he say?"

"He laughed it off, naturally. But sometimes a lesson can go too far. I get the impression that Frank Watts is a man who doesn't like to be let down."

"And you actually think—"

"Danny, I'm clutching at straws and I'm full of theories and speculations, none of which bears much scrutiny, I'm afraid. It's the absence of any evidence, it screws with my mind every time. Why don't killers leave clues anymore? I'm coming back."

"Sir?"

"Yes?"

"Your earlier ... appointment?"

"What about it?"

"Is she a looker?"

Tyler ended the call.

CHAPTER EIGHTEEN

Following the press release and media blitz, the rumours that had been circulating and steadily gaining momentum exploded.

Along with sales of the EP.

All Colours Are Blue was everywhere, on every playlist on every radio station nationwide. Johnny Richards was the news of the day, the week, the month. The story had captured the imagination of the public, the missing singer's face adorning the front of all the national newspapers, taking pride of place on the TV news channel networks.

The world loved a good mystery and speculation was rife. Was there a clue in the song? Was *All Colours Are Blue* a cry for help, a suicide note? *Or the work of a deranged killer?* Had Johnny Richards taken his own life after killing his old friend and original band member, Adam Lane?

And why?

The street corners, the pubs, the gossip columns were full of it. Everybody had a theory. At the same time, and much to the frustration of Chief Superintendent Graham Berkins, nobody was coming forward with any answers.

Tyler sat across the desk from Berkins and couldn't help wondering whether the CS had added an inch either side to his formidable moustache. Perhaps he had been in somewhere and had the thing straightened, to give the illusion of growth. Or maybe, like so many things in life, the growth had been a gradual phenomenon that had gone unnoticed until, for some reason, recognition had suddenly dawned.

Tyler forced his thoughts from the senior man's evident pride and joy, and tried to answer the question that the CS was putting to him. The difficulty being that Jim Tyler hadn't any answers to give CS Berkins. They were no closer to finding Johnny Richards, alive or dead, and no closer to finding Adam Lane's killer either.

The fact of the matter, according to Berkins, was this: the only result that the twin investigation had so far achieved had been a huge spike in record sales!

Tyler wondered if it was time for the nutshell. He was proved correct.

"In a nutshell," said Berkins, the first finger and thumb of both hands twiddling furiously at the ends of his moustache, "we are doing wonders for the local music industry but little for the safety and peace of mind of the general public."

Tyler could see how impressed Berkins was with his own summary of the situation, and at the same time how much frustration was boiling beneath the veil of cheap and easy humour. But still DCI Tyler had nothing to offer CS Berkins, and he refused to disguise the fact with an empty show of bureaucratic sophistry.

Berkins switched topics. "I understand that you walked out of a session with the staff counsellor."

Tyler didn't deny it.

"Was there any particular reason for your action?"

"Nothing that I would wish to make a formal complaint about."

Berkins raised an eyebrow, and its neighbour appeared tempted to follow. When Tyler declined the tacit invitation to elaborate, Berkins informed him that another appointment would have to be made, and promptly. "I take the welfare of my staff very seriously, you know that, Jim."

Tyler couldn't muster the will to argue. If it kept Berkins off his back, he would sit out a session. In the meantime, an endless series of interviews and appeals to the public for information appeared to stretch to the horizon.

They needed a break; someone to come forward. Berkins agreed. "... You don't need me to tell you, Jim. Sometimes we have to make our own luck. You're one of the best officers we have, and I have every faith in you. But I need you at full strength."

Tyler endured the speech and wondered if it might culminate in a second nutshell. Then Berkins' phone rang, and the DCI found himself ushered from the room. He wasn't disappointed to leave.

Entering the CID office he found Mills wearing a set of earphones and jotting down lines on a notepad. Every so often Mills would tamper with the device to which the earphones were connected, with a distinct air of impatience. Seeing that the DCI wanted his attention, Mills finally took out the earphones.

"Reliving a scene from childhood?" asked Tyler.

"Giving that song a listen," said Mills. "Blue is the Colour - I mean, what's it called ..." Mills checked his notepad.

"A telling remark," said Tyler. "I think you might be referring to *All Colours Are Blue*."

"That's the one. Thought there might be a clue in the lyrics."

Tyler held up a finger. "I've had a thought. The case last year, the *Red Is The Colour* case." The case Tyler was recalling had involved pupils at the same school that Johnny Richards, Adam Lane and Billy Steele had attended. A historic case - the death of a schoolboy back in 1972. Missing for thirty years.

"I wonder," said Tyler. "It's probably something and nothing." He glanced at the notepad. "So, did you discover any answers in the song, then?"

"Maybe we could nail it between us, sir?"

The detectives looked over the lyrics together, indulging in a few minutes of unadulterated amateur sleuthing and pop psychology before pulling themselves up sharply. "Song lyrics could mean anything," said Mills.

"Or nothing," said Tyler.

"I don't see a suicide note."

"So, your conclusions?"

"I don't think I'm qualified to draw any."

"Is anybody?" said Tyler. "We're talking about art, not science. I can't fault you for trying though."

"What did you mean about last year's case?"

"Like I say, it's likely something and nothing. But it drew a lot of media interest. Most people in this city at least would have heard about it. And with Richards and Lane being at the same school ... I think it's a little bit too coincidental, that's all: *Red Is The Colour, All Colours Are Blue*. It may not mean much, but I think the writer, Richards or Lane, had something in mind. Of course, we might never find out."

Mills didn't say anything. He looked again at the lyrics written down on the note pad, but there was no connection staring back at him. "Setting aside our attempts at lyrical analysis for the moment," said Tyler, "let me ask a detective's question. Who would stand to gain from the disappearance or death of Johnny Richards?"

"That depends on whether Richards is dead or missing."

"It does. In one sense. What you are saying is that Richards might stand to gain the most, if he is alive. Yet some people choose to find fame and glory in death, apparently. He may have written the song as a farewell to a cruel world, had it recorded, released and then topped himself to cash in on the eternal, posthumous acclaim. That's if he wrote it at all, which opens up another can of worms."

Tyler shook his head. "I don't know about you, but that doesn't work for me. I want to know who gains materially from a record that is now selling bucket loads. I want to know who has the rights to the song. And if they belong to Johnny Richards, regardless of who actually wrote it, I want to know who benefits in the event of his death."

"Apparently," said Mills, "there are rumours of a forthcoming album."

"You astound me. But as you were. Same rules of policing apply."

CHAPTER NINETEEN

"Well," said Tyler as Mills drove across town, "our efforts appear not to have been entirely wasted after all."

"Really?" said Mills.

"Apparently our investigations have pushed the record to the top of the charts. Some achievement, I would have to say."

"We should ask someone for a percentage, sir."

"Trouble being, we have yet to work out who."

"You sound surprised," said Mills.

"That the record's doing well off the back of adverse publicity? That a murder and a missing person has caught the imagination of the public? No, sadly I'm not. And I get less surprised about a lot of things with every passing year."

"It's called life, sir."

"You philosopher you."

Mills pulled up on the car park of the Thirteen club on Trinity Street. "Ever had the pleasure?" asked Tyler. Mills shook his head. "I never was a big one for gigs. Beer and football was always enough for me. Still is, when I get half a chance."

"The red and white stripes of Stoke City left little time for other pursuits, then?" asked Tyler.

"I had a little spare time to look for a wife, now you mention it."

"And to work on your career, of course."

"Of course, sir."

Tyler got out of the car. "I'm looking forward to a second opinion here, so keep your wits about you. Shall we see how Frank Watts is celebrating the *success* of his latest signing?"

The detectives found Watts down in his office, concluding an angry phone call.

"I believe congratulations are in order," said Tyler.

"I take it you are referring to *All Colours Are Blue*. Pity we can't capitalise with a tour and a follow up."

"I'm told there are rumours of an album," said Tyler.

"There are always rumours."

"You've still hit the jackpot, though."

"Depends what you call a jackpot. Look, I have a busy day ahead of me, so if you could—"

"Cut to the chase? It would be my pleasure." Tyler gestured towards a vacant chair. "May I?"

Watts nodded, and Tyler took a seat while Mills remained standing. "I understand," said Tyler, "that you funded the recording, is that correct?"

"It is, yes."

"I assume there is an existing contract?"

Watts looked at Tyler for a moment. "You assume correctly."

"And that the song has a copyright?"

"Yes."

"Who wrote the song, Mr Watts? Or, more to the point, who owns the copyright?"

"The song was written by Johnny Richards."

Tyler retained a poker face. "And he owns the copyright on the material?"

Watts didn't answer.

"Mr Watts?" prompted Tyler.

"The copyright is owned by myself," said Watts.

"Ah, I see. An interesting arrangement."

"Not particularly. It was agreed that, as I funded the recording and agreed to manage and promote the band, I would naturally take the larger percentage of any proceeds from sales of the recording."

"Agreed by the band?"

"Agreed by Johnny Richards."

"But you own the song?"

"That's correct."

"And what about the other three songs on the record?"

"Johnny has copyright on those."

"You mean on two of them?"

"I mean on all three. I'm not a greedy man, Inspector."

"If you say so."

"What's that?"

"And what does Billy Steele think about this arrangement?"

"What does it have to do with him?"

"Billy Steele is not credited with writing any of the songs on the recording?"

"I've told you, they were written by Johnny Richards."

"All of them?"

Frank Watts' face clenched into a scowl. Tyler glanced at Mills and discreetly winked. Then he turned back to Watts. "The song *Blue Murder* is owned by Johnny Richards?"

"Yes! Are you going to keep asking me the same question for the rest of the day?"

"That depends."

Tyler was about to say something further when Watts said, "You're probably getting confused because of the printing error. On the initial batch Steele was mistakenly credited with writing that song. The mistake has now been corrected."

The scowl had been replaced with an expression of cordial geniality. "I hope that clears up any misunderstanding. Now, if that's all—"

"What about Adam Lane?" asked Tyler.

"What about him? I don't know him, I never met him. I heard he was in the band prior to Billy Steele replacing him, but that's about all I do know."

"I see," said Tyler, and the edge to his comment was clearly not wasted on Frank Watts, who was trying hard to maintain his cool and not allow himself to be riled by attempts to unsettle him. But the DCI had played the game more times than he cared to remember, and he wondered how much practice Frank Watts had racked up.

"So," said Watts, gathering up papers from his desk, "if you've got what you came for, I have other appointments."

"Billy Steele seems to be believe that he wrote *Blue Murder*."

"Then," said Watts, "Billy Steele is clearly ... mistaken." Watts continued to gather items from his desk, with a contrivance of purpose to what he was doing.

But Tyler wasn't having any of it. "Furthermore, Billy Steele also believes that the song *All Colours Are Blue* was not written by Johnny Richards."

"Oh, really?" said Watts. "Steele's claiming that one too?"

"It doesn't seem so. He believes it was written by Adam Lane."

Watts stopped what he was doing. "Then he's mistaken on two counts."

"You know," said Tyler, "varicose veins can be terrible things."

"What are you talking about?" asked Watts.

"I'm talking about varicose veins. They can strike at any age, male or female. DS Mills suffers beyond words, and standing for long periods is the worst thing in the world." Tyler stood up and gestured for Mills to take his seat. Then the DCI perched on the desk, at the side of Frank Watts, and looked down on him.

Watts nodded, as though an answer had already been given. "Billy Steele," he said, "is full of it."

"You don't like him?" asked Tyler.

"I never liked him. I never trusted him. But it's Johnny's band at the end of the day. So Johnny decides who plays and who doesn't."

"Any particular reason for this dislike, this lack of trust?"

"I don't like the company of people who have a chip on their shoulder," said Watts.

"And what would Billy Steele have a chip on his shoulder about?"

"Do I look like a psychologist or a social worker?"

"I'm told they come in all shapes and sizes."

The scowl was back. "Steele's not someone I've taken that much interest in, but I'm not a stupid man. I could see straight off he wanted to be top dog, and that Johnny had his work cut out."

"Top dog?"

"Steele wants all of his own songs in the set, and on the record."

"And in the end he gets nothing?"

"Nothing? He got to play on a record that's topping the charts! There's a million hopefuls out there who'd give the skin off their backsides to be in his position. You call that nothing?"

"Billy Steele thinks he wrote *Blue Murder*."

"He can think what he likes."

"Are you saying he was mistaken?"

Watts looked almost stunned. "Are you kidding? People make up all kinds of stuff when there's money and success involved. Would you like me to lend you a book on the history of rock and roll - or on the entertainment industry in general? You might find it informative."

"I'll get back to you on that," said Tyler. "In the meantime ... if I'm understanding you correctly, Billy Steele is claiming that he wrote one song that he never wrote, and claiming another of Richards' songs for Adam Lane?"

Watts looked again at his watch, but Tyler wasn't finished.

"Okay, you're going to have to help me out here, Mr Watts. I can see why someone might try to claim a song for themselves, but why claim another on behalf of Adam Lane? What's the angle for Billy Steele in that?"

"Sour grapes."

"What kind of sour grapes?"

The flicker of a grin crept into the eyes of Frank Watts, though it was concealed well enough to leave adequate room for doubt. Watts looked again at his watch, this time standing up as he did so. Then he delivered his punch line.

"Steele was about to be thrown out of the band. And what's more ... *he knew it.*"

CHAPTER TWENTY

The following morning Tyler sat, for the second time that week, in a small room with a smart young woman separated from him by a frail wooden table. The woman, Theresa, wanted to know how he was feeling today. She smiled, and there was, thought Jim Tyler, genuine warmth in that smile, if no trace of seduction. Theresa understood that it isn't always easy opening up about the things that might be troubling us, and he couldn't argue with that.

She spoke for a minute or two, and it was easy enough on the ear. Then she brought the preliminaries to a close and gave him the stage.

But Tyler was thinking about Frank Watts and about Billy Steele. He was trying to figure out how credible it was that Steele might kill Adam Lane, and possibly Johnny Richards too, because he was to be thrown out of the band and/or because he was being cheated out of royalties for his contribution.

Was *Blue Murder* Billy's song in the first place? Did he know he was being cheated, and to be replaced by Adam Lane? All questions that he would have to put to Steele, and soon.

The woman in front of him was saying something, but Tyler didn't catch enough of it. He asked her to please repeat what she had just said, and for a moment her words and the movement of her mouth appeared out of synch.

"Are you okay?" she asked him. "You appear very distracted today."

"Distracted? Well, yes. I suppose that I am a little distracted. You see, I am in the middle of a murder investigation."

Tyler stopped, letting the swell of anger surge through him; trying to breathe and not speak. To not let Theresa take the force, the tidal wave of feelings that had swelled within, threatening to drown the two of them in its outpouring.

He stood up, glancing at the clock on the wall as he did so.

This time he hadn't even managed seven minutes.

Tyler and Mills rode out to Penkhull to visit Lane's parents for the second time. On the way Mills asked the DCI if he was alright.

"The question of the day. I will be, just as soon as this lot adds up to something."

"You spoke to Steele again?"

"I like the coffees over in Trentham. While I was there I asked him two questions and he gave me two answers. He didn't know that his song had been credited to Richards, along with all the others. And he didn't know that there were plans for Lane to rejoin the band, leaving him out on his ear."

"Do you believe him?"

"I don't trust him. It's one of the few things I have in common with Frank Watts. But then I don't trust a lot of people. I don't, for example, trust Frank Watts."

As they pulled up at yet another set of temporary traffic lights, Mills could practically taste the boiling fumes of frustration steaming off his colleague.

"Is there anything you would like to talk to me about, Jim? I mean ..."

The thick silence gave way. "I would like to talk to someone about why they have to dig up every road in this city at exactly the same time. I would like to talk about ... I would ... I don't trust Steele. He tells lies, and when people tell lies I find myself unable to tell the difference when they happen to tell the truth, and even liars tell the truth sometimes. But I'm disregarding my lack of trust until I have clear grounds for it. And at the moment I don't have any.

"CS Berkins would be proud of me. I'm ditching intuition and placing everything on evidence. In other words, I'm doing my job."

The traffic moved and Mills pulled out again.

Tyler closed his eyes and saw himself as Billy Steele. The old skin and bone Jim Tyler, the outsider, the afflicted. The orphan and victim. A part of him wanted to like Billy Steele, and heap the troubles of the world at the feet of Frank Watts. A part of him wanted to land everything at the door of a *real* villain, an exploiting devil; the bully robbing the poor to feed the fat stomachs of the rich.

Tyler would have given everything, his pension and his badge, to lay it all on Frank Watts. But sometimes you couldn't make the world the way you wanted it to be. Sometimes the Billy Steeles were really not worth saving, if that could ever be said of anybody.

"Dammit!" screamed Tyler, smashing a fist into the glove box, denting it.

"Sir? I'll pull over."

"Don't you dare. I'm sorry, I'm okay, really."

"Are you sure you ought to be at work?"

Tyler laughed at that, a low chuckle, devoid of any joy. "It's all I have, Danny. It's the only path to redemption that I know."

They pulled up a few minutes later outside the home of the Lanes. Mr Lane ushered the detectives through to the living room, where they found Mrs Lane in her customary seat by the window. She didn't acknowledge their presence, continuing to stare out through the window in an attitude of vacancy. Mills wondered if she had moved since their last visit.

Mr Lane appeared glad of the opportunity to make some drinks, while Mills attempted, unsuccessfully, to engage Mrs Lane in small-talk.

When everyone was in the room, and the seating arrangements agreed on, Tyler manoeuvred the conversation to the subject of their lost son. Mills couldn't help but admire the skill, the sheer tact and sensitivity with which his colleague raised all the pertinent questions. If it had been captured on video, thought Mills, it could have served as a training resource for years to come.

Tyler's questions weaved across a broad spectrum, unpacking aspects of Adam Lane's short life, moving deftly from his relationships to his songwriting, and any plans he might have had about rejoining the band. Questions made to sound like natural avenues stumbled down in the course of a casual conversation.

Mills sat spellbound. Even the way Tyler accounted for the visit, touching base, checking they were okay and if there might be anything they hadn't thought to mention, or something that had more recently occurred to them - *consummate*. Light strokes, finely judged and perfectly executed; a master of his craft. Danny Mills doubted he had ever come across one so talented, so empathetic, and at the same times so haunted and troubled. It would be a crying shame if Jim Tyler let his demons destroy him.

In the car, as the detectives headed back towards Hanley, they picked over the fruits of the visit.

Neither bereaved parent had been aware of any plans that their son might have had to rejoin the band. He certainly hadn't mentioned anything about that, in fact he hadn't mentioned Johnny Richards in any capacity for quite some time. As far as they knew, Adam was concentrating on his studies, with his university finals fast approaching. Regarding his songs, they didn't know if he ever made any recordings of the material he had written. But Mr Lane mentioned that his son had kept notebooks, and jotted down bits of poetry and lyrics that he was working on, occasionally trying them out on his parents.

Tyler had managed to make the suggestion seem completely innocuous, wondering if any of Adam's ideas had landed up in the songs making a stir on the EP. He didn't specifically mention *All*

Colours are Blue. Sowing the seed had been enough and he left it at that. The Lanes would no doubt be checking out their son's notebooks before the day was done.

Arriving outside the flats close to the canal, overlooking Hanley Park, Mills wondered how Jim Tyler would ask the questions this time. There were different reasons for subtlety here. Something less innocent, he thought, about Daisy Finch.

Finch looked surprised to see the detectives again so soon, and she asked if they had any news. Tyler informed her that they had not, and Mills saw the disappointment etch painfully across her bloodless face. It was only later that it occurred to him that her question had come without a reference. *Was she asking for news regarding the investigation into the murder of Adam Lane, or about the search for Johnny Richards?*

Inside the flat appeared as chaotic as it had done on the previous visit. Finch asked if the detectives would like a drink. "I've even got some biscuits," she said. Mills was licking his lips when Tyler said, "Thank you, but this is a flying visit."

Tyler cut to it. Was she aware that Adam might have been thinking about rejoining the band?

"It's news to me."

"He didn't mention the possibility?"

"No, he didn't."

"Do you think it likely that he might have considered rejoining?"

"I wouldn't have thought so. And anyway, I can't imagine Johnny Richards wanting someone as talented as Adam back in the band."

"I would have thought Richards would want the very best."

"Most people would, I'm sure. But Johnny Richards wasn't like that. He was an ego-maniac. He wouldn't want the likes of Adam usurping his position. Has someone suggested that Adam had been approached?"

A light appeared to have entered the woman's eyes, and Mills caught it. *Is she seeing an angle?*

Tyler was busy batting off Finch's question, and contriving a casual conversation about Adam Lane's songwriting. That it was all hands to the deck getting top material if the band was about to take off. Mills watched shadows and shapes shift between the lines of Daisy Finch's curious expression. At one point she seemed about to ask something, but held back. A period of silence followed, and it felt to Mills like a stand-off. Were they all itching to ask the same question: Did Adam Lane write *All Colours Are Blue?* And if so, when it was recorded and started to get airplay, did Adam want it back?

The stand off endured and Tyler at last stood up to leave. As he did so Finch asked the detectives if they were sure they didn't want a biscuit and a drink to go with it. Mills heard a sympathetic growl rise up from his belly, earning him a cautionary look from the DCI.

Out in the car, Mills said, "Maybe we ought to have asked her directly." Tyler shook his head. "She anticipated the question, but wanted us to ask it. She knows the situation alright. Anyway, I fear you are mixing up two kinds of curiosity."

"Sir?"

"Your mind wanted to know what perhaps she cannot truthfully tell us, while your stomach was more concerned about the contents of her biscuit barrel."

"You've got me all wrong."

Tyler checked his watch. "That's as may be. But more to the point: if you drive without concern for personal or public safety, I might just make my appointment with Berkins."

CHAPTER TWENTY ONE

CS Graham Berkins was unusually agitated. As chief superintendents go, Tyler had no doubt that Berkins was about the best he had ever worked with. The man knew his stuff, was supportive of his staff and didn't attempt to micro-manage the men and women appointed to serve as officers of the law in North Staffordshire. It didn't get much better than that.

But still, the man was prone to stress; and the deluge of the stuff he was under was threatening to burst the banks by the look of things. Not good for Berkins, and not good for anybody else, either. Because, in the time-honoured tradition of any organisation, when the pressure was on the likes of CS Berkins, the entire department knew it.

The meteoric rise to fame of the missing singer, Johnny Richards, had pushed that case, along with the attendant investigation into the murder of former band member Adam Lane, to unprecedented notoriety. The entire world, it seemed, wanted to know what had happened to the singer; and whether the fate of Richards bore any relation to the dead man.

Tyler took his place before the stressed-out chief superintendent. Before Berkins got on to such grave matters as murder and missing singers, he wanted to address another area of concern. With his thumb and forefingers tapping away at the respective ends of his moustache, he addressed Tyler in solemn tones. "I believe, Jim, that you have walked out of a second appointment with the staff counsellor."

Tyler began to speak, and Berkins responded, letting go of one side of his moustache to hold a raised forefinger at the DCI. "One moment, please. Let me finish." The speech followed, and it came as a source of great disappointment to Jim Tyler. He had expected more from a man like Berkins, not the rehashing of tired clichés that ought to have been retired and out on a boat somewhere enjoying their dotage.

Tyler let the long sentences roll over him. He tried not to appear disgusted at the lack of effort, the sheer absence of imagination on the part of the CS.

... The testimony to how high DCI Tyler was held in the esteem of the chief superintendent, and the department as a whole ... the challenges faced by any detective working in the cities of Great Britain these days ... the political context ... the economic context ... the toll that the job could sometimes take on an officer, particularly an officer as senior as Detective Chief Inspector Tyler ...

He tried to give Berkins the benefit of the doubt. The man was tired, distracted, tearing his hair out and clearly not operating anywhere near his best. Still, some things were destined never to change, and Tyler could feel the nutshell coming.

"In a nutshell, Jim. We all need help at times in our lives and in our careers. You are no different in that respect. You are a man, and an officer, of the highest integrity. It is not always easy to acknowledge what others might, ignorantly, perceive as weakness."

Tyler tried again to interject. And again the CS silenced him.

"Some things need saying, and without further delay. Now, there is no shame in addressing your issues professionally, no shame in that whatsoever. I value you beyond measure, but you are no good to me if you are firing on anything less than all cylinders."

God, the man's tense, thought Tyler. Probably more in need of counselling than anyone in the building. He doubted such advice would be accepted graciously.

The speech appeared to be winding up.

" ... So, perhaps you would care to tell me, Jim. Do you have a problem with that particular professional? I don't expect you to betray any confidences, naturally. What happens in there is of course between you and the counsellor - unless of course an issue arises that threatens the safety and well being of either yourself, your colleagues or the public at large."

"I'm not planning suicide, or to kill any fellow officers or members of the community, if that's what you mean," said Tyler.

He watched the agitation sitting opposite him slide up another notch, and he studied it with regret. "I have no issue with the woman. I'm sure she is perfectly capable."

"But?"

"I'm working things out myself."

"Are you, though?"

"I don't drink. I haven't punched anyone for ... how long is it now?"

Unable to help himself, Tyler looked at his watch to complete the joke. But Berkins didn't look at all amused.

Tyler sighed. "Look, Graham. I've got everything under control. If I'm a little tense some days, well, aren't we all?" He aimed his chin slightly in the direction of the chief.

Berkins glowered back. The CS appeared to be practicing some breathing techniques of his own, or else preparing for the onslaught of a full-blown panic attack. Tyler didn't care much for his colour.

"Either you will request to see a different counsellor, Jim, or else you will make an appointment with the same one, in your own time, within the next five days. Understood?"

"Better the devil you know."

"What's that?"

"Consider it done."

"Good man. Perhaps a good sort out is what the doctor ordered. It might clear your head sufficiently to make some progress on your current enquiries."

Tyler let it go. Stress was a killer, and he didn't wish to be responsible for another death in the neighbourhood. And anyway, Berkins was about to ask for an update on those *current enquiries*, and unlikely to be much impressed with what he was about to hear.

Having updated CS Berkins, Tyler awaited the eruption. He didn't have to wait long. The agitation had reached critical. A full blown hysterical breakdown, or else an immediate sacking, appeared imminent. The man was officially apoplectic.

Unspoken bile filled the room. Then a voice, restrained but quivering with frustration, ushered in: *Was the DCI seriously wasting valuable police time trying to decide who wrote a song?* "I have to make a statement. Within the hour I have to face the media and present them with reason to make this city confident that everything is being done to bring our enquiries to a satisfactory conclusion. Perhaps I can tell them that we are very close to establishing who wrote the song in question!"

A hand smashed down on the desk, and was instantly regretted. That hurt, thought Tyler, but the man won't show it. "Would you have me go out there and make a fool of myself, and make a fool of this department? Charles Dexter is already on the war path, and he wants results. Yesterday!"

And what Dexter wants, Dexter gets, thought Tyler. No higher authority in the county. Perhaps Dexter could leave the golf course or the business lunch early and pitch in. God once sent down his only son to get his hands dirty, but Charles Dexter stood in a higher realm than that.

Tyler thought back to his time in London, of his nemesis, Greenslade, the bully who had provided the last straw. The perfect excuse to let it all fly. Greenslade, who had come to stand for everything Tyler had ever despised. Who had finally coaxed the long promised punch out of an aching fist, earning Jim Tyler this exile in the City of Stoke on Trent. Greenslade, who had taken on the face of all bullies: at the care home where Tyler had spent his early years; at school and on the force.

But with the likes of Charles Dexter, the rank of a mere detective chief inspector could not expect to lose his rag and survive. Greenslade, yes, at a pinch and at a price; the price of a northbound ticket into the valley of the shadow of death. But Dexter? Not a chance in hell. Those were the rules. There had to be an ultimate sanction, an off-limit to any amount of reasonable justice, or else so-called civilisation could not reasonably be expected to survive. Charles Dexter was the strap in the hand of the house parent at St. Saviour's, and the stick in the hand of the headmaster on the same sick estate. You punched them and they had you flayed alive.

"Are you okay?"

Tyler heard the voice but for a moment couldn't place it. He looked again and saw Graham Berkins sitting there. Beneath all of the layers of fear and stress and responsibility that the chief superintendent was suffering under, humanity was still just about recognisable and holding sway. And for Tyler clarity was again restored; he could see that this man was not Greenslade and not Charles Dexter, and he deserved better.

CS Graham Berkins deserved the best.

Regaining his composure, Tyler smiled into the question-mark that sat looking back at him. "I will solve this case," he said. "Have faith in me, Graham. I will find Johnny Richards, one way or another, and I will bring to justice whoever killed Adam Lane."

For a few moments neither man said anything. Then Berkins nodded. "We'll leave it at that for today, then."

CHAPTER TWENTY TWO

Mills took the call. Mr Lane had found a page of lyrics, hand-written by his son. Lyrics to the song *All Colours Are Blue*. He asked Mr Lane if his son wrote only lyrics, or complete songs. "Oh, he writes the lot." The man corrected himself. "He *used* to, I should say," the sorrow in his tone close to unbearable.

"Did Adam make recordings of the songs he wrote, Mr Lane?"

"I don't know. I don't believe so. But still, doesn't this mean that my son owned at least half the rights to the song on the radio?"

"It might," said Mills, less than clear on the law when it came to music copyright. It would be a matter of proving ownership, he knew that much. Arguments over who had written what had been known to rage on for years. High-profile copyright cases he had seen on the news from time to time revealed clearly enough how dirty and protracted that business could be. "We can certainly look into it, Mr. Lane."

When Tyler emerged from his meeting with the CS and entered the CID office, Mills was waiting with two mugs of tea and a look of expectancy that required no translation. "The drink is very welcome, Danny, but as far as your question goes, let me put it like this. Berkins wants me to do something that I have no intention whatsoever of doing."

"I see."

"What do you see?"

"I'm not altogether sure."

Tyler took the drink from Mills. "Best that we leave it like that, then. Anything to report?"

Mills informed him of the call from Mr Lane. Tyler thought for a minute. "We're putting a tail on our three favourites so far."

"Favourites?"

"Frank Watts, Janine Finch and Billy Steele."

Late that evening Tyler put on his running clothes and set a course through the streets of Penkhull. It was a mild night, and dry. There could be no excuses. He ran through the lanes, along Thistley Hough, across Lodge Road, down through Hartshill and all the way into Newcastle. He wondered if he was still running away from those same memories, or else towards something that glittered and shone on the far, unseen horizon.

As the thoughts crowded in on him, Tyler ran faster, as though he was attempting to outrun thought itself.

Heading along the A34 he passed through Hanford, close to the house where Mo Richards lived and where Johnny had lived with her. Easing the pace, the thoughts came once more, battering through the roadblocks, and this time with greater sparkle, if to little avail. He thought of everything that might have happened to Johnny Richards; and every combination of events that could have led someone to take the life of Adam Lane. Theories, motives; ideas clashing, sometimes merging, but producing nothing but sound and fury and chaos in the mind. No genuine clarity, merely a lame approximation of it, no matter how hard he made the blood pound through his brain.

The solution might be a mere beat of blood away; a change of pace, a sudden burst of speed that would bring the picture into focus; but until the pieces fell into place, all that remained in Tyler's mind was a confusion of faces and voices.

He ran on to the Trentham Gardens roundabout, and through the village of shops and cafes, all closed now for the evening. He passed the Reality cafe where Billy Steele worked. *Billy Steele.* There was no evidence against him, or against anyone else, for that matter. There was nothing. He had left Graham Berkins to face the hounds with an empty hand, and it didn't feel good.

Tyler ran on into Trentham Park, following the path that led up to the Seven Sisters, the hills that Mills had pointed out when they had first driven towards the Trentham Estate. Feeling close to exhaustion Tyler paused to look down on the lake below. Panting for breath he observed the faces swimming through his mind, and tried again to make sense of the picture. Frank Watts, Billy Steele, Daisy and Janine Finch, Mo and John Richards and the Lanes. He conjured the photographs of the living Adam Lane, and the grotesque image of the dead young man, and the images of Johnny Richards.

Johnny Richards may be alive or dead, but one thing is certain: Frank Watts is laughing. Watts has hit the jackpot.

Tyler began running once more, back along the ridge of the Seven Sisters, back through the park, out onto the A34, heading through Hanford, Trent Vale, at last towards the final hill of Penkhull. Taking him to the place that he was still learning to call home, in the city that had adopted him and accepted him, stranger though he was.

His money was on Frank Watts, with a rider on Billy Steele. He had backed an outsider too. Yet it was all instinct tinged with wishful thinking and an ounce or two of dread. He couldn't make the sums add up.

It was late when Tyler finally crawled into bed, weary but still wired. He was finally closing his eyes to yield to beckoning sleep when the phone rang.

Mills had taken a call. Janine Finch had been out to visit Frank Watts.

"At the club?"

"No," said Mills. "At his house."

"What time is it?" said Tyler, his eyes adjusting to the unexpected brightness in the room. As he asked the question he checked the clock. It was early morning already; the night had been and gone. And the outsider had come in.

Janine Finch had been out to visit Frank Watts and she had stayed the night.

CHAPTER TWENTY THREE

"I'm not certain that it actually constitutes a criminal offence," Tyler told Mills as he waited outside Berkins' office.

"Janine Finch sleeping with her missing boyfriend's manager, you mean, sir?" said Mills. "And with Johnny Richards' song topping the charts!"

The detective sergeant's deadpan delivery cracked Tyler up. The door of Berkins' office opened without warning, finding Tyler doubled over.

"Glad you've found something to laugh about," said Berkins, ushering the senior detective in and closing the door unceremoniously on an unsurprised Danny Mills.

"Charming," the DS muttered to himself, before effecting a sharp about turn. "Know your place, Sergeant Mills. Left, right, quick step ..."

He marched away in parade ground fashion, grinning as he went.

Berkins looked to be teetering on the edge of something, a coronary or a stroke being the most likely contenders, thought Tyler. He wanted to offer comfort to the distressed chief superintendent, but knew well enough that kind words were not what Graham Berkins wanted to hear.

"I believe you have requested a warrant on a property belonging to Frank Watts. Can you explain your reasoning?" As Tyler explained the logic behind his request, Berkins' face darkened to a deeper and more dangerous shade of red. "So, let me clarify: are you now pursuing Richards as a suspect in the murder of Lane, or in the interests of popular culture?"

Tyler could see how pleased Berkins was with his pithy remark. *Let him have it*, thought Tyler. A line or two of good old-fashioned sarcasm is medicine for the soul. A lifesaver, in fact. *Take it with my compliments.* Mills was better at it, though. Mills was something of an artist when it came to delivering a dark stab of sarcastic wit without betraying a semblance of intended humour. The chief had a long way to go to catch up with DS Mills, though it was good to see that the man was at least trying.

Tyler spoke up for his own defense. "I am following up a number of lines of enquiry. It is possible that Richards fled into hiding following an altercation with Adam Lane, planned or otherwise. The timeline is tight, but not entirely out of the question. Watts may have wished to protect his valuable asset."

Berkins made no immediate comment, though his expression tightened another notch.

"It is also a possibility, of course, that Richards is dead. Janine Finch and Frank Watts could be co-conspirators, involved in the deaths of both young men. It is also possible—"

"Anything's possible!" spat Berkins. "But you don't have any evidence, otherwise I assume that you might have mentioned it by now."

"With respect," said Tyler, "that is why I requested the warrant."

"It sounds too much like conjecture to me."

The following morning Tyler was again awoken by an early call from Mills. Janine Finch had been keeping nocturnal company again. *Frank Watts*. Mills, as it happened, did not live a million miles from what he now referred to as "the scene of the crime."

It was still early when Tyler pulled up outside the neat semi-detached house in a quiet cul-de-sac close to Cheadle. He remembered when he had first met Danny Mills, and how the DS had still been coming to terms with his relocation out of the city and into the Staffordshire countryside. Mills hadn't exactly taken to the move, feeling something of a fish out of water away from the city streets and pubs and oatcake shops that he had known all of his life.

Tyler empathised, at least with the sense of dislocation. He had left the Big City for the relative backwater of Stoke on Trent, though in very different circumstances to those responsible for Mills' relocation. For Tyler it had been the price to be paid for finally giving a piece of dirt the kicking it deserved, and that many others might have delivered, had they the bottle for it. A multitude, by all accounts, had secretly applauded, though few had shaken his hand publically. It had almost cost Tyler his career, and would have if Greenslade hadn't settled for seeing his adversary leave his long-held position under a cloud of shame. There had been other perks, too, for that living piece of trash, and Tyler had to suffer the further indignities of knowing that the gloating would never end, and that he could never return.

Stoke on Trent hadn't held much appeal on first acquaintance. Tyler had found the place dull and filled with a redneck attitude that belonged way back when the land had been all forest and swamps. Yet, little by little, things had started to change. The hidden beauty of the place had stolen him, inch by inch, and a peculiar honesty and compassionate understanding from a significant proportion of its residents had done the rest. It had become a place that, some days at least, he could call home, and Danny Mills a colleague he was more than proud to call a friend.

So suck on that, Greenslade.

Mills had struggled in those first days, and Tyler had recognised the man's fears. This new DCI up from London, with new-fangled methods and a kick up the arse to any backwater attitude. Mills, and not only Mills, had been protective of his heritage, sensitive beyond belief. The locals could put the place down, and did so, many times and in many ways, and even appeared proud to do so. But if anyone from outside tried it, the ranks closed, and the tribe moved in on them.

Mills came out of his house and got in the car. "Froghall," he said.

"And good morning to you, sergeant."

As they drove through the countryside Tyler recalled how the stunning landscape surrounding the city, together with its inner lungs of greenery, had been one of the first things that had caused him to reevaluate the tired old cliché of a dark, drab industrial town that had lost its glory; the splendour of a world-famous pottery industry now merely a miserable collection of dislocated towns.

Arriving at Froghall, they crossed the railway lines and Mills pointed over to a large house at the edge of a wood. "I believe that's the Watts mansion."

"Trying hard to be a mansion," said Tyler. "Still, impressive enough. I didn't imagine such riches could come from running a small venue in Stoke."

"Watts has his fingers in many pies," said Mills. "He knows a lot of people."

"Sounds to me like a remark that carries hidden treasure."

"Watts has made a few enemies along the way. We're trying to get in touch with some of them."

"Good work," said Tyler. "You have been busy."

"I do my best."

"Not that we leap to premature conclusions."

"Your teachings have not been wasted," said Mills.

"So, Janine Finch, since we put the tail on her, has spent two nights in that house. We have 'no evidence on which to request a warrant with any credibility', and yet everything tells me that we have to get inside that property." Tyler glanced at his watch. "I make it about time for a cuppa. Do you reckon our Mr Watts keeps in a good supply of refreshments?"

"Only one way I know of answering a question like that, sir."

Tyler drove up to the house and parked in the spacious front driveway. There was no reception committee or obvious curtain twitching evident. "Shall I do the honours?" asked Mills.

"Be my guest."

The detectives got out of the car and walked up to the large and highly polished black wooden front door, on which a brass knocker was gleaming in the early morning sunlight. A doorbell had also been provided, but Mills went for the knocker, and used it resolutely, three times in quick succession.

A downstairs curtain twitched at last, and then the door opened. Frank Watts stood looking out on his visitors. "Was I expecting you?" he asked Tyler.

"Not unless you have been at the crystal ball. Or have friends on the force," Tyler added, pointedly. "You never know who knows who, these days."

Watts ignored the remark. "You've only just caught me," he said.

"We won't keep you long, sir," said Mills.

"What can I help you with?" asked Watts.

"Just a few questions, sir."

"Make it quick." Watts didn't move from the doorway and gave no sign of invitation.

"May we come in for a moment?" asked Mills.

"Is that necessary?"

"We don't usually conduct delicate business on doorsteps, if we can help it, sir."

Despite Mills doing the talking, Watts was keeping both eyes trained squarely on Tyler. At last Watts moved back inside the house and gestured to the detectives to follow him.

Inside, a large reception area greeted them, and Mills wondered if he had been in smaller stately homes. Then he wondered if he had been in any stately homes at all.

The reception area led into a sizeable living room, where Watts offered the detectives the opportunity to make themselves comfortable. Mills took a seat on one of the many chairs dotted around the room, while Tyler remained on his feet, looking around at the various furnishings and wall mountings, though not seeing anything that he felt inclined to comment on. The rich did not always lead such interesting lives, and so far he hadn't noticed anything in the house that contradicted that long-held wisdom. But Frank Watts certainly appeared to be rich.

"Please, take a seat," Watts said to Tyler. At last Tyler did so, joining Mills beneath the huge bay window that offered a stunning view of an idyllic England. Watts joined them. "You've got five minutes, then I really have to go. So, how can I help you, gentlemen?"

Mills asked how record sales were going.

"They are going well," said Watts. "But then I'm sure you know that already. I'm going to have to ask you to please get to the point."

"Janine Finch," said Tyler. "Johnny Richards' girlfriend, I understand. I wonder if we might have a word with her, if she's not too busy."

Watts stood up and was looking ready to remonstrate, when Finch walked into the room. Glancing at Watts, she took a seat opposite the two detectives. "You would like to speak to me?"

She was wearing the same boots, braces and combats that she had worn when Tyler and Mills visited her in Tunstall, and the same hard, uncompromising expression too.

For a moment the detectives were lost for words.

"You did want to speak to me?" she said.

"Does your boyfriend know about this cozy set-up?" asked Tyler.

"Right, that's enough," said Watts. "Your time's up."

Finch hadn't batted an eyelid. Mills stood up, but Tyler remained seated.

"Or *did* he know?" said Tyler, staring straight at Finch.

Something seemed to flip in Janine Finch, and without warning she launched herself at Tyler, fists flailing. Tyler was lightning quick, up on his feet, side-stepping and unbalancing the woman, restraining her despite the continued, frenzied attempts to lash out at him. Mills stood on hand to assist, but in the event wasn't needed. At last Janine Finch showed signs of calming down, though Tyler was taking no chances.

Watts stood watching, looking faintly amused.

"You can let me go now," said Finch. "I get a little uptight when people start accusing me of killing my boyfriend."

Cautiously, Tyler let her go.

She took her place at the side of Frank Watts and glared back at the detective. "So how did you dispatch Johnny Richards?" said Tyler, looking from

Finch to Watts. "And let me guess: fifty-fifty on the royalties?"

Watts looked at Finch. "Do you know what he's talking about?"

The fury in her appeared to have subsided, despite the provocation, and she laughed. "I haven't a clue."

"So," said Watts, looking at Tyler, "let me get this straight: you are accusing us of killing Johnny Richards?" Without waiting for a response, Frank Watts turned away, opening the door on the opposite side of the room and shouting, "Hey, have you got a minute." Leaving the door open, he returned to the side of Janine Finch and stood watching the detectives, grinning at them.

Tyler and Mills eyed the doorway, listening to the footsteps approaching. A few moments later a young man appeared, and entered the room.

Johnny Richards.

CHAPTER TWENTY FOUR

The three of them were taken to Hanley Police Station for questioning. Frank Watts and Janine Finch played it hard-faced all the way, making noises about solicitors and serious complaints, while Johnny Richards looked a safe bet to be the one who would give way and crack under pressure.

Richards, in skinny black jeans and a plain black t-shirt, sat in the interview room, looking nervously across the table at Tyler and Mills as the tape rolled. Watts had arranged a solicitor for Richards, and Tyler recognised the model: manicured and smooth and sharp as a razor; the kind the likes of Johnny Richards could never afford, unless there was anything left from the record sales once Frank Watts had finished taking his cut.

Tyler dispensed with the pleasantries. "Why did you kill Adam Lane?"

"I didn't kill anyone," said Richards. He looked edgy and at the same time subdued. Almost relieved, thought Tyler. A bundle of contradictions. Richards didn't abound with the nervous energy that seemed to be the constant companion of his band mate Billy Steele. There was a stillness, an assurance about him. A weird confidence. Yet the quick movements of the eye, the restless legs and the picking at the fingers nevertheless betrayed the jangling nerves that Richards couldn't altogether hide. Hardly unnatural, though, thought Tyler. When you've been taken to a police station and accused of killing your best friend.

Tyler spent the next few minutes riffing on variations on the theme of why Richards had killed Adam Lane. Why the two friends, so close previously, had fallen out so spectacularly. Artistic issues? Money? Women?

Richards was answering the questions with at least an appearance of candour, though he was still not saying much. He hadn't killed Adam Lane and they hadn't fallen out.

He wasn't coming across as someone with a dirty secret to hide, and accordingly the solicitor kept his own counsel, letting the circular examination go around a couple of times, and fruitlessly. He was getting paid to sit there watching the merry-go-round, after all, and his client appeared to be in no imminent danger from the questioning.

Without warning Tyler suddenly changed tracks. "Was Frank Watts keeping you against your will?"

The solicitor seemed to flinch at the question, though he still didn't respond formally. Richards shook his head. "Mr Watts has been kind to me. I stayed there because I wanted to. I didn't know what else to do."

"Why did you fail to turn up for the gig at the Thirteen club?"

Richards looked at the solicitor, who merely nodded.

"I ..."

"Yes?" said Tyler.

The words didn't want to come out. Richards' fingers were drumming on the table in front of him, his face the colour of a ripe tomato that had ambitions to become a beetroot.

"If you could please answer the question," pressed Tyler.

"I - bottled it," said Richards at last.

"You *bottled it*?" repeated Tyler. "Could you please explain what you mean by that." Richards glanced towards his solicitor, who again nodded his approval. "I couldn't face it. I don't know, the pressure got to me and I bottled out. I've never felt like that before. I just couldn't face it."

"So what exactly did you do? At what point did you 'bottle it'?"

Richards started from the beginning. Tyler and Mills had to agree, when they discussed the interview afterwards, that the account was nothing if not exhaustive.

The night before, following the rehearsal at the Liverpool Road studios in Stoke town centre, Johnny had stayed with his girlfriend, Janine. He had been okay during the band practice, but afterwards, when the band had all gone their separate ways, he began to feel edgy. Janine had picked up that something was wrong and he talked about his feelings with her. According to Richards, she had been nothing but supportive.

"She always supported me, behind me one-hundred percent in everything I'm doing. She said it was natural that I was nervous. The gig was a big moment in my life, and for the band too. A lot was riding on it.

"In the morning I got up for work. I knew I couldn't go through with the gig, but I couldn't tell Janine."

"Were you afraid of Janine?" asked Tyler.

"I didn't want to let her down. She had so much faith in me. I didn't want to let anybody down. I couldn't explain how I was feeling, not even to her. I had to ... get away."

And so Richards had gone through the motions of leaving for work. He didn't drive, and had taken his usual bus into Stoke. But on that day, instead of alighting on London Road, close to the factory, he had remained on the bus, getting off a few stops further on. "I just walked. I didn't know where I was going, I needed to keep moving. I walked all day. I didn't know where I was in the end. I found a pub and I started drinking."

He didn't recall how many drinks. At some point he left the pub; it was coming into evening by then. He knew that there was technically still time to get a taxi and make it to the gig. "So I started walking again, trying to get so lost and late that I could never get there in time even if I changed my mind. It was like there was two of me, fighting it out.

"I don't know how to explain it," he said. "I've never felt like that before."

Richards went on, recounting how eventually he came across another pub. "I had no idea where I was. It was late when I finished drinking. They wouldn't serve me any more and I asked if they would call me a taxi. When the taxi came I didn't know where to go. I had the address of Mr Watts in my head and I asked the driver to take me there."

When they arrived at Watts' house, there was no-one home. Richards hadn't enough money on him to pay the fare.

Tyler caught Mills' eye, and then the eye of the solicitor. A tacit agreement appeared to pass between the three parties, and Johnny Richards continued with his tale: The taxi driver threatening to call the police; Johnny begging him to wait until the owner of the house returned; Frank Watts returning home, paying the fare, giving Johnny shelter; telling him that he could stay there for as long as—

Again catching the eye of Mills and the solicitor, Tyler finally called time on the account.

"Mr Richards, you have a very vivid imagination. However, we only have so much recording tape available. Now, I would like you to tell me the truth. I would like to hear what actually happened."

The calm centre that appeared to have been holding Johnny Richards, collapsed. Tyler wondered if it had been an illusion all along; a thin, if reasonably presented, charade.

"But I've just told you ..."

"Mr Richards, please. You have been missing for days. Appeals and descriptions have been circulating on the television, in newspapers, and on the radio. Your photograph has become so familiar throughout this land and doubtless other lands beyond, that I doubt even the Royal Family have been getting your levels of coverage lately."

Tyler saw the eyebrows of the otherwise expressionless solicitor rise a fraction.

"I'm sure that you must be aware of your celebrity status. So, if you wouldn't mind: the truth, please." Tyler's voice was rising with frustration and Mills could feel the tension flooding through the room. Richards looked frightened.

"You caught a bus, you walked for miles, you stopped at two public houses, got so drunk that they refused to serve you, and then you had them call you a taxi. The taxi driver threatened to call the police."

Tyler paused for a few breaths. Tried to shake the shapes of fists from his hands.

"And yet, in the end, despite your subsequent notoriety, neither the taxi driver, nor anyone else whom you encountered on your extensive travels that day, has thought to *actually* call the police. Do you really think that is credible? Or would you like to reconsider your version of events?"

The solicitor took Richards to one side and whispered in his ear. A short break was requested and agreed on.

In the CID office Mills said, "For my money, Frank Watts set this up as a publicity stunt. He pre-arranged for Johnny Richards to 'bottle' the gig."

"And had Adam Lane killed to ramp up the media angle?" suggested Tyler, a wicked glint in his eye. "That would be some stunt. I'm not sure even the likes of Watts would ... but then again. You know, Watts as good as suggested it the first time I interviewed him. Not killing Adam Lane, of course. But providing the notion that Richards' disappearance had been good for business. A deliberate stunt."

"A double bluff, you mean, sir? Making a joke of it? Bit of a dangerous trick to try and pull off, though, wouldn't you say? Unless he was protecting himself, shifting the responsibility onto Richards."

The interview resumed, Tyler returning to the subject of the two once-great friends and fellow band members falling out. But according to Richards, it hadn't been so much a falling out as a drifting apart.

"You won't believe this," said Richards.

"You can try us," said Tyler.

"I asked Adam to rejoin the band."

"Go on."

"Billy wasn't right for us. It wasn't working out."

"Not working out?" said Tyler. "A successful record, a showcase gig?"

"Adam and I were like brothers. We had been, anyway."

"You mean like Cain and Abel?"

"Who?" asked Richards.

"Two brothers from the Old Testament who didn't get on. One wound up dead. It doesn't matter. It's a very old story. You were saying ..."

"I regretted Adam ever leaving and I wanted him back. Sometimes you don't know what you've got until it's gone."

"I think there's even a song about that," said Tyler, looking unconvinced and equally unimpressed.

"Maybe it was one reason I bottled the gig. I needed Adam, we used to be there for each other. I never felt that with Billy. I didn't want it to go any further with Billy - the band, I mean."

Tyler looked hard at Richards, as though studying a specimen under a microscope. Trying to identify exactly what he was looking at.

"While you have ... *been away*, I understand that your record has sold extremely well."

"That's not what this is about. If you think - if you think I did all of this to sell records ..."

"I want to know the truth, Johnny. That's all I want."

At that point the solicitor again leaned across and spoke quietly into his client's ear. It occurred to Tyler that whatever Richards was about to say, it had already been vetted, and possibly by Watts himself.

Men who never get their hands dirty. The rich, the powerful, the invulnerable. And the likes of Johnny Richards, talented or otherwise, merely pawns in the game.

Richards told his tale a second time. The revised version. It hadn't been Frank Watts that Johnny Richards had been protecting with his earlier account, but rather his girlfriend, Janine. The night before his disappearing act, in the early hours of the morning, he had confided in her, telling of his predicament. And in the end she had accepted it. That as things stood, he couldn't go through with the gig.

"She could see what state I was in. She could see there was no way I could play that gig. Better that I bottled it and didn't show up than screw up on stage in front of all those people."

"And you didn't think to inform your mates?" said Mills. "Or your parents, who have been worried sick? All these days and nights and you didn't come forward - why?"

"I should have done, I know that. And I would have."

"What stopped you?" asked Mills.

"I heard about what happened to Adam. It came on the news. I was scared that people would think I'd killed him. That's why I stayed in hiding. It was nothing to do with selling records. I was afraid I would go to prison for killing my best mate."

"Okay," said Tyler. "So, even if that part has any truth in it, why didn't you tell the band at least that you were bottling the gig?"

"I don't know. I couldn't face it. I couldn't face them. I felt ashamed, stupid. I wasn't planning any of this."

"And Janine wasn't trying to persuade you to change your mind?" asked Mills.

"I think she thought - if she didn't put any pressure on me, I might come round. She was giving me time and space. She knows me. She wanted what was best."

"And so what happened next?" asked Tyler.

"Janine wasn't at work until that evening. She stayed with me. I couldn't face going to work. At some point she knew that I really was bottling out."

Tyler measured up the question. It was, he knew, the hinge on which everything was about to swing. "Who contacted Frank Watts?"

Tyler watched the possible answers somersaulting through the mind of Johnny Richards; watching in fascination through the young man's rapidly blinking eyes. At last Richards said, "Janine rang him."

"Janine?" said Tyler.

"She got Mr Watts to come and see us play in the beginning. She knew Mr Watts is a reasonable man, and that he would understand."

"And did he?"

"After she rang him, she drove me out to his house. I didn't see him until late that night. He was angry, and I was scared at first. But he saw I was genuine, that I wasn't playing games. He could see the mess I was in.

"He said that I could stay at his house and that we would talk about where to go from there."

Richards went silent.

"And ...?" said Tyler.

"And then the news about Adam came out."

Tyler looked at Richards, at the mute solicitor, and at his own conjured image of Frank Watts. He allowed the scenarios that Richards had described to play out in brief within the confines of his imagination.

Then the solicitor clapped his hands loudly, once, and regained his powers of speech. "So: do you have any further questions to ask my client?"

Tyler looked at Richards. "*All Colours Are Blue* appears to be selling in vast quantities."

Richards nodded, but betrayed no emotion.

"Who wrote it, Johnny?"

He again looked at the solicitor, who nodded in his customary fashion. Turning back to face the DCI, the tears welled up, suddenly overwhelming him. Tyler watched and waited, Mills too. As the sobs abated, Richards wiped his face and said, "Adam wrote it. He wrote it for me."

CHAPTER TWENTY FIVE

Tyler and Mills relocated to the interview room that was temporarily housing Janine Finch, and asked for her version of events. Everything corresponded with the details given by Richards in his later account. When the brief representing Finch requested, on his client's behalf a short comfort break, Tyler and Mills adjourned to the CID office where they tried to answer the conundrum.

"Am I missing something, sir, or am I just plain stupid?"

"How long have I got?"

"It's just that ... Richards, Finch and Watts have been in that house together long enough to get their story straight, and yet Richards goes off on some imaginary tale of buses and taxis and pubs. He must have known that we would be asking his girlfriend - and Watts - the same questions, so why would he do that?"

"And the answer, my friend, is that you are neither stupid nor missing something. Unless of course the same applies to myself, which of course is blatantly absurd. Isn't that right, sergeant?" Tyler's eyes narrowed. "The creative imagination can be a strange beast. I don't know, maybe fear sent him off into fantasy land - I don't think we can rationalise it, if that is what you are looking to do. Perhaps there is something very wrong with Johnny Richards. I'm requesting a psychiatric report, though I'm not hopeful it can tell us a great deal. In fact, I'd put money on it."

The interview with Finch resumed.

When they quickly reached the stage of treading water, Tyler let loose: the feud with her sister; her fear that Adam might return to the band and usurp Johnny's position as leader and star; Watts conspiring with her to have Adam Lane killed because Lane wrote the song and would be wanting his share of the profits; Watts arranging the murder and Johnny Richards knowing about it. He didn't bottle the gig, he bottled being a party to the murder of his best friend and he fled into hiding as a result.

Did Watts expect the gig to go ahead as planned, after arranging Adam Lane's murder? Not telling Johnny of the plan but not counting on Johnny bottling the gig; then giving shelter, waiting to see how it played out; seeing the angle on the publicity as an unexpected bonus. Maybe Johnny Richards could end up taking the rap after all, instead of, as originally planned ... Billy Steele?

He was firing off rounds like a Western hero, but Finch and her brief kept their silence and appeared content to enjoy the fireworks.

"Was Adam demanding his share - was that why he was approached about rejoining, to appease him, while all the while behind his back the knives were being sharpened?"

Finch's solicitor, no doubt another member of the Frank Watts team, thought Tyler, at last called a halt. He asked the DCI if he had any evidence with which to back up his wild accusations. Tyler was about to speak when Finch said, "I wasn't aware that Adam Lane wrote the song."

"Is Frank Watts aware?"

"How the hell should I know? Have you asked him?"

That hard faced confidence. She was made of stronger stuff than her boyfriend. Again thoughts of Lady Macbeth came into Tyler's mind. *The king maker, wanting her man to take his place on the throne so that she might become queen.*

Frank Watts, flanked by his solicitor, gave a corresponding account. He spoke with confidence but without swagger, appearing untroubled, if a tad concerned for the welfare of Johnny Richards. He feared that the young man may be suffering with depression. But in saying that, Watts insisted, he spoke only as a layman and a concerned friend and not as a professional.

Tyler considered the comments for a moment before accusing Watts of conspiring with Richards and Finch to have Adam Lane killed. The objection from the solicitor followed swiftly, and Watts didn't bat an eye through any of it. Why would he have a man killed that he didn't know and had never even met? That wasn't the way he went about his business. It wasn't the way any sane person went about their business.

"The song," said Tyler. "*All Colours Are Blue.* Who wrote it?"

"I thought we were in a pub quiz there for a minute," said Watts.

"Do you think any of this is funny?" asked Tyler.

"No, not really. I understood that Johnny Richards wrote that one," said Watts. "And he wanted Adam back in the band."

"Why? Because Adam Lane had in fact written the song and wanted his fair share of the proceeds from sales?"

Watts laughed. "Now that I do find funny. You really think that Lane was killed over a song? Do me a favour! Johnny wanted his mate back in the band because they worked well together. He didn't think Steele was right for the band and that's all there is to it, as far as I know."

"You once suggested that Richards going missing might be a publicity stunt, Mr Watts."

"Did I? And you believed me? Maybe I was being sarcastic."

"But you didn't think to inform me that Richards, a missing person wanted in connection with the murder of Adam Lane, was in fact living under your roof?"

"I was concerned for Johnny's well being. If I had for one second thought that he had killed somebody I would have been on the phone to you like a shot. Do you really think that I would have risked everything I've worked for to harbour a killer? Why would I do that?"

Tyler eased back in his chair.

"Johnny was in a right state over the gig, and an even worse state when it came on the news about his mate."

"You don't think that he might have been *in a right state* because he had killed somebody, or been a party to it?"

"No, I don't. Not for a second."

"Were you not angry with Richards for letting you down?" asked Tyler. "Risking your *reputation*?"

Watts appeared to weight the question carefully. "With almost anyone else, in any other circumstances, that would have been that, no question about it.

"But then Johnny Richards is a remarkable talent. You don't come across the likes of him very often, and I was prepared to make an exception. I could see he was genuine. He convinced me that Billy Steele was wrong for the band, and that with Adam back in he could move forward. It's a tragedy what's happened and I hope that you can bring the killer to justice."

Tyler locked eyes with Watts. "Oh, believe me, Mr Watts. We will."

The interviews wound up, Tyler and Mills taking their thoughts back upstairs to the office. They talked over the case, considered the angles; but whichever way they looked at it the same conclusion reared its ugly head: they had reached a dead end.

They had found Johnny Richards, but were no further forward in finding Adam Lane's killer. Richards' alibi for Lane's death wasn't watertight any more than Billy Steele's was, though in both cases it was pretty close to being so. And unlike Steele, Richards had to make his way without a car, as Janine Finch had been working. Giving him even less time or demanding an accomplice. Or risk leaving a traceable loose end.

Watts. Frank Watts. He was like a bad tooth that the DCI couldn't leave alone.

Did Watts expect the gig to go ahead ... not telling Johnny of the plan ... not reckoning on Johnny bottling the gig ... giving Johnny shelter ... waiting to see how it played out ... the publicity an unexpected bonus ... Richards taking the rap instead of ... Billy? ... Watts didn't like Billy ... was it all planned out ... or none of it ...?

Tyler was going back around in the same old circles and his head was bursting with it. At last he gave it up and Mills couldn't help but look relieved. There were no new leads, and no-one else in the frame to talk to. "We need a break, something new, or somebody. A development. We have to make something happen. There's nothing else for it, Danny. We shout louder. All eyes on this city."

"Sir?"

"We are going to have to tell the world, or at least Berkins is. *Johnny Richards, alive and well.*"

"Alive, at least," said Mills.

"Correction accepted."

"At this rate," said Mills, "that record's going to end up selling more copies than *White Christmas*."

CHAPTER TWENTY SIX

In the interview room housing Johnny Richards, the brief was getting tetchy. How much longer were they planning to keep his client without a shred of evidence against him? Were they charging him or letting him go?

Everyone in the room knew the answer to that. But still Tyler wanted to ask one more question before turning the newly appointed superstar free to face his adoring fans.

"You have admitted that the song, *All Colours Are Blue*, was in fact written by Adam Lane. Do you intend making that fact public, ensuring that Adam Lane is properly credited with writing the song, and consequently that all royalties from sales of the record will then pass to Mr Lane's next of kin?"

"Of course," said Richards.

"Why," said Tyler, "was that not done originally?"

The solicitor started to interject, but Johnny Richards cut across him. "I never intended doing Adam out of anything, it never crossed my mind. Adam wrote that song for me and I used to love singing it. When we went our separate ways, I stopped singing it because I knew it was his song and not mine."

"So, what changed?"

"I'm not sure. One day I was going over material and I dug out the song and started singing it again. I realised what a great song it is, but also how right it is for me, for my voice. But more than that."

"What are you saying?" asked Tyler.

"The song is about me. When I rediscovered it, I realised that. It was written out of love. I saw what Adam had done, and how deep our friendship really was." The solicitor coughed, but Richards hadn't finished. "I'm gutted, what's happened. If Adam had come back to the band, as I wanted, do you think I would have kept the proceeds from the song?"

"Are they yours to keep?" asked Tyler.

Richards was floundering.

"Frank Watts took ownership of the song, and any proceeds generated from its sale. But it wasn't yours to give away, was it, Johnny? And now neither you, nor Frank Watts - and sadly, not even your *friend* - will gain a penny from sales. His family will benefit though."

The venom in that last line seemed to coat the room, and the dark silence that followed it was fierce.

Richards was free to go.

Along the corridor, in the next interview room, the detectives again took their places in the company of Watts and his brief. Tyler ask the same question that he had put to Richards: Was he prepared to make Lane's ownership of the song clear, signing a legal document to ensure that full copyright be made over to Adam Lane?

Watts agreed. He had accepted the deal with Richards in good faith. He had not been aware of Adam's authorship of the song.

It was left to the solicitor to pour on the mockery, suggesting that now the simple misunderstanding had been cleared up, people might be allowed to go home and get on with their lives. No deceit had been intended by anybody, and by any reasonable standards the whole business hardly constituted a credible motive for murder.

Finally, the two detectives sat across the table from Janine Finch. But this time Finch was the one asking the questions.

Was *her Johnny* going to receive a full apology for being accused of a crime he hadn't committed? For being *dragged* to a police station to be humiliated, because the police, like so many other people in the city, couldn't bear to see a genius like Johnny Richards finally getting the recognition he deserved?

When the tirade had finished, Tyler said, "Are you aware that the song that appears to have made *your Johnny* famous, was in fact written by his 'friend' Adam Lane? That copyright of the song will now be restored to its rightful owner and that the beneficiaries will be Lane's family?"

If it had been a reaction Tyler was angling for, he got it. Finch moved to her feet and raised a finger like a gun, pointing it right into the DCI's face. "You've done this out of spite. You just can't stand to lose, can you? You don't know who killed Adam Lane and you can't pin it on Johnny, so you want to take what you can from him. You make me want to puke!"

"Adam wrote the song," said Tyler. "You don't think it fair that the least his family deserves is the money that would rightfully have been their son's?"

"It's Johnny's song!" she screamed.

Mills, along with the solicitor, pleaded for calm while Tyler sat steely-eyed. When Finch had returned to her seat, the DCI said, "Johnny himself has admitted that Adam wrote the song. We didn't beat the admission out of him. He gave us the information, in the presence of legal representation, entirely of his own volition."

"It doesn't matter, you stupid—"

The solicitor advised Finch to show restraint.

"*It doesn't matter.*"

"How so?" asked Tyler.

"Even if it was written by *him*, it was given to Johnny. It belongs to Johnny now."

"You knew it was written by Adam?"

Finch didn't answer.

The solicitor asked if his client could go.

The interview was over.

"Nothing fits or adds up to anything," said Tyler to Mills as the two of them shared a hot drink in the CID office. "Finch wants the world for her boyfriend. But if she had played any part in the death of Adam Lane, I don't imagine she would have sounded off like that. Call me old-fashioned. And Richards might already have told her the song was written by Lane - I'm not sure there's anything in any of that."

Tyler thought for a moment. "Richards, through his own naivety, has ended up in the clutches of Frank Watts. He could have become a huge star, he still might, but Watts would have stood to make all the money. It's an old story, and you could no doubt fill Wembley a thousand times over with young hopefuls who have fallen foul of the man in the suit promising to make them rich and famous."

"I don't doubt it for a moment," said Mills.

"Finch worked at the club, worked for Watts. She got Watts to take a look at the band, and that led to him offering one of his shady deals. Fair enough so far. Adam Lane is out of the band by then, and Billy Steele is in. I don't trust Watts as far as I can throw him, but is he going to risk everything by arranging the murder of Adam Lane over the ownership of one song? I doubt that very much. So, tell me, Danny: what does that leave?"

"Steele killing Lane because Lane was being asked back into the band to replace him?" suggested Mills. "Richards killing Lane because Lane wouldn't rejoin, and threatening to expose the theft of his song?" Mills spoke the words without any conviction.

"But can we prove it? Do we even for one second believe any of that is credible?"

"I think that depends, sir. I don't think it's the kind of behaviour you would expect from a normal person. I think it depends on how sane, or else unhinged, we think Richards or Steele are. Have we got anything back on the psychiatric assessment?"

"Nothing of any interest. And there's nothing in the background on either of them. I don't see Richards as the killer, Danny. It doesn't fit. If Watts had any notion that Richards had blood on his hands ...

"No, that man has too many secrets of his own, we'd all put money on that. No way would a guy like Watts give shelter to Richards if he thought he'd killed someone. On the contrary, I imagine he would have relished the additional media coverage. I think he would have shopped Richards faster than you could say his name. He'd have worked out the angles with the newspapers and the television networks - in some ways Frank Watts' dreams would have come true.

"I think he realised that it simply wasn't credible. I'm inclined to the notion that Richards really did bottle the gig and Watts came to believe him - and when the news broke about Lane, I'm sure that Watts would have interrogated the living daylights out of him."

Mills looked at the DCI. "So what about Billy Steele?"

Tyler sighed. "I look at Steele and what do I see? I see *victim.* I see the me that I don't want to see and some days he's too close for comfort. Some days all I feel is resentment and anger and on those days I could kill to stop the pain and be filled, not with remorse, but with righteous indignation."

Mills looked at his colleague and friend with nothing but compassion. "Do you think, Jim, that it's time you talked to someone?"

"I'm talking to you, aren't I?"

"I mean—"

"I'm making you nervous?"

Mills started to say something.

"It's alright, Danny. I appreciate it. Your concern, your friendship. And you are right, I will talk to someone. Because people like you don't deserve to bear the brunt and to keep on bearing it. So either I hand in my notice or I clean up, once and for all."

Tyler looked at the clock on the wall.

"Let's call it a night, shall we?"

CHAPTER TWENTY SEVEN

Tyler lay on his bed, tired and restless. Too wired to sleep and too fractured to put his thoughts into any kind of order that made sense. His thoughts were raging, moving like a wild fire, out of control, consuming all that stood in the way. Attempting to keep a focus on the case, he tried to narrow his inner gaze as the faces rose up, kindling to the flame, to be quickly devoured, leaving nothing he could use. Watts, Richards, the Finch sisters, the Lanes, Steele - nothing remained still for long enough. The image of Frank Watts segued into the playground bully, becoming the man in the black cloak, the head master, the house master, building empires on pain and grief, becoming Greenslade back in London.

Tyler's thirst for alcohol was growing like a curse as he lay on the bed longing for oblivion; something, anything, to kill all of this.

To lay it finally to rest.

He got dressed into his running clothes and set out into the night. Every road in Penkhull that wasn't a hill had a hill leading off it, and he had a mind to tackle every last one of the bastards.

Tyler circled the streets, finding new avenues, routes that he had not ventured down before. A labyrinth of possibilities, up hill and down again. As he worked through the miles, tracing the borders with Hartshill and Stoke, Oakhill and Trent Vale, he allowed fatigue to reach deep down to the core, until finally he was ready to begin the climb back towards the village square and home, this new found home.

The square was empty. Tyler walked the perimeter of the churchyard, getting his breathing back under control, beginning the warm down, weary again to the brink of exhaustion, yet somehow more alive than he had felt in a long time.

He stood under the hot shower until the skin was practically scalded off him, and then he took a hot drink to bed.

Within seconds of closing his eyes he thought of Kim back in London, now married with children. Sleep transforming the once love of his life, the lost love for whom he had placed a stake through his own heart, turning her now in dreaming, exhausted and pitiful sleep into ... *this* ... this new creation, this dim horizon of new possibilities, this woman he had come close to reaching out to last summer ... *Alison Hayburn* ... and he had let her down ... because Kim had left with that stake still piercing him ... refusing to come back and rescue him ... forever unlovable ... but Alison Hayburn was looking for him, in this crazed fairy tale she was out there and hunting him down ... to save his soul ... not out of mere compassion ... but the stirrings ...

... *of love*?

Tyler turned over, the dark side of the coin waiting to reveal itself. He *was* Billy Steele. But not here in Penkhull; not here in Stoke on Trent. Back in Leicestershire, on the estate, in the care home. The orphanage of lost hope.

St. Saviour's.

In trouble again, speaking out of turn ... demanding a loving embrace, once in a while. The housemaster responding with a whipping for impertinence ... the small, skinny figure no longer Jim Tyler, but now Billy Steele as the belt thrashed down on his fragile frame, the silent screaming rupturing his insides, still bearing scars.

Tyler stirred but sleep still held sway, taking him back to a dozen classroom episodes of a fist here, a kicking there. A headmaster who told the boy that he was not unsympathetic to his situation; that every young man needed a father, and that he, the man in the sinister black cape and dark beard would be his father now, a father with a grievance, a shepherd who taught his lost sheep with a shepherd's crook, done for love, the same grim scars but formed in a different image, the rampant headmaster becoming every bully, every figure of authority abusing its power, bearing down on the bent figure of the boy Jim Tyler, the stick rising and falling and the laughter at the windows echoing through the years ...

Tyler sat bolt upright, the sweat pouring from him.

One day I will nail those devils and hang them all from the same cross.

Bringing his breathing back under control he leaned back slowly on the pillow. *But for now ... justice for Adam Lane. Nothing more than that ... and nothing less.*

Tyler awoke with sunlight pressing in through his bedroom window. It was early and yet he felt strangely refreshed, ready to do battle. At the police station Mills updated him. Richards was back home with his mother, keeping a low profile despite the clamour of a nation's-worth of insatiable fans; an adoring public that would not be denied.

The latest press release announced to the world that Johnny Richards had been found safe and well but that he was taking some time out. He had asked that the privacy of his friends and family be respected.

The press conference had thrown up a myriad of questions. Was Johnny being investigated in relation to the death of Adam Lane? Was he a suspect? Had he been attacked himself? Kidnapped? Had a ransom been paid and if so how much? Was the song really a suicide note? Was there a tour, an album to be announced?

"Some folk can't lose for winning," said Mills. "Richards and Watts might lose a small fortune on *All Colours*, but they stand to make an absolute killing on future releases and tours."

"You don't say," said Tyler. "I hope that you are not suggesting that any of this was foreseen when the ownership of the song was so generously revealed."

"Nothing further from my mind, sir."

"Has Berkins shown his face this morning?"

"Not as yet, as far as I know."

Tyler frowned. "Give me five minutes."

There was no sign of Berkins, though he had been expected at the station early according to his diary. His secretary hadn't been instructed of any change of plan, and Berkins had never been one to ring in sick.

Heading back towards the CID office Tyler thought, *Something's wrong. I would have put my pension on Berkins wanting to see me first thing.*

Mills greeted him with a concerned look. "Is anything the matter, sir?"

"Yes, as a matter of fact. I don't know what exactly. But something."

"There has been a development," said Mills. "Daisy Finch."

"What about her?"

"Taken to hospital. It sounds like she's had a right battering."

"Do we know who was responsible?"

"We have our suspicions, sir."

CHAPTER TWENTY EIGHT

Janine Finch opened the door of her flat. Finding Tyler and Mills on her doorstep she rolled her eyes. "My lucky day. I suppose you'd better come in."

The detectives followed her inside.

There were swellings around both her eyes, and dark bruising prominent around her right cheek. Mills could see scratch marks on her neck and on her hands and arms. He recalled an occasion from his schooldays, girls fighting, not a pretty sight. The boys always said that girls' fights were the worst. They weren't as hard as the boys, of course, according to the wisdom of the day. But they were reputed to be the more vicious when it came right down to it.

Finch didn't deny that she had been in a fight with her sister, and her flat also bore the hallmarks of the altercation. The place looked, thought Mills, as though a burglar had undergone a psychotic episode. Everything seemed to be broken and displaced, though Finch herself appeared the very definition of calm.

"Would you care to tell us what happened?" asked Tyler.

Daisy had come to Janine's flat late on, and when she answered the door her sister had pushed her way in and attacked her. "She went crazy. I could hardly contain her. She was smashing up my things and when I tried to stop her she was swinging at me. What choice did I have? I had to defend myself."

"I believe," said Mills, "that your sister has sustained a broken wrist, three cracked ribs and severe bruising to her face and abdomen."

"I don't look a pretty picture myself. I gave as good as I got, that's all. She would have killed me."

Janine had managed to manhandle her sister from the property. Nobody had called the police, and Daisy hailed a taxi and returned to her flat. It was only later, after experiencing severe abdominal pains, that Daisy called for an ambulance.

"Did she give any reason for attacking you?" asked Mills.

"She was looking for Johnny. She'd heard he'd been found and that you lot had released him. She thought he'd be here. She was banging on about how it was Johnny who killed Adam. I told her she was talking out of her arse, that Johnny would never harm a fly and that deep down she knew it. But you couldn't reason with her. She needs taking in somewhere. She needs a fucking lobotomy."

"If she blamed Johnny, why did she attack you?" asked Mills. "Why didn't she go looking for Johnny elsewhere?"

Janine tapped the side of her head. "Because she's nuts, that's why. She turned on me, said it was my fault Adam was dead. I told her to make her mind up. I'm not taking the rap for this, I tell you. I was defending myself and my property." She looked around at the state of the place. "What's left of it. That bitch wants locking up, I'm not kidding."

"Are you intending to press charges?" asked Mills.

"What's the point? No-one believes me, just like they don't believe Johnny. Everyone thinks Adam was a saint and that bitch sister of mine too. They could both put on that angelic butter-wouldn't-melt act and it's bullshit. No, I'm not 'pressing charges' - but she still wants locking up, for her own safety and everyone else's."

Daisy Finch was discharged home later that day and Tyler and Mills thought it rude not to visit the convalescent. Finch answered the door looking about fifty years older than when the detectives had last visited her. She had clearly taken the worst of it. Her face was a mass of bruised swellings, one eye almost closed. She moved around the flat like a geriatric, bent and wincing with every step. Cracked ribs were nobody's idea of fun.

Easing herself onto a chair, she offered a painful smile. "I'll be okay," she said. "My sister thinks she's tough, but it would take more than that cowbag to put me out of action."

Looking at her, Mills doubted that. But he couldn't deny that the young woman had spirit. There was no trace of self-pity, or any attempt to garner sympathy. Indeed, the opposite: she appeared to wear the wounds of battle with a certain pride, he thought.

"Why did you visit your sister's flat last night?" he asked.

"I went looking for that lump of trash."

"Which *lump of trash* would that be?" asked Tyler.

Finch gave him a look, and Mills saw the hardness, the toughness beneath suddenly exposed to the light, savage and raw. Daisy, slighter in build, more delicate in features, appeared the tamer, more fragile, gentle version of her sister. But in that flash Mills recognised the presence of the same seething heart that might rip worlds apart.

"I was looking for *Johnny Richards*," she said, almost spelling the name out.

"And what would you have done had you found him?" asked Tyler.

"Are you joking?"

"I am asking you a question. If you had found Johnny Richards last night, what would you have done next?"

She started to laugh, until the pain pulled her up short. Both hands nursed at her abdomen. "I would have asked him if he had any plans for a world tour. Maybe his autograph, for my darling little sister. I would have asked him if he had any more records coming out - and then I would have ripped his head off."

"You believe Johnny Richards killed Adam?" asked Mills.

"Miss Finch?" said Tyler.

"If it wasn't for him, Adam would still be alive."

Tyler pressed the point. "Miss Finch, do you believe that Johnny killed Adam?"

"I don't know if he actually killed him. But it's because of him."

"Can you explain what you mean?" said Tyler.

"I've lived with Johnny. I've seen what he's like, what he's *really* like. Everyone sees a dreamer, a harmless dreamer. Cute little Johnny Richards. Someone not of this world, floating somewhere above it. But when things aren't going Johnny's way you'd better watch out."

"But things were going his way, surely?" said Tyler. "And I understand that he wanted Adam back in the band."

"That was just smoke and mirrors, that's all that was. Adam wouldn't have gone near it. It was obvious, Johnny was scared of Adam, scared of him taking over, because Adam was the one with the talent and they both knew it. But Johnny knew it the most. He was making it look like he wanted Adam back, but it would never have happened."

"Why would he do that?" said Tyler.

Finch looked sharply at the two detectives. "I don't know exactly how that bastard's mind works, no-one does, even if they think they do. Maybe he meant it to look like he wanted Adam back, so no-one would be looking his way when Adam was killed. I wouldn't put anything past him. He didn't want Adam anywhere near his band. I don't know, maybe it was about the song. So Adam wouldn't kick up a storm over who wrote it."

"And would he have? Was he doing?" asked Mills.

Finch shook her head, the effort appearing to make her wince.

"Are you okay?" asked Mills.

"I will be," she said. "Adam wasn't that type. He was too easy-going. He actually found it funny that Johnny was recording a song chronicling his own depression - a song that Johnny hadn't even written! But there was more than that. Adam believed it helped Johnny. He didn't bear a grudge, he was not the kind. He believed the song helped Johnny recognise he had a problem.

"But even so, he still deserved recognition for what was rightfully his. Exposing Johnny as a thief - yes, I think that's why Adam died."

A snarl of bitter laughter followed. "That *is* ironic, don't you think?"

Tyler's face assumed the shape of a question mark.

"I mean," said Finch, "that even Adam didn't realise the extent of the problems Johnny Richards had, or how dangerous that made him. I think my sister would have killed to protect her *precious Johnny*. They really are two of a kind."

"So now you believe that *Janine* killed Adam?" asked Tyler.

"I don't know who killed him. I wasn't there. That's supposed to be your job, isn't it? Isn't that what you are paid for - to find out who killed Adam?"

A trickle of tears coursed down over the bruises and swellings.

It was time to go. Like her sister, Daisy Finch was not intending to press charges. Neither was she planning to attack Johnny Richards. Her anger, she said, had overtaken her, but it was spent now. She would wait for the police to bring the killer to justice.

Tyler and Mills together absorbed the scorn in those last words and said their goodbyes.

*

Out in the car Mills observed the grim mood that had again overtaken the DCI. He waited for Tyler to say something. At last Mills said, "Are you alright, Jim?"

It was, thought Mills, as though the demons that possessed the Finch sisters, Daisy and Janine, had passed on their spite, transferring the malignancy, and it had taken hold of Jim Tyler. *Have we ceased to become detectives, getting nowhere on the case, adopting the role of exorcists?*

Tyler, becoming aware of the scrutiny, looked back at Mills, his expression haunted, fuelled with rage. "I will," he said, "find the killer, whoever it is, and for whatever reasons they did what they did. I will find them.

"I will find them and I will bring them in if it kills me."

CHAPTER TWENTY NINE

Chief Superintendent Graham Berkins had suffered what was being described as a 'coronary incident.'

"A heart attack?" Tyler asked the desk sergeant.

"Sounds like it to me. But coronary incident is what they're calling it. They never call anything what it is, these days. Poor sod."

"Quite."

On the way up to the CID office Tyler said, "Wife and two kids, I believe."

"Same as me," said Mills. "Same age as you."

Tyler didn't respond to that.

Following the briefing, someone asked for the latest on Johnny Richards.

"Selling records by the shit load," said Mills.

Laughter shook the room for a few seconds, and then quickly fizzled out. The feel around the place was tense, particularly in the presence of DCI Tyler.

The news about Berkins had cast a further, denser cloud over the mood of the team. Berkins could be a stickler, no-one argued with that, and in his position he had to be. That much was acknowledged and generally accepted at Cedar Lane. But Berkins was considered a *reasonable* stickler, a fair man. Liked and trusted, or at least as far as any high-ranking figure could be. Tyler had said as much already and Mills hadn't found fault with any of it.

The entire team wished Berkins well, all of them genuinely rooting for him.

Johnny Richards was about to give his first public interview since returning home. In the CID office the team gathered around the radio.

At three minutes and thirteen seconds into the interview, Richards took an audible breath. And then he stated to a listening nation that the song, *All Colours Are Blue,* had been written by his late friend, Adam Lane. Lyrics and music, all down to Adam.

He sounded emotional as he spoke about how deep their friendship had been; of how his friend had written the song for him, a song about his - Johnny Richards' - depression. About his - Johnny Richards' - struggle with drugs. It had not been Johnny's suicide note, as many had suggested, but Adam's wake-up call to his best friend. Johnny was clean now, one-hundred percent, though continuing to battle with depression.

The interview became, finally, a public appeal for information. If anybody knew anything, had seen anything, that could help lead to finding the person responsible ...

The interview was given an upbeat coda; a few questions about what Johnny Richards had planned. A tour was on the cards, and the band would soon be starting work on an album. "We need to get back to it," Johnny Richards told the nation. "We need to move on."

"Well, I don't think Richards' admission is going to harm sales," said Tyler, switching off the radio. "On the contrary. Though I wonder if the band may undergo a change of personnel."

"Billy Steele?" suggested Mills.

"We will have to wait and see," said Tyler.

The feeling around the team suggested that it was only a matter of time before someone came forward with the vital piece of information that would break the case open. The world it seemed was aware of the situation, and most of its population owned a copy of the record, judging by the volume of sales. Everybody had heard of Johnny Richards, and everybody knew about the death, the murder of Adam Lane. The stroke of luck that could bring everything else tumbling into place - it was coming and everybody sensed that it was coming. It was just a matter of waiting for the door to swing open or the phone to ring.

A get-well card for Graham Berkins was doing the rounds and the team all signed it. When Tyler had finished adding his own best wishes for a speedy recovery, he handed the card to Mills. Then he picked up the phone and, in front of the bemused DS, made himself an appointment.

Ending the call, Tyler looked at the gob-smacked sergeant. "Earliest they can see me is tomorrow. I will try to remain sane until then."

"You can only do your best, sir."

Tyler stood up. "Don't get me wrong, Danny. I may have ulterior motives."

Mills didn't appear altogether surprised to hear it. "Well," he said, "I did say that she's a bit of a looker, by all accounts."

"I didn't mean those kind of motives! If I'm the one taking Berkins the flowers I need to be able to give him some good news."

The following morning, as good as his word, Tyler sat once again opposite the woman tasked with putting him back together again - or at least with spending a few minutes in his company before his customary early exit.

The woman appeared nervous and Tyler was hardly surprised. But he had no reason to make anybody's job more difficult than it need be, and no intention of doing so. He remained in his chair for the full fifty minutes, and he even threw the young lady's day out of kilter by throwing in a full five minutes overtime, clocking off from the session at five minutes to the hour. He knew, of course, that it could do no good, any of it. But still he took it through the motions. It was the least he could do.

He started at the beginning.

Growing up on a rough estate in Leicester. He had never known his father, and his mother died when he was young. Enter St. Saviour's. A place of wailing and gnashing of teeth. Monsters coming out of the brickwork, bullies of all shapes and sizes; the running away, recapture, punishment; school becoming an extension of those sufferings, with teachers and headmasters promising to be the *father you never had*. Cue more wailing and further gnashing of teeth.

A chance encounter; an aunt and uncle who had lain dormant for all of his life up to that point. A lot of catching up to do. The chance to go to college. A flame ignited and the rebellion showing the first signs of dying down.

Learning, education, ambition. A new mantra, and one that he could embrace. The father he never knew had been a police officer, though not a particularly good one. Another seed sown, and one that would remain forever ambivalent; that would not grow altogether straight but not grow crooked, either.

The move to London. The love affair with Kim, and the breaking apart. The moving through the ranks, working, always working; still trying to outrun the past, and working out on the running track and in the gym. Hiding the skinny frame that the bullies had loved to beat, and covering it with a wall of muscle.

Enter Greenslade. The one who proved to Jim Tyler, beyond all question, that not all the wickedness had been left behind. That the eternal story of good and evil, heroes and villains, had never been that simple: Life, he had discovered, was far more nuanced than that, and the cardboard cut-out, one-dimensional goodies and baddies lived only in the pages of fiction or else on the screen, large and small. In real life the forces of good came with embedded demons, the same as the disciples had come with Judas Iscariot.

Greenslade had come to stand for them all.

He'd been drinking quite a bit for some time by then, and it wasn't doing a thing for his anger management. And then the day arrived when it all came together. When the face of every playground bully, every stick and strap wielding devil formed into the shape of DCI Greenslade, and the punch was fired, all the way from the shoulder, and it could never be taken back.

Exile. Stoke on Trent. The story so far.

He had given up drinking but he hadn't given up feeling angry. He was out running through the streets of his new city when he wasn't working; when he wasn't trying to bring justice to the streets of that same city. He was as home as he had ever been or was ever likely to be. He had known love and he had blown it. Not so long ago he thought that he had come close to finding it again, only to blow it again. It was getting to be a habit, and one that he doubted he would ever be rid of.

Some things, perhaps, were never meant to be. Not everybody on the sad planet did find love, and even fewer had the sense or good fortune to keep hold of it when they did. Maybe he didn't deserve to find it, he was willing to concede that much. And meanwhile he was running to escape the past, over and over, time and again and running to keep the hounds of anger and resentment at bay. Some days it worked and some days it didn't touch the sides. And still he fought against authority - whenever the need to arose, and occasionally even when it didn't - and he hoped that he always would do.

Jim Tyler had a case to solve, and he had made for himself a promise that was not his to make: solve this one, bring the culprit to justice, and the gods looking down and moving the pieces around like figures on a chess board will call it a day. Some remote, unsigned debt paid in full. Greenslade, and all the others that he had come to represent, could filter back to where they belonged, in the forgotten cesspits of memory and imagination to lie there and rot.

And give Jim Tyler his life back.

His autobiography completed, or at least the skeleton of it, he thanked the counsellor for listening. He thought that she looked sad, but at the same time he knew that she needn't. He threw in an apology for the way she had been forced to listen to a man wittering on who ought to know better; taking her way beyond the call of duty. She might wish to consider, he suggested, having the room fitted with an ejector seat should she ever have the misfortune of encountering his like again.

Then, checking his wrist, making certain that he had served his time - indeed overrun it - he made his way from the room as though re-entering the light.

CHAPTER THIRTY

Johnny Richards' father didn't seem any different, thought Mills. The last time the detectives visited, his son had been missing, and no-one seemed to know - or at least were not admitting to knowing - whether he was alive or dead. It was hard to see that a weight had lifted at all, or if one had been there that required lifting.

Tyler set about the questioning with gusto. Had Mr Richards been aware that his son was suffering stage-fright? That he was bottling the gig? That he was safe and well, taking refuge in a mansion belonging to the man taking all the profits?

No, he hadn't been aware - on all counts. Sometimes these things happen, Mr Richards had said, with a shrug. Like it was no big deal that his now-famous son had gone missing for days. That Johnny had been under suspicion for the murder of his friend. That Frank Watts had given him shelter.

Sometimes these things happen.

"Do you think, Mr Richards, that this entire episode might have been a publicity stunt, arranged by Watts and your son?" asked Tyler.

John Richards laughed and began to roll another cigarette, coughing in anticipation.

"You don't believe that's likely?" said Tyler.

Richards' eyes widened and he chuckled some more, then focused his attention squarely on the cigarette.

"Did you know that Adam Lane wrote *All Colours Are Blue*, Mr Richards?" asked Tyler.

"I've heard about it."

"And what do you think about it?"

"What am I supposed to think?"

"Did you know that your son was depressed? That he had a drug problem?"

Richards shrugged again. "Everyone's depressed these days, and everybody's doing drugs. That's just the world we live in. But Johnny's a survivor. He'll always come through. So, he bottled the gig. He'll come back stronger."

"What do you think about Frank Watts?"

"I don't really know him. Johnny seems to like him, so perhaps he's alright. He stood by my son when Johnny was desperate, so he can't be that much of a twat, can he?"

Tyler weighed up the remark. "Are you not disappointed that Johnny didn't come to you?" The DCI saw the anger flicker in John Richards' eyes, but then quickly die down again.

"I've come to realise the truth about myself, Inspector."

"And what's that, Mr Richards?"

"I'm a poor attempt at a father. I was a poor attempt at a husband too. I know a few chords on the guitar and I can roll a decent joint, and that's about it. Johnny can't learn anything worth knowing from the likes of me."

Billy Steele's shift was due to end. As the detectives travelled along the A34 towards Trentham, Mills said, "I think John Richards knew what was going on."

"Do you? That's natural enough."

Mills asked what Tyler meant.

"I mean," said Tyler, "that it is easier to assume that Richards knew his son was safe, than to imagine that he couldn't have cared less either way."

"You think that's a possibility?"

"A lot of things are possibilities. I wonder if Mr Richards isn't past caring about anything. If his son really is depressed, I can see where he gets it from. The rock and roll life, eh?"

Arriving at the Trentham Estate, Mills parked up. The cafe where Steele worked was almost empty. The mild weather was holding up and threatening to announce the unequivocal arrival of spring any day now, and the detectives took seats at a table outside, as was their custom.

Steele had seen the new customers and was heading for the door, hesitating when he realised who the two men at the table were. "Imagine," said Tyler, studying Steele's uncertainty with interest. "A young man with a father who's past caring, and another who might have settled for any kind of father."

"Sir?"

"I'm thinking aloud. Don't mind me."

Billy Steele was coming towards them.

"We orphans," said Tyler. "We don't stick together."

"I heard an unsavoury expression the other day," said Tyler as he watched the young man head back towards the cafe. "Shaking like a shitting dog."

"We do have that effect on some people," said Mills.

When the drinks arrived Mills asked Steele if they might have another word or two, in private. The young man's eyes questioned what the police wanted him for this time, but his lips remained sealed. He merely nodded, before retreating back towards the safety of the cafe.

By the time the detectives had finished their drinks, Steele's shift was over, and once again he sat in the back of the unmarked police car with two plain-clothes officers for company. Mills took the lead, asking how things were going. Was he was continuing in the band? Had he met with Richards since the singer had been found?

Steele's answers were nothing if not succinct. Despite his nervousness, or perhaps because of it, he didn't waste a word. Yes, he was continuing in the band, why shouldn't he? He had spoken with Johnny Richards and they were alright, why shouldn't they be?

"There were rumours," said Mills, "that Adam Lane had been approached about rejoining the band. Replacing you."

"Who cares about rumours? You just have to get on with it."

"How do you feel about Richards going missing?"

"How do I *feel*?"

"About him messing up the gig?"

"I'm glad he's okay. He was under a lot of pressure. Now we can carry on making records and get back to gigging."

"You don't feel any resentment?"

"Why should I? Because of some stupid rumours?"

"Richards seems to be taking all the glory, doesn't that bother you?"

"He's the singer. Singers always take the limelight, that's how it is."

"What if he bottles another gig?"

"It could happen to anyone."

"Do you think Johnny killed Adam Lane?"

"No."

"How can you be so sure?"

"He had no reason to."

"He stole his friend's song. Suppose Adam was going public on that? Suppose Adam wanted his share?"

"I don't think he killed him."

"Who, then?"

"I don't know."

"Richards seems to make a habit of not crediting songwriters with their work. He's done the same to you."

"There was a misunderstanding, that's all."

"So, you didn't write the song, *Blue Murder*, after all?"

"I did, sort of."

"*Sort of*, Billy?"

"I came up with the chords and some of the words. But then Johnny changed it around a bit. He came up with the title."

Tyler, silent up to that point, was watching Billy Steele carefully, trying to weigh him up. Listening to the words, and the pauses in between; trying to suck everything out of what was being said, and what wasn't.

Why would Steele disown his song? Why would he play down any rift between him and Richards? Was that the deal? To stay in this band, you do as you're told? Was Billy Steele so desperate to remain a part of it? Richards had Watts on his side, and the other two, drums and bass, seemed happy to go along with anything so long as they were making music and appearing to be getting somewhere.

Tyler said, "Have you met Johnny's dad?"

Steele looked puzzled by the question. "Once or twice," he said.

"What do you think of him?"

"He's alright."

"Johnny's mum?"

"She's okay, too."

"What about Adam's parents?"

"Why are you asking me all this?"

"I'm interested, that's all," said Tyler.

"I've met them but I don't know them very well."

After they had let Billy Steele go, Mills said, "What was that last bit about?"

Tyler shook his head. "I can't make him out. But something isn't right."

Mills thought carefully about what he was about to say. "You think Steele has issues, because he's an orphan?"

Tyler didn't respond.

"You think that because Adam's parents were there for him ... and Johnny's dad teaching his son the guitar, his mother welcoming to all Johnny's friends ..."

"Go on," said Tyler. "I'm interested to hear how your theory will develop."

"I don't have one. I'm trying to move away from amateur psychology."

"What's that supposed to mean?"

"It isn't supposed to *mean* anything. I'm inclined to agree with Berkins, that's all."

"What's he got to do with it?"

Mills' jaw dropped. "I happen to agree that we look for evidence."

"And in the absence of evidence?" Tyler looked hard at Mills. "Well?"

When Mills didn't respond, Tyler said, "I wonder why children can't play nicely together. Like undertakers we will never be out of work. You and Berkins are right, though. Evidence is the name of the game."

"How is Berkins?"

"About ready to accept the bouquet of flowers and the cards, I understand. Though not quite ready to step back into the fray. I suggest that we call on the great man before we go back to school."

"You mean—"

"Berkins first."

CHAPTER THIRTY ONE

Chief Superintendent Berkins was sitting out of bed on the side ward at the City General hospital in Hartshill. He looked tired, thought Mills, though hardly at death's door.

Berkins was alright. He looked a bit of a tit with that moustache, but there were a lot worse than him doing the rounds. It came from the heart when Mills wished the CS a full and speedy recovery.

"Any developments on the Lane murder?" Berkins asked Tyler.

"Are you sure you ought to be discussing work?"

Berkins winked, and it was the first time Tyler or Mills had ever seen the man do that. "I won't say anything if you don't," he said. Then he winked a second time. The effect was distinctly unnerving. Perhaps looks are deceptive, thought Mills. Perhaps the 'coronary incident' had damaged Berkins more than anyone realised.

Tyler told the CS that the team were still following up leads, though in truth not many. He was confident that a breakthrough was around the corner.

"Just the sort of hogwash I would be putting in my statement to the media, if I wasn't sitting here," said Berkins.

Mills let out a sigh of relief. Berkins was still intact. In need of surgery above that top lip, and in need of a quiet word on the whole issue of winking, but otherwise still a full shilling.

When a lull entered the conversation, Tyler was about to suggest that they get on with cracking the case and let the CS get some rest. Berkins was tapping two fingers on the table next to him, the table that was littered with cards and flowers and grapes and the essential bottle of Lucozade. He was mumbling something too.

"What was that?" asked Tyler.

"Eh? I was miles away," said Berkins. "This *episode* I've had appears to have temporarily affected my powers of concentration."

"Nature's way of giving you some time out," suggested Tyler.

"Perhaps so," said Berkins, his fingers continuing to drum as he hummed along to a familiar tune.

Mills smirked. "It's getting everywhere," he said.

"What's that?" asked Berkins, looking drowsy suddenly. "These darned tablets they're pumping into me."

"The tune you're humming. *All Colours Are Blue*, if I'm not mistaken."

"What? Oh, I see. Hospital radio. I don't know why they don't just poke me in the eye and done with. The most effective methods of torture, I find, are the simple ones."

"So much for getting away from work," said Mills.

"I'll give that Johnny Richards his due," said Berkins. "He can put together a catchy melody.

Though I haven't a notion what the Dickens he's singing about."

"Maybe that doesn't really matter so much, after all," said Mills. He looked across at Tyler, who was gazing back at him with an expression that was hard to call.

"I'm likely to be out of action for a little while, I expect," said Berkins, as the two detectives got up to leave. "Charles Dawkins paid me the honour earlier."

"Golf course closed for the day?" muttered Tyler.

"What's that?"

"Is he keeping well?"

"Tasking one of his chums to keep an eye on things until I'm back."

"Anyone we know?" asked Mills.

"David Rogers, I believe."

"I see," said Mills, trying to smile politely but instead giving a first-rate impersonation of a man with toothache. "*Great!*"

As the detectives made their way back towards the car park Tyler asked Mills about David Rogers.

"Been on a secondment for a while. Pity he couldn't have made it a permanent post."

"Not a fan?"

"I've not met any of his fans."

Getting into the car, Tyler said, "Interesting conversation about that song."

"You mean Berkins not being up to date on who wrote it?"

"I think, under the circumstances, we can allow some leniency on that score, as well as for having an old guy's take on *not being able to make head nor tail of these modern pop tunes what they come out with today ...*"

"He's only your age, Jim."

"My point is, what you said: that maybe it's not about the words at all."

"Most pop music isn't, in my opinion. It's something to whistle along to when you're driving, that's all."

"That's as maybe. But leaving aside this old farts take on popular culture for a moment, what I mean is ..."

"Yes?" asked Mills, awaiting revelations.

"Oh, just drive," said Tyler. He switched on the radio. "Let's see if we can find you something to *whistle along to.*"

The sound of *Johnny Richards and The Swamp Seeds* filled the car.

"Wouldn't you know it! Some days I feel like I'm the band's chief publicist. I might come out and ask for a cut and done with."

Mills glanced across, wondering if the DCI might switch the radio off or at least change stations. But Tyler did neither. When the song finished, the DJ paid homage. What a tune, and what a fascinating lyric. He fell short of any suggestion that the fascination of the lyric might lie in recent events surrounding its singer and writer, one back in the land of the living, the other gone forever.

After fuelling speculation of the rumoured tour and album, the DJ moved on to the next item on his busy itinerary, and Tyler came out of his reverie.

"I'm on the panel," he said. "It's Saturday night, I've listened to the song, and now the nation waits to hear my verdict."

"Sir?" said Mills driving through the gates of River Trent High school.

"Don't you want to hear my verdict, Danny?"

Mills pulled up on the car park and gave Tyler his full attention. "I'm all ears, sir."

"I give the song five out of ten for lyrics, possibly a six point five going on seven for melody. But I give the guy in charge of publicity a definite ten."

"Take a bow, sir."

In spite of himself Tyler couldn't help but smile.

CHAPTER THIRTY TWO

School was finishing for the day. The detectives made their way to the main office where Tyler asked if Miss Hayburn was available. The secretary checked, and then informed him that the headteacher could spare a few minutes if the officers would like to go through.

Approaching the now familiar door, Mills asked if he should wait outside.

"You imagine," said Tyler, "that I'm here on anything other than police business?"

"Of course not, sir. The thought never occurred."

"I think that, for rank insubordination, you ought to wait outside. And think hard about your behaviour, young man."

Tyler disappeared inside, while Mills stood, as though on sentry duty, trying to stifle a schoolboy grin.

Miss Hayburn was sitting behind the usual mountain of paperwork, her head and shoulders barely visible above it. Without looking at the DCI she gestured to him to take a seat.

"Perhaps our jobs are not so dissimilar," he said, nodding at the stack of papers and files dominating her desk.

"How can I help you today, Detective Chief Inspector?"

"I would like another word with Mrs Statham and Mr Linsell, if they are available."

"Can I help at all?"

"In a manner of speaking."

"Fire away."

He hesitated.

"Is there something the matter?" she asked him.

"Actually, yes, there is."

"I see." When Tyler again hesitated, she said, "Have you made any progress?"

"How do you mean? On the current enquiry, or …?"

"*Or?*"

"I'm getting there. On both counts. Slowly."

"I'm pleased to hear that. *On both counts*. And I am happy to help, as far as I can."

"I'm sorry I messed you around."

"You've already apologised. There's nothing more to be said."

"Am I forgiven?"

Miss Hayburn, still appearing focused on the paperwork in front of her, said, "You are forgiven."

Silence swallowed up the moment.

"Can I ask," he said, "what forgiveness means?"

At last she gave the DCI her full attention. "That is a rather profound question."

"I meant … in terms of where *we* might stand."

Miss Hayburn looked at her watch. "If you are hoping to catch Mr Linsell and Mrs Statham, now might be your best time. Good luck with your enquiries."

As the detectives made their way along the corridor, Mills asked how the meeting with the headteacher had gone.

"Isn't it obvious?" said Tyler. "The fact that we are walking through the school would suggest that my request to speak with members of the teaching staff has been granted."

They continued walking, deafened by the sound of their own footsteps on the uncarpeted floor. Approaching their destination Tyler said, "As far as any other business is concerned, not that there is any, you understand ..."

"Perfectly, sir."

"Then I would have to say: *as well as can be expected*. The case for the defence has been made."

"And?"

"The jury is still out."

Mr Linsell was organising his classroom for the following day and Mrs Statham had started on a pile of marking. Tyler asked if they might assemble together as he wanted to brainstorm on their old charges.

In the music classroom the four of them sat together. The teachers had of course heard the news and were relieved that Johnny Richards had been found alive and well. They asked if the police were any closer to finding out about Adam Lane, and Mills answered like a budding bureaucrat, saying nothing beyond the fact that enquiries were still ongoing.

Over the course of a laborious few minutes it was re-iterated that Johnny and Adam had been extremely close friends during their time at school, but that friends fall out, people change, circumstances arise; five years is a long time, particularly in young lives, a lot can happen ... they were going around again, despite everybody's best efforts, and coming up with nothing new. Linsell and Statham seemed to be questioning the purpose of the repetition when Tyler mentioned Billy Steele.

Mills smiled to himself. He knew the tactic well enough by now. Switching subject-matter, Tyler was hoping to catch some fresh, unguarded insight; something out of the blue. Mills had seen it work famously. It could be a highly effective ploy in the hands of Jim Tyler.

Billy, according to both teachers, had been something of a loner, as had already been documented. An outsider, trying desperately to get in. But had he been closer to Johnny or Adam? Could he have driven a wedge between the two friends?

Mills was listening attentively, though nothing was emerging. He was wondering if Jim Tyler's powers were deserting him when the breakthrough came.

A new name to conjure with. It had come from Mrs Statham.

Lizzie Butler.

In the last months of school, Billy and Lizzie had started to hang around together. "I'm not sure that it was a relationship, as such," said Statham, "though of course it might have been. What drew my attention, as I recall, was a certain discretion between the two of them."

"Discretion?" asked Mills.

"I could sense a warmth, an affection. Those little giveaways that we women tend to notice. But it was as though they didn't want to be seen as friends. Like they were hiding it. It's hard to explain, but I think that is what drew my attention in the first place." Mrs Statham thought for a moment. "Whatever they had together, it seemed to have a positive effect on Billy."

"In what way?" asked Mills.

"He seemed less alone, I suppose. A little more self-reliant. Less in the shadows of the other two. I understand that Lizzie was at the same care home as Billy."

Mr Linsell was nodding, as though he had finally caught up with the conversation. "I remember Lizzie," he said. "I would never have put her and Billy together, though. They must have been discreet."

"They were," said Statham. "Extremely. But some of us notice these things."

"I was their form teacher in that final year."

"But also a man," observed Statham.

"Charge accepted," said Linsell. "She was a curious girl, was Lizzie."

"Curious?" asked Mills.

"Odd, in some ways. A bit like Billy, now you mention it. A bit of a misfit - yes, two of a kind, thinking about it. I didn't have a lot to do with her. She was very quiet. Perhaps they didn't parade their friendship due to being at the same home - I mean, not wanting to make it obvious they were different - oh, I'm not sure what I'm trying to say."

"Actually, I think that you may have a point," said Statham. "We had a few children from the care home over the years. Some would stick together, and some actively detached themselves from the others who lived there with them. I think it did affect the dynamics, in some cases."

"Did Lizzie Butler have much to do with Adam or Johnny?" asked Mills.

The two teachers looked at each other, and shook their heads. "Not as I recall," said Linsell. "Johnny was in his own world, when he wasn't talking about music with Adam or Billy. Adam was more gregarious, but he hung around with Johnny mainly. I don't recall him being friends with Lizzie Butler."

"I'm not sure that we've been much help to you," said Mrs Statham. "I do hope that you manage to find who did this dreadful thing. I'm so glad that Johnny's safe and sound though. I do believe that young man has a very bright future ahead of him - and Billy too, for that matter."

Walking back towards the car, Mills concluded that they had not exactly stumbled onto the mother lode. Tyler didn't respond, appearing to be deep in thought. "Still," suggested Mills, "it wouldn't hurt to have a word with this Lizzie Butler. If we can find her. Get a bit more perspective on Steele, and on Richards and Lane too."

As Mills pulled out of the school gates, he said, "The care home is just around the corner, sir. We could call in and see what they remember about Steele and Butler." Tyler, still appearing somewhat distracted, merely grunted.

Mills swung the car down the hill before turning immediately right into a tree-lined cul-de-sac. Chamberlain Drive. A few yards along, a large building came into view on the right-hand side of the road, a discoloured local authority sign indicating, *The Meadows*. Mills was about to drive into the adjacent car park when Tyler held up a hand. "Here will do," he said. "For the moment."

The detectives sat in the car, looking across at the home. "I was in a place like this, once upon a time," said Tyler. "Back in Leicestershire approximately a lifetime ago."

Mills waited to see if Tyler would say more. When he didn't, Mills said, "We could leave it for today, sir. Or I could call back later. Whatever you prefer."

"You think I'm feeling haunted, Danny? Old ghosts rising? You think I'm afraid of confronting something?"

"I'm not saying anything, sir."

"Well, you should be. Because you'd be bang on the button. We have to face our fears, though - isn't that what the psychologists are always telling us to do? And I will, don't you worry about that.

"But first up I think we would do better to find out where Lizzie Butler is living. I prefer to keep the preconceptions at bay, for the moment. Person first, background second. It works for me. Now, if therapy's over for the day, I suggest we head back to Hanley and go from there."

"Whatever you say, sir."
"That's the spirit."

CHAPTER THIRTY THREE

Mills was tasked with tracking down Lizzie Butler, while Tyler was given the unexpected pleasure of a meeting for senior officers with David Rogers.

Rogers had been chief superintendent prior to Berkins, but had more recently been seconded out as a county-wide trouble-shooter. Mills had never come across anybody who said that they missed David Rogers, and few seemed to relish spending time in the man's company.

It took Tyler around fifteen seconds to confirm that the man was a born again twat. The arrogant but ultimately lame attempts at charm, along with that heavy-handed authoritarian bullshit, was apt not to bring out the best in the DCI. As far as Tyler was concerned, Rogers was Greenslade all over again, and that working relationship hadn't exactly ended happily.

He listened to what the man had to say. Everybody listened to what the man had to say. Rogers was the type who loved the sound of his own voice and despised the sound of everyone else's. In Jim Tyler's experience it was usually prudent to let that sort get on with it, and then disregard them at will. It took up too much energy engaging in unnecessary warfare; better to save the bullets until they actually started shooting at you.

Tyler caught up with Mills back at Cedar Lane. The DS was in the CID office and it looked like he was the bearer of good news.

"We've found our Lizzie Butler," he said. "She lives in Trentham, out on the old Barlaston Road. She's happy to talk to us and she remembers Billy Steele. Do you know what the first thing she said was, when I rang her?"

Tyler appeared to ponder. "Now, let's see: how about ... *he isn't in trouble, is he?*"

Mills looked taken aback, and then the sarcasm registered.

Tyler grinned. "Elementary, Danny Mills. Well, we are the police, don't forget. Or do you mean that she sounded ... maternal?"

"She didn't mention anything like that," said Mills, trying to give as good as he was getting. "How did you get on with Rogers?"

"I can see why people are wishing Berkins well."

"Not great company is he."

"I've seen worse back in London. Everything's a little dirtier back there, though."

"So I've heard."

"Rumours, I take it? Of course, you've never set foot outside the Potteries, have you?"

"None of us have," said Mills. "We are not encouraged to fraternise with the outside world. When you're born in Stoke you are expected to die here, and not make a fuss about it either."

The two officers looked at each other, with mock-stern expressions, before folding into hoots of laughter that earned them looks of concern from the other members of the team.

"Is Lizzie Butler expecting us?" said Tyler.

"She's ordering in the biscuits as we speak, sir."

"Come on, then. Enough of this frivolity. Let's see what she can tell us."

Lizzie Butler was living in what had once been the family home. Her mother had left when she was young and she had lived with her father for much of her childhood.

Until one day he stuck a shotgun into some people's faces and demanded money. If he'd done that kind of thing before, he had got away with it, though it wasn't clear where the gold was hidden. Still, suspicions were rife, if as yet unproven. His imprisonment for armed robbery had led to Lizzie, his only daughter, spending her final school years at The Meadows, where she had met Billy Steele.

Mills cast his eyes around the spacious semi-detached property, and he couldn't help wondering, as others before him had done, how a twenty-one year old without a mother, and with a father serving a stint, had done so well for herself.

The young woman was nothing if not forthcoming. The house, which she had previously occupied with her father, before he stormed into a post office one bright summer's day brandishing his firearm, had, along with a considerable sum of cash, been secured legitimately. The family solicitors had satisfied many an enquiry into the matter, though a lot of people were still asking a lot of questions, if by all accounts receiving very few answers.

On her eighteenth birthday, Lizzie Butler had returned to her family home with a pile to live on that had been signed over to her by her loving dad.

"It was a bit rubbish being at The Meadows," she told the detectives. "They were alright with us, they were not cruel or anything like that. But it wasn't like being with your family. It was bad enough having to go to school and mix with strangers, but when you're with strangers 24/7 it gets a bit much."

"You made friends with Billy at the home?" asked Tyler, recalling his own poor efforts at finding friendship back in those dark days on the Leicestershire estate.

"I hit it off with Billy. I thought he was alright. He could be a bit intense, but then so could I. It felt a bit like we were kindred spirits, and we could talk to each other. I didn't fancy him, nothing like that. I don't think he fancied me, either. He didn't seem that sort, somehow."

"You mean that Billy was gay?" asked Mills.

"Good question," she said. "I never found out. He just didn't seem interested in that sort of thing. Bit odd, I suppose, but there you go. It helped though."

"Helped?" asked Mills.

"Sex always complicates things. I didn't have any of that complication with Billy. We were just good mates, and we knew that we could trust each other. We could talk about anything, and in total confidence. I think we helped each other through a difficult time."

Mills asked her about Johnny and Adam.

"I've seen it all on the news, otherwise I wouldn't have known anything about it. I haven't seen either of them much since I left school. The odd gig, and that's about it."

Mills asked how she recalled the two of them.

"I didn't have a lot to do with them, really. Or with anybody, apart from Billy, like I said. From what I remember, Johnny was a bit full of himself. He was quite good looking, though. If I had been looking for a boyfriend, I could have fancied him a bit." She smiled. "But I would definitely have tried to bring him down to size."

"And Adam?"

"Funnily enough, the same. He wasn't a bad looking lad, either. He was a bit aloof, like he was better than everyone else, same as Johnny. They were a pair together. I knew they had all these great ambitions to be in a band, because that's all they ever talked about. I didn't pay a lot of attention."

"Was Billy good friends with Adam and Johnny?"

Lizzie Butler thought for a few moments and Mills watched her closely.

She was a thoughtful young woman, observant; knew her own mind, comfortable in her own skin and quietly confident. She was different, exuding a quiet wisdom that Mills warmed to. It was hardly her fault if her father had taken up armed robbery for a living.

"I think Billy tried hard to be friends with those two," she said at last. "Billy was really into music, and he had the same ambitions. I think he imagined that Adam and Johnny were super-cool guys, and he wanted to be a part of that. He was trying hard to find himself, find out where he fitted in, if you know what I mean."

Mills nodded and he noticed that Tyler appeared absorbed by Lizzie Butler too. She was an attractive woman, if a bit on the skinny side for Mills' tastes. He sensed deep waters. "Do you have any thoughts on what happened to Adam Lane?" he asked her.

"I have no idea. How could I? Is that why you've come to see me? I wondered if you might think that Billy had something to do with it."

"Why would you think that?" asked Mills.

"Because you asked about him over the phone, I suppose."

"Of course," said Mills. He glanced across at Tyler, and tried to ride the blushes.

Tyler took up the reins. "When did you last see Billy?" he asked her.

"We kept in touch for a while after we left school."

"You remained at the home until you were eighteen?"

"I did, but you were classed as being more independent when you reached sixteen, and I didn't spend as much time there. So I wasn't as close to Billy then. I've seen him around, but not much since I moved back here."

"Three years ago?" asked Tyler.

"That's right."

"And you've not kept in touch?"

"I'm the world's worst at doing that, to be honest with you. And Billy must be as bad as I am. I wish him well, though. I hope that he's not in any trouble."

"Would you expect that he might be?" asked Tyler.

Butler cast the DCI a knowing look. "I wouldn't have any reason to think he would be. I never heard that he got into any trouble. Billy was a lot like I am, he liked to be left alone."

"A bit of a loner, would you say?"

She appeared to hesitate. "Where we differed is that I can take or leave people, full stop. I don't run around after anyone, and I never have done. I'm as independent as they come. It's no problem to me."

"But Billy?" said Tyler.

"I used to hate the way he would run after those pair. It did piss me off a bit. I wanted to tell him to go his own way, not try to be like them. If people sense that you're desperate, they try and use you. As good as begging them to let him be in their little band, he was. I wanted to say, you don't need the likes of them, you have enough brains and talent of your own. And he had. I think people underestimated Billy."

"Underestimated?" said Tyler. "In what way?"

"What I knew - what I saw - of Adam and Johnny, I don't think they had time for anyone but themselves. I don't think they were the kind to recognise what others might have to offer. Billy was a lot sharper than many people realised, he just didn't go around showing off like some I could mention."

She paused for a moment. "But when he was around them, he tried too hard, and then he wasn't himself. I think he wanted them to acknowledge him - acknowledge that he had something to offer. It frustrated him. Billy wanted to fit in but he didn't know how. The harder he tried the less he had to offer, if that makes sense."

She laughed. "Listen to me! I mean, what do I know? Billy's in a band that's all over the radio and looking set to be huge. He's going to be a star, what a pisser. Good luck to him, he deserves everything he gets." She shook her head. "I thought he should steer clear of the likes of those pair and look at him now: taking over the world in a band with Johnny Richards! Who knows anything? I certainly don't."

She asked if they would like a drink. Mills was about to decline, thinking that they'd wasted enough time already, but then Tyler surprised him, taking up the offer. While Butler was busy in the kitchen, Tyler answered Mills' unasked question. "I want to spend a few minutes getting her into free-fall," he said. "It might be nothing, let's see."

When the young woman returned with the drinks, Tyler struck up a conversation about schooldays and life at The Meadows. He asked what she thought of Penkhull, indicating that he was fairly new to the area. Once again Mills admired the skilful way that his colleague weaved the topics, leaving ragged openings, invitations to say something. Possibilities for contradictions to arise that might prove significant.

This is turning into a proper game of chess, he thought. Butler was appearing open and conversational, yet at the same time there was something guarded about everything she said.

Mills tried to disregard the knowledge that her father was doing time for robbery; tried not to let the sins of the father affect his interpretation of the daughter. It was too easy to conclude that she might have been raised with a tendency for remaining artfully tight-lipped, particularly in the presence of police officers. But was he doing her an injustice, thinking like that? Perhaps she simply didn't have that much time for small-talk, not everyone did. He wasn't the world's greatest fan of it himself.

At last Tyler indicated that it was time they were on their way. He thanked the young woman for her time, and before leaving he asked if it would be alright if they called to see her again. Butler looked puzzled. "Is there anything else you wanted to ask me?" she said.

"Not at present, though something might occur at a later stage," said Tyler, and rather clumsily, thought Mills.

"I can't imagine what. I haven't had contact with any of them for ages, like I told you." But Tyler pressed the point. That in the course of the investigation, something might arise. Was there a problem? Butler laughed off the suggestion: No, of course there wasn't any problem, and of course she had no objection if they wanted to talk to her again.

She showed the detectives to the door.

Out in the car Mills looked quizzically at Tyler, but the DCI didn't say anything until they were almost back at the police station.

As they pulled onto the car park at Cedar Lane he broke the silence. "There's something that I'm not seeing, Danny."

"That makes two of us," said Mills. "You think she's not on the level?"

"For some reason, I don't buy that she has had no contact, at least with Steele."

"Why should she?"

"They had too much in common."

"People drift. Circumstances change."

"I know that. But these two were close. They had a bond."

"What if they have kept in touch? It's hardly a crime."

"Then why lie about it?"

Mills conceded the point, but maintained that there was nothing to prove that she had, for whatever reason, lied.

"I want to check the tail on Steele."

Mills raised his eyebrows.

"Less of the smut," said Tyler. "This is still a filthy town, for all its 'heritage' and attempts at moving forward."

Mills checked out which officers had tailed Billy Steele, and he asked for a detailed report on who Steele had visited, and where, giving a description of Lizzie Butler. The immediate feedback didn't reveal anything of interest. During the time Steele had been tailed, he had certainly not made any visits to Butler's address. His life appeared to consist of working at the cafe and playing with the band, with no detours down the old Barlaston Road. And neither had anyone fitting Butler's description visited Steele's home address in Longton. In fact, Steele hadn't received any visitors at all.

Then one of the officers who had been tailing Steele got back to Mills with something that did appear interesting, or that might turn out to be.

Sometimes, after his shift at the cafe, Steele would walk into the Italian Gardens close to where he worked. It was on the Trentham Estate and these days you had to pay for the privilege. Sergeant Stephanie Osgood had noted that while Steele had always been on his own when he left the cafe and headed towards the visitors centre, on a couple of occasions she had spotted him in the company of a woman as he had made his way over the bridge into the gardens.

Mills asked Sergeant Osgood if the woman could have been Lizzie Butler. From the description Osgood thought it a possibility, though she couldn't be certain. The age, height and build sounded about right. The woman, however, always wore a hat, as Osgood recalled, and so hair style and colour could not be corroborated.

Mills had a lot of time for Sergeant Osgood. If he hadn't been happily married himself ...

He quickly packed up the thought and stored it where the less trustworthy part of his mind couldn't easily gain access. He'd seen only too often what thoughts like that could do. For all his grievances about being moved out into the country, away from the beloved city, Danny Mills loved his wife and his children, and he had no intention of letting those kinds of speculations compromise all that he held dear. Focusing again on the matter in hand, he asked Osgood if the pair appeared to act like a couple when she had seen them entering the gardens.

"Actually, that's hard to call. They were not exactly all over each other. It wasn't obvious. But they were close, if you know what I mean."

"Close?"

"Not strangers. It wasn't a blind date. They walked ... *close*. They were at ease with each other."

Mills thanked Sergeant Osgood.

"You could check out through the estate office," she said.

"What's that?"

"Billy Steele, being an employee, would have free access to the lake and gardens. But anyone else would have to pay. The woman - if she's not an employee herself, of course - may have an annual pass, if she's a regular. We could check the dates and times when any card in her name was used, and I can check that against the log I kept when I spotted Steele with company."

It didn't take Osgood long to complete the task, and she rang Mills straight back. "We have confirmation," she told him. "Both times it was Lizzie Butler. She visits the lake and gardens quite often."

"Good work," said Mills.

"It's odd though, isn't it?"

"Odd?" said Mills.

"I mean, if they're regularly seeing each other, how come she didn't meet him at the cafe? Or go to his home address, or he to hers?"

And more to the point, thought Mills, why would she deny having seen him? "Did their meeting have a—what's the word I'm looking for ...?"

"Clandestine?" suggested Osgood.

"That's the one. Did it have a *clandestine* quality?"

"Not in a third rate spy movie kind of way, if that's what you mean. They weren't constantly looking back over their shoulders and acting suspiciously. They appeared entirely natural. It didn't raise my suspicions, anyway."

Mills found Tyler at his desk tearing through reports and statements, looking harassed and frustrated. After listening to Mills' update on the movements of Steele and Butler, he said, "I want to call again on Daisy Finch. I'm keeping the tail on Steele and extending it to Ms Butler. Who've we got available?"

"I can certainly recommend Stephanie Osgood for the job," said Mills. "I have to say that I've been rather impressed—"

"If she's available then go ahead."

CHAPTER THIRTY FOUR

Daisy Finch appeared to be making good progress following the beating she had received at the hands of her sister. She was moving around the flat more easily now, breathing without wincing. She asked what progress the police were making. Were they any closer to finding out who had killed Adam?

Tyler parried the barbed remark with a bureaucratic line, and Mills presented the convalescent with a couple of packets of biscuits and an unspoken plea for a brew to wash them down with.

While they sat drinking tea, and Mills made a start on the biscuits, Tyler brought the subject of Billy Steele into the conversation. Mills noted once again the subtlety in the DCI's strategy, and at the same time detected a flicker of interest in the eyes of Daisy Finch at the mention of Billy Steele.

Tyler waited to see if the name might draw any comment. When it didn't, he embarked on the charade of casually wondering aloud whether Steele had any girlfriends. Another game of chess, thought Mills. But, curiously, he observed, Tyler didn't seem to be at the top of his game. And Daisy Finch was clearly no fool. She seemed to detect that something was loaded inside the unformed questions. After circling each other for a few minutes, Finch appeared to grow tired of the game and asked straight out why Tyler might want to know about Steele's girlfriends.

Tyler tried to shrug it off as merely being interested in what makes people tick. But Finch had clearly sensed an opportunity. The detectives waited in vain for the name Lizzie Butler to come up, but Finch merely stated that she wasn't aware that Billy had a girlfriend. The stalemate ticked on and then Tyler went for it, raising the name to see what might come back.

Daisy Finch appeared to ponder. "The name does ring a bell," she said. "I can't place her, though. Has Billy mentioned her?"

Tyler was cautious. More cat and mouse, thought Mills. But he could see that Tyler's patience was running low. A brittle tension had entered the fray, and Finch was feeding on it.

"Do you still believe that Johnny Richards killed Adam?" asked Tyler.

"Yes, as a matter of fact I do."

"Over the song?"

"I don't know the details."

"But you knew that he wanted Adam back in the band."

"I knew he'd said as much. But I don't believe it. I don't believe that he really wanted Adam back."

"Then why ask him?"

"To pacify Adam? Who knows with a screwed up guy like Johnny Richards?"

"Pacify him - because of the song?"

"Maybe. I don't know. He's warped. You could say he has a lot of problems. Most are of his own making. He has to have everything his own way - I've said all this before."

"Adam turned him down, then?"

"I don't know if he ever gave him an answer."

"Where would that have left Billy? If he thought that his days in the band were numbered, how would he have reacted?"

"Are you asking me if I think Billy killed Adam?"

"Do you think it's possible?"

"I suppose it is."

Tyler paused for a moment. "Did *you* tell Billy that Johnny approached Adam?"

"Why would I?"

"Perhaps you didn't like the idea of Adam rejoining the band."

"It wasn't down to me. Adam was free to do whatever he wanted. If he had decided to rejoin, that would have been up to him."

"It could have been a big opportunity for Adam, surely. After all, the band were finally getting somewhere ..."

"Like I say, it would have been Adam's decision. But I didn't talk to Billy about it. You think I was trying to make trouble?"

"What do you think of Billy Steele?" asked Tyler.

"In what way?"

"Did you have much to do with him?"

"Not really. He seemed okay. I don't really know him."

Mills was closely observing the exchange, an unfinished digestive biscuit trapped tightly between thumb and forefinger. *There's something you're not saying*, he thought.

"Did Adam like Billy?" asked Tyler. "He must have mentioned him, given that he replaced Adam in the band. And they used to hang around together at school, I understand."

"He didn't say a lot about him. Billy had been around them at school, like you say, and he could play guitar and wrote a bit. He was keen. I suppose Adam thought he was an obvious choice."

"Adam was fond of Johnny, wasn't he?"

"They *had* been good friends. But Adam was finding him difficult to be around. He was becoming too much of a pain in the arse and Adam didn't need any of that. That's why he left the band. He wasn't bitter. He had other strings to his bow. Uni, for one thing. He wrote the song for Johnny, he wanted to help him. He wished him well."

"Did Adam want recognition for writing the song?"

"It wasn't a big deal for Adam. I think Johnny ought to have acknowledged who wrote it, but Adam wasn't like Johnny. He was genuinely easy-going, not just when it suited."

"But if Johnny suffered with a serious depressive illness - he couldn't help his moods."

"That still doesn't make him a good person to be around. Anyway, *serious depressive illness* - is that what he's telling you now? She laughed. "Throwing tantrums when you don't get your own way, and smoking too much weed isn't the same as having a 'serious depressive illness.' He really is full of shit, you know. But Adam wished him well, like I say. He didn't make a big deal about having his song nicked, either."

"Which means that I'm struggling to find a motive for Richards killing him!"

The words came out hard.

"What are you saying?" she asked Tyler.

"I think, Ms Finch, that you would like to believe that Johnny Richards killed Adam. I think that you feel a lot of anger towards him."

"And that I want to make trouble and, what, ruin him?"

"Do you?"

"I want justice for Adam, that's all I want. Johnny could be nasty when he didn't get what he wanted. I was with him long enough, I should know."

"Why did you tell Billy that Johnny wanted him out and Adam back in?"

"*I didn't*. Look, I'm not feeling well, you're harassing me. I want you to find who killed Adam, but I can't tell you any more because I don't know anything."

"What about your sister?"

"What about her?"

"She attacked you. Could she have attacked Adam?"

A faint light, heavily curtained, glowed briefly, and Mills caught the dim rays.

"She's off her head. I wouldn't put anything past her. Janine and Johnny are made for each other."

"So, you believe she could have killed Adam?"

"Like I say, it's possible. Have you asked her?"

The irony was heavy, and clearly meant to be. It came down like a rock, leaving echoes in the ensuing silence.

Tyler was the next to speak. "But it leaves us with the same problem."

"What problem?"

"Janine and Johnny having the same motive. Killing Adam over a song - unless your sister has other motives that you are not telling us about."

"Like what—what are you saying?"

"I'm not saying anything. I'm asking you to tell us what you know. Anything that can help to establish who would kill Adam and why."

"Janine wouldn't have wanted Adam back in the band."

"Why not?"

"Because she was afraid that Adam was the real star and she couldn't bear the thought of that. The thought that my man was the one with the talent."

"Let me get this straight," said Tyler. "You believe that your sister might have killed Adam ... to keep him out of the band?"

"I haven't got anything to prove anything," she said. "But Janine would stop at nothing to hurt me."

"Even kill your boyfriend?"

"Yes, even that."

Outside the flats Tyler stood perspiring. "Watts is set to lose a fortune on that song, but hoping to make long-term gains. If Richards and the rest of his band have anything about them, they will secure a better deal before making another record or playing any more gigs. Richards has found his fifteen minutes of fame and can stick or twist though I suspect he might twist.

"In the war between the Finches, Janine, at least for the time being, has won. Janine didn't kill Adam Lane, her alibi is watertight. But Daisy wants blood. She wants her sister's blood and Johnny Richards' blood - I wouldn't put anything past her.

"And Billy Steele is still in the band."

"Sir?"

"Adam Lane is dead but Johnny Richards is alive. Daisy Finch, it could be argued, has reason to want Richards dead. And Lizzie Butler has lied about not seeing Steele."

Mills waited, sensing that Tyler hadn't finished.

"Are we dealing with the aftermath, Danny, or are we in the midst? Are plans being unfurled, or could no-one have foreseen what would happen to Adam Lane, or to Johnny Richards for that matter? A random attack, a robbery gone wrong coinciding with a bottled gig? Is that naive nonsense?"

Tyler started to walk towards the car. Mills followed, glancing back at the flats.

CHAPTER THIRTY FIVE

A statement had been released on behalf of the band. *Johnny Richards and the Swamp Seeds* were back in rehearsals, with a tour to be announced any day now and an album in the pipeline. *Watch this space!*

Sales of the EP hadn't slowed down, far from it. It was looking to be a strong contender for biggest selling record of the year. If the band never recorded, never played again, their place in musical history was already assured.

Frank Watts had been asked, and more than once, about a rescheduling of 'The Gig That Never Was' as it was now being referred to. He had quipped that, to accommodate the clamour for tickets, the band would have to agree to a year-long residency at The Thirteen club. "I'm giving that possibility some serious consideration," he added, though it was hard to judge whether the comment was meant to be taken seriously.

Tyler had been summoned to a meeting with David Rogers. He had never imagined how much it was possible to miss a chief superintendent, and would have gladly given a year of his life to have been sitting in front of that ridiculous moustache, waiting for the nutshell. Instead, DCI Tyler found himself sitting before the reincarnation of a man who wasn't even dead, as far as he knew. It might have been Greenslade sitting across the desk, clean-shaven and humourless, dripping in the will to power. Pig eyes and in-bred superiority, like an old headmaster he used to know and whose dark shadow he had been condemned to sit in. Back in Leicester, late sixties, early seventies. A man who would conduct an interview with sober austerity and solemnity, and then give himself away with the merest flash of a hidden, well-kept smile in the final few seconds before he took the stick down from the wall.

It was like this: Rogers wasn't a happy man. Tyler's investigation had spluttered out, and the eyes of the world had come to focus their hungry gaze on the latest rock and roll superstar—and all happening right here in Stoke on Trent! "We appear to have inadvertently conspired to turn a local bunch of chancers into the new Beatles. And a small venue on Trinity Street into the new Cavern club."

Tyler maintained a fixed expression, giving nothing away.

"Richards hasn't been charged with anything. His manager, Watts, similarly."

"Any suggestions?" asked Tyler.

Rogers' eyes grew smaller still, the glare from those venomous points of light becoming suddenly more dangerous. "Do I have to tell you your job, Detective Chief Inspector?"

"Perhaps you do."

The frozen silence had turned into a wasteland. Back in the headmaster's study, this was always the worst part. The final waiting, wanting it to be over.

Tyler couldn't stand it. The urge to bring it on was overwhelming. "Are you intending to take disciplinary action against me?" he said.

Rogers didn't answer.

Tyler, in no mood to play the games that senior personnel sometimes revelled in, said, "I think you need a fall guy. I have been offered staff counselling, and I haven't engaged. You can switch the emphasis from a stretched department and heap the troubles on a copper who came up from London. I'm about ready for a rest."

Rogers laughed, but the laughter contained neither humour nor pity. "Not so easy, I'm afraid. You think I'm proposing to sit you on the bench, collecting your considerable salary while others take the strain on your behalf? Think again, Detective Chief Inspector Tyler. I'm demanding that you go up a gear. In fact, make that a couple of gears."

"Meaning?"

"Instead of pissing around while the likes of Frank Watts makes fools of us all—"

"So you've cracked the case already? I wish you'd said something earlier."

The venom was almost frothing on the lips of the senior man, but Rogers held back.

"You think Frank Watts killed Lane? Or organised it?" spat Tyler. "You think I haven't considered that? You don't think I would want to nail Watts? That I would have any reason not to, or that I might be working towards doing just that?"

"We haven't seen many signs, it's true."

Tyler checked his own rising anger and began to laugh. "Go on, say it."

"What's that?"

"I heard about your comments. The case last year. You think I'm afraid to go after the big guys.

You think I'm swanning around looking for an angle on a handful of youngsters caught up in petty squabbles rather than gunning for Frank Watts. You've got a list on Watts, and you want this case to bring it all home. If that's true, maybe it's time you shared what you know, or what you think you know. There are a thousand and more like Watts, scumbags to the core. Sycophants robbing the poor to keep themselves rich, and operating just inside the law of the land."

Rogers didn't say anything.

Tyler waited.

At last Rogers said, "I want to see someone brought to justice for the death of Adam Lane. I have no other agenda."

"Bullshit."

"You might care to rephrase that comment."

"And I might not."

"You are continuing with your counselling sessions now, I understand?"

"That's irrelevant. I'm fit for purpose or I'm not. What do you imagine they can do, mend me?"

"I doubt that."

"For what it's worth, I will tell you how it is. I'm going to find the killer of Adam Lane, whoever they are."

"If it takes the rest of your career to do it?"

Tyler shook his head. "You don't have to like me any more than I like you. If I find Frank Watts at the bottom of it then I will crush him without hesitation."

The look of doubt and condescension from Rogers flicked a switch in Tyler, and he saw, in the slow-motion frames of his inner-eye, the transformation as David Rogers became Greenslade. He felt the punch release all the way from the heart, splitting the face in two, then the figure of himself pinning down the prone frame, pummelling it until the blood-stained image beneath him had become unrecognisable.

A voice was calling him from a distance.

David Rogers.

But there's nothing personal here. Rogers, Greenslade, there's no grudge. Not really. They hate everyone who doesn't doff a cap, and everyone who does, too. You cannot possibly win. That's the whole point. Personalities rotten to the core, holding power - a bad combination.

Rise above it.

Rogers wants results. He just doesn't know the best way of going about it. He won't go down, no matter how bad things get. That's what the troops are for, the cannon fodder. His arse is always well protected.

Tyler was back in the room, his breathing fully under control. His fist was not bruised and the face of David Rogers bore no scars from the imaginary battering that it had taken. He drilled a look into Rogers, penetrating deep and hard. *We do have one thing in common, you and I. We have a loathing for the likes of Frank Watts.*

Something in common? Tyler thought that he might throw up. *Something in common with that?*

Corruption in high office has one redeeming feature, he thought, still looking straight at Rogers.

You get to nail one of those. And there's nothing finer.

So don't ever slip off the track, Rogers. Because if you do, the likes of me will be waiting. Stick to being a bully and leave the really nasty stuff to those with greater intelligence. The dogs of this world who would chew you up and spit you out.

"Do you have anything else to say?" asked Rogers.

"Just this, for now. I'm planning to nail a killer. If that's good enough for you and your department, then I suggest that you let me get back to it. Otherwise, do whatever the fuck you like."

Jim Tyler left the room, closing the door behind him.

"How did it go?" asked Mills, back in the CID office.

"They have enough to get rid of me, if they choose. But that's up to them." Mills looked uneasy. "Tell you what," said Tyler. "I don't know if you fancy taking in a band this afternoon, seeing as we don't have very much else on."

"I think it would be rude," said Mills, brightening, "not to support local talent. Shall I book us in on the guest list, sir?"

"Don't you dare. It will be a nice surprise for them."

The rehearsal room upstairs at the Thirteen club was reasonably well sound-proofed, though there was still some faint leakage that the local traffic on a busy afternoon could not entirely conceal. Tyler and Mills got out of the car and stood listening to the sounds of stardom in the making.

"They would seem to be playing nicely," said Mills.

"All friends together again. Are you surprised?"

"Not entirely."

"Under the watchful eye of Mr Watts, I have no doubt. Shall we?"

They went inside.

Watts was in his office and didn't appear concerned to see the detectives again. Tyler answered the man's question of how he might help the officers today, suggesting that he had come to speak to one of the band.

"I'll show you up to the rehearsal studio," said Watts. "You can take a listen to the future of rock and roll."

"No change in personnel, then?" said Tyler.

"None necessary. Why tamper with a winning formula?"

"It was my understanding that you don't like or trust at least one of the band."

Watts smiled. "Sometimes people get hold of the wrong end of the stick. Then you get things out in the open, talk things through ..."

As they walked upstairs the unmistakable sound of Johnny Richards' voice was belting out above the guitars and drums. He was no connoisseur, but it didn't sound bad to the ear of Jim Tyler. Whether or not it was the future of rock and roll, though, was another matter.

The song was finishing as Watts opened the door and led the officers inside, applauding as he went. "We have a couple of keen fans here, boys," he said. "I think they're hoping to bag a few autographs."

The presence of Tyler and Mills in the room drew mild curiosity from the drummer and the bass player, while Johnny Richards appeared to recognise old friends. Only Billy Steele looked at all concerned.

"What do you think?" asked Richards. "It could make the album, I reckon, with a bit of work."

"Rehearsals going well?" said Tyler, scanning the faces in front of him. "Mind if we sit in for the next song?"

The band kicked in again, and Tyler observed the dynamic of the band, if not the song itself, with a close attention to detail. Was tension evident between them? It didn't seem so. It wasn't obvious, at least. Steele looked uncomfortable in the presence of the detectives, though, continually glancing over towards them.

When the song finished, Richards said, "That one could do with a *lot* more work." Tyler saw him glance over at Steele. "I don't think we were all focused that time."

Steele looked back at Richards but didn't say anything.

A hint of unrest?

Watts, appearing to sense the subtext, asked if the detectives would like a drink. Tyler licked his lips, eyeing the bar in the corner of the room lined up with optics, the beer pumps beneath them. He felt the thirst reaching down deep. "Whose songs are those?" he asked.

"Guilty," said Richards.

"I see," said Tyler. "Perhaps you are due a break," he said, somewhat ambiguously. Richards took off his guitar, signalling to the rest of the band to take five minutes. But as Richards walked towards the officers, Tyler looked at Steele. "Could we have a word, please, Billy?"

They took Billy Steele out to the car. It was like old times.

"I believe," said Tyler, as the three of them sat in the unmarked police car, "that you are friends with Lizzie Butler."

They had been together at the home. They had attended River Trent High school. He hadn't seen Lizzie Butler for years.

Funny, thought Mills. *The way neither wants to be associated with the other. What are they hiding?*

Tyler kept the card up his sleeve for the moment, and asked about Butler's father. Billy didn't know anything about him. Lizzie had never mentioned him. Yet Billy's nerves seemed to stretch significantly at the mere mention of the man's name.

Trevor Butler.

The DCI looked at Mills and handed him the reins.

"So, how's it going with the band?" asked Mills.

"It's going okay."

"You've patched things up with Johnny, then."

"We're cool."

"No hard feelings?"

"Hard feelings?"

"About him stealing your song?"

"No, nothing like that. There might have been some misunderstandings, that's all."

Mills eyeballed him. "But one big happy family now?"

"We get on great. I need to get back—"

"And Frank Watts? What's he like to work for?"

"He's okay."

"You're lying, Billy," said Tyler, cutting in. "I will ask you again about Lizzie Butler. Try your best now. I want you to recall if you might have seen the young lady recently."

Steele swallowed hard.

"Something stuck in your throat, Billy?"

"I might have seen her."

"You might have?" said Tyler. "Interesting. So, when do you think that you might have seen her, and where exactly?"

Steele looked from one officer to the other while seeming, thought Mills, to be engaged in frenetic mental activity. Trying out scenarios on the inside of his head, perhaps.

"I think I may have bumped into her, near where I work."

"May have bumped into her?" said Tyler. "Not arranged to meet with her?"

"I shouldn't think so."

"I think that there's something you're not telling me, Billy."

Steele was starting to sweat.

"Billy?"

"I don't know anything. Why won't you leave me alone?"

"Are you protecting somebody - Frank Watts, Johnny - who are you protecting, Billy?"

"I'm not protecting anyone, I've told you. I don't know anything."

"Listen to me," said Tyler. "If anything should occur to you, anything at all, about why someone should choose to cave in Adam Lane's skull and leave him to drown in the canal, you *will* let me know, won't you? Anytime, day or night?"

Steele nodded.

"Good," said Tyler. "Sorry to have kept you."

Steele got out of the car. The detectives watched him hurry back inside the club. "Where do we go now?" said Tyler, turning to Mills. "Is that your question? Well, I'm out of ideas. I could retire to see my shrink - or staff counsellor, if you prefer - and watch the rise and rise of Johnny Richards and Frank Watts. Or else I can go around in circles for bit longer, until the likes of Rogers finally calls me in."

The sound of music was striking up again from inside the club. Mills watched as Tyler slowly turned his head in its direction.

CHAPTER THIRTY SIX

Billy Steele sat across from the detectives as Tyler announced for the tape that the interview was commencing. Mills noticed the solicitor sitting next to Steele; one of the duty solicitors, not part of the clan that had represented Watts, Richards and Janine Finch. Frank Watts' generosity clearly had limits.

He thought back to earlier, sitting in the car outside the Thirteen club. Listening to the band striking up again had triggered something in Tyler's mind, and the DCI had marched back in to arrest Billy Steele for the murder of Adam Lane.

Watts had been there, though he hadn't put up a fight on behalf of a member of the band he was managing, far from it. Watts hadn't appeared at all concerned. Had this been part of the plan, or a convenient addendum to it? The police tidying the mess up for Watts and Richards, getting Steele out of the way?

Mills had put that to Tyler, but the DCI had remained tight-lipped on the matter. "Let's see what unfolds," is all he had offered by way of reply. Mills had heard of playing your cards close to your chest, but this was becoming ridiculous. They were supposed to be a team!

The DS observed as Tyler took charge of the interview.

"... How did you feel, Billy, when you heard that you were about to be replaced by Adam Lane?"

Steele looked close to tears. Tyler repeated the question. When Steele still didn't answer, Tyler said, "You were aware of the plan to replace you?" Steele looked to the man sitting at his side, who widened his eyes in a gesture that suggested that he get on and answer the question.

A rush of words followed, as though Steele wanted rid of them. Yes, he had been told about Adam returning to the band. But he had asked Johnny Richards about it and Johnny had denied that there was any truth in it.

"And you believed him?" asked Tyler.

"Johnny said he would never have Adam back. He said he would sooner jack in the band than do that. Yes, I believed him."

Tyler frowned. "So, who told you that Adam was going to rejoin?"

Steele glanced again at the silent brief, and Mills saw the recognition dawn: Billy knew that he was as good as alone in that room.

"It was Daisy Finch," he said.

The name appeared to confirm something in Tyler's mind, and Mills finally caught a glimpse of what was going on. "Did Daisy suggest why Adam might be rejoining the band?" asked Tyler. Asking the question, the DCI leaned forward, his nose twitching as though he was smelling blood. When Billy didn't answer, Tyler said, "And why did she take it upon herself to inform you that Adam was coming back?"

The youth's meagre frame filled with all the air that it could take on, and another outpouring followed. "She told me it was only fair that I knew. She said that she didn't want Adam back in the band or anywhere near Johnny. I thought she was telling me because she wanted me to confront him about it so that Adam wouldn't end up rejoining."

"You thought it would play out like that? You went to see Johnny to plead your case for staying in the band?"

"I wanted to know where I stood. Daisy said a lot of hurtful things and I needed to know the truth. I needed to hear it from Johnny himself."

"What did she tell you, exactly?"

"She said it was because of the song, *All Colours*. That Johnny told Adam he'd rediscovered it and realised how his friend had nailed it."

"Nailed it?"

"Nailed how Johnny was feeling. About his depression. Johnny realised how strong their friendship had been and he wanted them to get back as friends, and back together in the band."

"And where would that have left you?" asked Tyler.

"Daisy said Johnny didn't think I was up to it. That my songs were second rate and that I couldn't play like Adam. She said Johnny reckoned I tried hard but had no talent."

"That must have hurt," said Tyler. "Did you believe that Johnny would say such things?"

"I didn't know what to think. Johnny had been acting strange. He'd wanted me in the band, so I knew he must have thought I was good enough. I needed to talk to him, and I did."

"And he denied saying any of those things?"

"Yes, he re-assured me. He said that Adam had made it all up because he was jealous about the band doing well after he left."

"How did that make you feel about Adam?"

"I was angry that people were trying to make trouble."

"You were angry with Adam?"

"Of course I was."

"Angry enough to kill him?"

"No!"

"Did you kill Adam Lane, Billy?"

"No! I believed Johnny. I wouldn't have stayed in the band if I didn't."

"Really? You would have every reason to want to stay in the band, even if you weren't getting on with Richards. Even if you thought he really did want to replace you with Adam. The band were on the cusp of success. You were going places. All your dreams were coming true. You killed Adam to keep your place in the band, didn't you?"

"I swear, it wasn't like that."

"What was it like, Billy?"

"Johnny assured me that Adam would never play with him again. That I was in the band for keeps. I believed him, I still believe him."

"You didn't decide to have it out with Adam? After all, wouldn't that be the logical thing to do? You hear the rumour from Daisy, Johnny denies it and so you go and see the man himself. You go and see Adam."

"That isn't true. It isn't what happened."

"Are you telling me that you weren't just a little curious? All this trouble being caused ... wouldn't you want to know what was going on, what Adam was playing at?"

"I didn't see him, I've told you."

"I don't believe you, Billy. Daisy goes to the trouble of alerting you to what is going on and you expect me to accept that after a few words from Johnny you were prepared to carry on as though nothing had happened?"

Taking a break, Tyler told Mills to grab his jacket. They drove out to find Johnny Richards.

Richards was at his mother's house in Hanford. She was out shopping at the supermarket, he told the detectives, before cautiously welcoming them inside.

You don't seem so relaxed today, son, thought Mills. *You look to me as though you're carrying the weight of the world on your shoulders.* Mills asked if everything was alright, and Richards replied that he was concerned about Billy Steele. He wanted to know if Billy was okay, and if he had admitted to anything?

"Are you expecting him to admit something?" asked Tyler.

"I don't know what to expect anymore," said Richards.

Tyler asked if he had allayed Steele's fears about Lane rejoining the band.

"We had a conversation. He got it in his head that Adam was about to come back. I told him it wasn't true."

"But you did want Adam back in the band."

"I didn't want to hurt Billy's feelings."

Tyler wanted to punch Johnny Richards, and not just once. "You don't think it might have hurt Billy's feelings when he eventually found out?"

"I wasn't thinking straight."

"Do you believe Billy killed Adam?"

"Do you think I'd want him in my band if he had done that?"

"Do you like Billy?"

"He's okay. We've had our differences, but we can still work together. We're a good band."

"You wanted him out a few days ago and Adam back in!"

"I don't know."

"You don't know?"

"Like I say, I haven't been thinking straight."

"Are you thinking straight *now?*" Tyler waited for a few moments. "Does Billy have a girlfriend?"

Richards looked puzzled by the question. Then he shrugged. "I haven't seen him with anyone."

"Do you know Lizzie Butler?"

Richards blinked, and then blinked again. "I know the name. I think."

"Think harder, Johnny. You were at school with her."

"Yes, I remember," he said. "I didn't have anything to do with her, though."

"Did Billy have anything to do with her?"

"I'm not sure. Have you asked him?"

Tyler's eyes narrowed, issuing a warning. "I believe that she was in care with Billy."

"I'm sorry," said Richards. "I'm not being awkward, I don't know her, honestly. And I only see

Billy at rehearsals and gigs. I've never seen him with a girl, not that I can think of."

The detectives drove back towards Hanley. Tyler's silent rage filled the car and Mills couldn't wait to get out of it.

Coming off the roundabout, Mills was about to take the road back towards base when Tyler suggested instead the road to Penkhull.

"I'm in the mood for confronting ghosts," he said.

CHAPTER THIRTY SEVEN

The Meadows, on Chamberlain Drive, a few hundred yards from River Trent High looked nothing like St. Saviour's. Nothing like the hole in hell that Tyler had inhabited all those decades earlier. The Meadows was the place where Billy Steele had spent some of his formative years, Lizzie Butler too. There was no reason why this visit should be anything more than a dig into a past belonging to others.

Reminding himself of this Tyler stepped from the car and made his way, in the company of DS Mills, towards the main entrance of the building.

Entering through the front door brought confirmation to the DCI's thinking: that the past really was made up of different countries, not merely one. There might be sorrow here, and plenty of it; a share of pain too, no doubt. But the screams from his youth didn't have any echoes here; the bright faces of the staff, even the comforting tread of the carpets, suggested something very different from the haunted corridors and stark dormitories of his own past. At least some attempt at making a home, a real home, was evident here, and the coldness, the austerity that still lived in his memory, and the cruelty too, did not seem to be resident in this place.

After Tyler had made initial enquiries at the desk, a woman came through and invited the officers to join her in a small, comfortable office where they would not be disturbed. Tea and a plate of cakes and biscuits followed, and Tyler sensed no pretence in the hospitality or in the genial smile of Mrs Watson.

She looked to be in her mid-thirties, and had been working at The Meadows for almost ten years; a large woman with a round, red face that glowed when she smiled. She remembered Billy and Lizzie fondly.

Tyler noted that both Mills and Mrs Watson had a keen eye on the plate of snacks, and he sensed that a stand-off was already in play. But who would crack first?

He took the smallest biscuit on the plate and the action was like a starting gun being fired. The other two descended on the offerings with gusto, and by the time the preliminaries had been covered only crumbs remained, and not many at that.

She gave some background on both of her past charges. Billy had been at the home for a large chunk of his childhood. He had never been a cause of particular concern, and hadn't been in any trouble that Mrs Watson could recall. "I liked Billy. There was a lot to like. But you had to make the effort to get to know him. He was a little boy that you had to reach out to."

She spoke of a boy, and then a teenager, who seemed grateful for the smallest of mercies, and who tried to fit in. "I don't think I ever came across a child who tried so hard to be liked. He wasn't an attention seeker, don't get me wrong. That is not at all what I mean. Billy was very quiet and unassuming, actually. He just had that look about him, somehow. That *please like me, I'm really okay*, kind of look. I suppose it all comes down to his past experiences.

Being abandoned in life, in those early years, hardly does wonders for your confidence and self-esteem. I mean, how could it?"

Tyler asked her about Lizzie Butler.

"Ah, different kettle of fish. You never knew what was going on behind those eyes, not with Lizzie. Now Billy, he kept himself to himself, too. But there was more of a *what you see is what you get* with Billy. He couldn't hide his emotions the way Lizzie could. She was a one. Different background altogether, though. Different circumstances. I think they both had quite a streak of independence about them. Both tough nuts in their own ways, but Lizzie especially."

"Were Billy and Lizzie good friends?" asked Tyler.

The woman thought for a moment. "I only hesitate, because I think your question raises an interesting point."

"Which is?" asked Tyler, betraying a hint of impatience not lost on Danny Mills.

"I would say that they were very close indeed. It's just that they seemed to go to rather great lengths hiding the fact."

"Girlfriend and boyfriend?" asked Tyler.

"I'm not sure about that. More like brother and sister in many ways. Very defensive of each other, or should I say protective. I never saw any clear indication of romantic leanings. I did wonder if they might get together one day, but who knows."

She appeared to be framing a question, though not one that the detectives were in any position to answer. *Were Billy and Lizzie an item?*

"But, yes, very close," re-iterated Mrs Watson, once it was clear that she wasn't getting an update on any romantic gossip. Undefeated, she took another stab at gaining information. "I do hope that they are not in any kind of trouble?"

Mills answered her query by telling her nothing at all, indicating that they were merely looking to gain background information as part of an ongoing investigation. The way it came out, Mills wasn't quite sure that *he* understood what he had said. But the baffled, polite nod from Mrs Watson indicated that she wouldn't likely be asking anything further from the detective.

Job done, thought Mills.

With the refreshments consumed, and the closeness of Billy and Lizzie established - though leaving the question of romance still hanging in the air - Mills wondered if it was time to move. Tyler was thanking Mrs Watson for her time, and she was saying how she hoped that she had been of some assistance. Yet the DCI didn't appear anything like ready to go. More like he was settling down to the business at hand. Mills wondered how his colleague would shift the conversation forward without giving too much away. "I imagine, doing your job," said Tyler, "you must often wonder how things turned out for the children who passed through your care."

"It's true," she said. "You do often wonder. You know, I imagine that with a bit of fortune on his side, Billy could do quite well in life. I hope so. I can't help but feel a little bit, well, maternal towards that young man. He needs someone. I really do wonder if he and Lizzie ever did get it together."

She sighed and laughed. "Though I suppose it really isn't any of my business."

Tyler remained silent, letting the woman's thoughts roll out in their own time.

"Some people," said Mrs Watson, "have that self-assurance to make their way in life no matter what. I would put Lizzie in that category. But Billy - I think he needed to belong. To someone, or something."

Tyler's career, his love affair with Kim, flashed through his mind.

"Maybe someone to fight his corner. Oh, I don't know. But I wish him well anyway. And Lizzie too, of course, though she's one who can fight her own corner. I don't imagine anyone ever making a fool out of Lizzie."

"Did she fight Billy's corner?" asked Tyler.

"I can't think of an example of that ever happening. I think people sense things though. No-one ever tried to make trouble for either of them, as I recall. But, now you mention it, I reckon that if Billy had ever needed help, Lizzie would have been there. The other way around too, though Lizzie was always the stronger. Of course, I haven't seen either of them for so long now. They would make a formidable double act, if they ever did get together."

"What was their background?" asked Tyler, as casually as he could manage, attempting to conjure a sense of informality. But the woman still hesitated. "Of course," she said, "I would have to get access to their files."

"What do you recall, personally?" asked Tyler. Another level of bureaucracy he could do without was coming into play and he was keen to side-step it. "I may need to come back to you for more detail," he said, "but for now just a flavour of how they both ended up in the care system would suffice."

She thought for a few moments. "Billy was rather a sad case. That's why I recall the details so vividly, I suppose. He was taken into care quite young. His parents were both drug addicts and they more or less abandoned their son."

"Were there any siblings?"

"No, as far as I know Billy was an only child. The parents never visited. There was no contact at all."

"Had Billy suffered any abuse?"

"I'm not aware that he did, at least nothing physical or sexual. Of course, that isn't the entire picture, is it? In terms of emotional abuse, I can't begin to imagine what it must do to a young child living with parents who are too sick to care for you."

Mrs Watson's compassion for the suffering of the likes of Billy Steele, or anyone else in circumstances of abandonment and abuse, was clear enough. She appeared to exhibit a genuine mix of anger and sadness, and Tyler wished that someone like her had been around in Leicestershire, at St. Saviour's, all those years ago.

"Billy remained here until he was eighteen. He moved to our semi-independent annexe soon after he left school, to start preparing him for the outside world. It worked well, I think, for Billy. He was keen to get a job, and he found work at a few places as I recall. He saved his money, didn't smoke, drink or otherwise, as far as I know. He used to go to gigs, locally, but he was generally quite disciplined with his personal budgeting. He was keen to find his own place, if I remember correctly."

"And you were never aware of any problems at all?"

"I believe that Billy was something of a success story, as far as we are concerned. A good advertisement for the care system. He couldn't have had any quality of life with his natural parents, and to put it bluntly, he wouldn't have been safe with them any longer anyway. I'm not an advocate of removing children from their parents without very good reasons."

"Was fostering not an option?"

"I would have to get the file out to go any deeper into the case, I'm afraid."

"I understand," said Tyler. "And what about Lizzie?"

"Well, of course, she came to us much later. She was in her last year or two at school, if my memory serves me. Her mother had left home many years earlier and Lizzie had continued to live with her father. Then her father was sent to prison. But I assume that you know the details of all that."

"And you didn't have any problems with Lizzie?"

"Not at all. Actually, I suppose that in many ways, if anything was odd about Lizzie, it's the fact that we didn't have any issues. Your father goes to prison, your mother has already left home, you are wrenched from your surroundings at the age of, what, fourteen or so - you might expect a few ructions, to say the least.

"But no, she was remarkably well-adjusted, considering her circumstances. Remarkably mature. Strong minded, but no issues that I can bring to mind."

"Did she have many visitors? Any other family?"

"Again, without the file ... but I don't particularly recall her having visitors as such. I couldn't say for sure, not without checking."

"Did she talk about her father?"

"I don't remember her doing so. Like I've said, Lizzie kept her thoughts largely to herself. I vaguely recall prison visits being set up. They may have been fairly regular, thinking about it. I have the sense that she doted on her father."

"On what would you base that?" asked Tyler.

"Oh, I don't know. Perhaps a certain eagerness on visiting days? I'm not sure. More a feeling, really. It was quite a few years back."

"And she returned to the family home when she left here?"

"She was supported in returning home, as I remember. Again, I believe that the transition was fairly seamless, as with Billy. And like Billy, I think the care system worked to support her."

"Did Billy have a temper?" asked Tyler, switching subjects.

"He did have a bit of a temper on him, actually, did Billy. But I found that it generally didn't last. I could always coax him to calm down. I didn't see a lot of it, mind you. It wasn't as though he was an angry boy, or particularly aggressive. He just needed a bit of love and attention, that's all. And he always responded when he got it.

"You know, I think that we all respond to a bit of TLC now and again. I think we all need that from time to time. But I don't know if I ever came across a child who responded so strongly to it."

"Could you explain what you mean by that?" said Tyler.

"Well, what I mean is, Billy seemed so grateful, so ... responsive, I suppose. You spent a bit of time calming him down if he was upset over something, and he rewarded you. He had such a lovely smile. His face would light up like a Christmas tree."

Tyler thought how the same might be said of Mrs Watson, regarding the smile at least. Though he hadn't seen much evidence of that smile so far in the case of Billy Steele.

"I hope things work out for both of those kids," said Mrs Watson. "Mind you, they are hardly kids any more, are they. Makes me feel old." As though suddenly becoming aware that she was talking to two CID officers, she said, "I hope that they are not in any trouble. Are things alright with Billy and Lizzie?"

Tyler stood up. "As I indicated, these are routine enquiries. I am very grateful for your time today, Mrs Watson."

"Well, if you see them, please pass on my best wishes. They're both more than welcome to drop in any time."

"Do you get many dropping in?" asked Tyler.

"Some. But perhaps those two were just too self-contained to look back. Two of a kind in so many ways. I do wonder if they ever got together. I really could see them as an item, and, if I might say, I wouldn't like to be the one who tried to come between them."

Walking from the building, Mills noticed that Tyler seemed much easier, as though a weight had shifted.

"Interesting conversation wouldn't you say," said Mills driving back towards Cedar Lane.

"But at the same time speculative," said Tyler. "Let's see what Steele has to say, shall we?"

CHAPTER THIRTY EIGHT

In the interview room Tyler announced the resumption of the interview for the benefit of the tape machine. Then he took his seat and looked across at a frightened Billy Steele. "Okay, Billy. I want to know who you are covering for and I want to know now."

"I don't know what you mean."

"Then let me explain. If you didn't kill Adam Lane, you know who did. Either way, it's prison for you, unless you start giving me some answers. *Fast*."

Steele's solicitor looked about to say something, then reconsidered. To get more than a showroom dummy you had to pay the kind of money that the likes of Frank Watts could afford. Tyler wondered how far he would have to go to get this one to earn his fee. The thought sickened him.

"Okay," said Tyler, when Steele didn't respond, "let's say, for the sake of argument ... *Lizzie Butler.*"

"What?" said Steele. The fear was mingling with something else, and the cocktail of emotion produced an expression on the young man's face that was difficult to call. It didn't look pretty to DCI Tyler, though, and he wondered if he had hit the bull's-eye. "What's she got to do with any of this?" said Steele, his voice quivering.

"That's what I'm hoping to find out. Allow me to make a suggestion. You knew that your days in the band were numbered, and you didn't have the bottle to go and see Adam Lane to find out the truth. But you did talk to someone. You needed to *confide*. She was more than a listening ear, though, wasn't she? Lizzie Butler has connections, isn't that right?"

"I don't know what you're talking about."

"An armed robber for a father? I imagine she would know where to go to get a little job like Adam Lane done. Surprisingly cheap, these days, I'm told - getting a thorn removed from your flesh."

The solicitor coughed, but he still kept his thoughts to himself, if he was having any.

"Did Lizzie Butler take a cut, or was it done purely for love?"

Tyler watched Steele's face tighten, clenching into a foreshadowing of violence. Tyler knew that feeling only too well. He knew exactly how he would be feeling if their places around the table were reversed.

I would put a fist through the face of a bastard like me, he thought, compassion and self-loathing wrestling inside him.

"So, which was it, Billy? Did she - does she - love you enough to have a man killed, free of charge? Or did you negotiate mates' rates?"

Steele was almost out of his seat when the solicitor finally stirred into action. Putting out a hand, he pleaded for calm before suggesting that DCI Tyler act in a reasonable manner. Otherwise, he added, almost as an after-thought, the interview would have to be "halted immediately and an official complaint made."

Tyler didn't even acknowledge the interruption. He waited a moment for Steele to regain some composure, and then continued. "You have a temper, I see, Billy. I've heard about this temper of yours, though I've not witnessed it before. I can see that your feelings for Lizzie Butler run deep."

Tyler waited for a response. When it didn't come he said, "Anger can easily slip out of control, Billy, isn't that right? It can get the better of you. Adam wants your place in the band—"

"I've already told you, I spoke to Johnny about that."

"Yes, I remember you saying."

"Why would I need to talk to Adam when Johnny had already re-assured me?"

"You tell me, Billy."

"I didn't kill Adam. I had no reason to hurt him. And Lizzie didn't have any reason to get involved. There was nothing to get involved in."

"Then why the secrecy, Billy?"

"The what?"

"You and Lizzie seem to like to keep your *friendship* secret. Why is that?"

The eyes of the four men in the room narrowed, like gunfighters in a Western movie, waiting to see who would make the next move. A stillness descended. Tyler was about to come at him again when Steele said, "She has friends who don't like me."

"Lizzie Butler has friends who don't like you?"

"But that doesn't mean that she would have someone killed."

"What does it mean, Billy?"

"I like Lizzie, I always did. She was good to me, she was there for me, back at the home. She was the one I could always talk to. I wanted to stay friends with her. I wanted to be with her. She understands me, she knows where I'm coming from. She believes in me."

"And did you confide in her, Billy? Did you tell her about your fears - of being replaced by Adam? Of being thrown out, rejected?"

"I told her, yes, and she said that I needed to talk to Johnny, which I did. And then I told her that Johnny had put my mind at rest, and that's all there is to it. She was happy for me. She was nothing but happy for me."

The words tumbled out of him, suddenly, explosively. They didn't appear to have been considered or rehearsed and neither was there any hint of hesitation or fabrication. They came with a certain ring of truth that Tyler recognised.

But they still left questions that needed answering.

"You wanted to be with her, but you're saying that her 'friends' didn't like you?"

"Lizzie said it was better if we didn't see each other."

"When was this, Billy?"

"After we left the home. I wanted us to see each other. She said that she didn't want me to get hurt and that it was better that we didn't keep in touch. But I wanted to see her. I missed her."

"And so what happened? How did you make contact?"

"I found out where she was living and I got in touch. We saw each other occasionally, but someone saw us and she warned me off again. Then one night I was in my flat and two guys visited. They told me not to make contact with Lizzie again or else I would get seriously hurt."

"Who were they, Billy?"

"I don't know."

"Did they hurt you?"

"Not really. It was a warning more than anything."

Fear was at the root of Steele's sudden candour, Tyler was sure of it. He knew about Lizzie's father, and there were others, so-called 'family members' or 'friends' who appeared to have been tasked with keeping a close eye on any acquaintances of Lizzie, scaring them off. Particularly when it came to young men. *Suitors.* Getting too close, perhaps. Asking too many questions. Trying to lay claim to *complicated financial resources.*

Family business.

It came out straight and Tyler couldn't help but believe it. It answered questions, though not all of them.

"You didn't happen," said Tyler, "to be with Lizzie at the time Adam was murdered?"

He shook his head. "I've already told you. I was on my own and then I went to rehearsal. I don't know what Lizzie was doing. You will have to ask her that yourself."

"But despite the warnings and the intimidation, you have been *keeping in touch?*"

"I love her."

Three words and spoken like he had been storing them up all his life. As though in speaking them aloud, in the presence of others, he was admitting to the greatest crime of all.

"And does she have the same feelings for you, Billy?"

"I think ... I believe ... she cares for me, yes, I know she does. But we have to be careful."

"Can you go on like that?" asked Tyler.

"We don't have any choice."

They let him go, but not before Mills had reinstated the tail.

It took Sergeant Stephanie Osgood less than thirty minutes to make her first report back to Mills. Billy Steele had returned to his car, still parked at the Thirteen club, and driven to the flats to visit Daisy Finch.

Sergeant Osgood alerted Mills a short time later to report that Steele had left the flats and seemed upset and agitated; he was driving back in the direction of Longton.

Mills instructed Osgood to keep him informed, and updated Tyler.

"I am popular today," said Finch, answering the door.

"Don't knock it," said Tyler. "May we come in?"

"Be my guest."

She seemed, observed DS Mills, to be in a somewhat buoyant mood. Once inside the flat Tyler asked if she would mind telling him why Steele had visited her.

She grinned. "He's after advance orders on the forthcoming album. They're all going to be rich as well as famous now." The grin remained but her words came out sour and hostile. Tyler repeated the question. Sighing heavily, Finch gestured towards the seats. "Sit down, if you want to."

The detectives sat down and Tyler took the lead. "Why did you tell him that Adam had been approached about rejoining the band?"

She looked at Tyler and then at Mills, but she didn't say anything.

"Do you admit that you told him?"

"It's possible. I don't remember."

"We checked your phone records. You rang Steele a few hours before Adam was killed. He has confirmed that you told him about plans for Adam to rejoin the band."

Finch appeared to weigh up what the detective had said. "Okay, I admit it."

"Admit what?"

"Being nothing but a trouble-making cow! Is that what you want to hear? I was angry. I knew what Johnny was up to. I knew it was about the song - that he was using Adam, playing games. Trying to square the deal so it wouldn't come out who wrote it. Stopping Adam getting money for it - he was pulling the sentimental card, and I was afraid Adam would fall for it. Men can be so fucking stupid."

"And so telling Billy would achieve what, exactly?"

She took a deep breath, wincing as she did so. "I thought that Billy should be made aware. I thought he had a right to know what kind of a lowlife he was playing with."

"That was very public spirited of you. But are you sure that you were acting solely in his best interests?"

She glared at the detective. "Okay, so it was more than that."

"How much more?"

"I wanted to cause trouble, like I said. I wanted Billy ..."

"Yes?"

"I knew he had a temper."

"You knew that?"

"I'd never seen him actually attack anyone, nothing like that. But I can weigh people up. Billy was moody and people had said he could be volatile, one to watch out for. I wanted to cause some friction with Johnny. I wanted to get back at him and that stupid bitch he knocks around with."

"I take it you're referring to your sister?"

"It wouldn't surprise me if she hadn't put the idea in his head."

"I had the impression that Janine wouldn't want Adam within a mile of the band."

"She still wanted her precious Johnny keeping his hands on Adam's song, though. She wanted that, alright, the scheming ..." Finch bit her lip before carrying on ... "But even if he had rejoined, it wouldn't have lasted. As soon as it was convenient he would have been out on his arse again."

"So, again: what did you imagine Billy would do?"

"Well, I didn't imagine he would kill anybody, if that's what you're thinking. Like I said, I was angry and I wanted to cause as much trouble as I could. I also happened to think that Billy deserved to know the truth."

"And you expect us to believe that?" said Tyler.

"You can believe what you want. But that's all I can tell you." After a moment she said, "So why are you keeping tabs on me? You think I killed Adam now?"

"We're checking that you're okay," said Tyler.

"Yeah, right. *How kind*."

"Did Billy say where he was going after he left here?"

"Why would he? What business is that of mine?"

"You seem to have a habit of making things your business. Why did he come here today?"

"Do you really want to know the answer to that?"

"If it's not too much trouble."

"He wanted to know what I'd told you. He said you'd had him in again. That you wouldn't leave him alone. He wanted to know if it was something I'd said."

"And?"

"I told him I didn't believe he killed Adam. If I'd thought there was any danger of him doing that, do you think I would have told him that Johnny wanted him out of the band and Adam back in? I wanted to make trouble for Johnny Richards, and that's all I wanted. I wanted Billy to have it out with that two-faced piece of ..."

"He did confront Richards," said Tyler. "And Richards convinced him that you wanted to make trouble."

"That's Johnny Richards for you."

"But if he convinced him, why would he hurt Adam?"

Tyler glanced at Mills, and then looked back at Daisy Finch. "The night Adam died, you called him, telling him about Adam rejoining. You told him what Johnny Richards really thought about him, and in no uncertain terms - about him not being good enough.

"According to your statement, Adam went out to meet his friend, Ian Taylor. But Taylor has no recollection that he was due to meet Adam that evening."

Finch shrugged. "Taylor's three sheets to the wind, I said that."

"Yes, you did," said Tyler.

"What's that supposed to mean?"

"Could Adam have made different arrangements?"

"What are you trying to say?"

"I'm merely trying to establish the facts."

"No, you're not. You're trying to suggest something. Adam said he was meeting Taylor, and Taylor's too out of it most of the time to have a clue what day of the week it is."

Observing her escalating anger, Tyler timed his question to perfection. "Adam couldn't have been meeting someone else?"

CHAPTER THIRTY NINE

As Mills drove back to Cedar Lane his mind whirled over the case. Looking across at Tyler, he was startled to find the DCI staring at him.

"Let's hear it, then," said Tyler.

"Sir?"

"I can practically see the cogs turning. And I can smell burning. Is your brain on fire? Do we have a solution?"

Mills pulled the car over to the side of the road and parked it. Taking a moment to collect his thoughts, he said, "As I see it ... if Finch wanted to hurt Richards ... if her plan backfired and Steele ended up killing Adam instead ..."

"Then we are dealing with a situation that takes on the gravity of tragedy." Tyler shook his head. "I don't believe it for a second. It might look good on the TV, but it doesn't add up.

"Look: Finch tells Steele that Richards is about to ditch him, hoping that Steele, known to have a temper, will hurt Richards. Even kill him, for God's sake! It's a bit of a leap, in my opinion, but let's stick with it for a moment. And so what does our angry Billy do? He only goes and kills Adam Lane instead, kills the love of Daisy Finch's life - and all over a place in a band?

"It might go down well with a bucket of popcorn on a Saturday evening, but it doesn't work for me. It's cute but it doesn't work."

"Pity," said Mills, "because nothing else works, either. Unless ... "

"Yes?"

"You asked about Lane seeing somebody else that night, using the arrangement with Ian Taylor as cover."

Tyler nodded. "I still wonder about that. And from the strength of Finch's reaction, I don't imagine that we're the first to consider it. But where does it lead us, Danny? If she suspected that Adam had made other arrangements - ones that led to his death - wouldn't she want to tell us of her suspicions?"

"Unless she really did take matters into her own hands."

"But I keep coming back to Frank Watts. He wanted Lane out of the way because he threatened to expose Johnny Richards over the song. Watts stood to lose a fortune."

"We don't know that, sir. We don't know that Lane made any threats against anybody."

"I don't trust Watts. But then I don't trust Daisy Finch. Or Billy Steele. Maybe I don't have a very trusting personality."

"You think that Finch put Lane up to it? I mean, threatening Richards or even Watts?"

"It wouldn't surprise me if she wasn't pulling the strings. I'm just not certain exactly what the strings were attached to. You see, if we're dealing with high Shakespearean tragedy, then I'm back to Macbeth. Lady Macbeth. The king maker.

"Except that what we may have here are three Lady Macbeths. Three king makers. Three women all rooting for their men and Frank Watts rooting for himself."

"Daisy and Janine and *Lizzie Butler*? You're saying that Butler put Steele up to killing Lane to assure his place in the band?" Mills fought to restrain his laughter.

"Getting silly, isn't it? But hear me out on this, Danny.

"Watts sets Billy up as the fall guy to take the rap for Lane's death. Two birds with one stone, because Watts didn't like, didn't trust, either of them. Lane dead, Steele locked up - free to bring in a new guitar player, someone without the complications, Johnny the star, fame and fortune waiting."

"Except that Steele is still in the band, sir."

"And why? Because we are failing to do our jobs, Danny. Our part in this was to nail Billy Steele and clear up the mess. Plain and simple. Oh, and to encourage sales by providing more publicity than ..."

Tyler looked at Mills. "I can't make it fit. I'm trying too hard, and likely missing what's right under my nose."

"Going back to Finch," said Mills. "Suppose she really did find out that her boyfriend was seeing someone else and using Ian Taylor for cover?"

"And followed him and murdered him - or else got Billy Steele to do the dirty work, for whatever reason? I don't see it. Maybe there's a connection between Watts and Lizzie Butler."

"Nothing on either party, though, sir. We've gone over Watts' business with a fine tooth comb.

Unscrupulous, but always on the right side of the law, just about. His accounts and legal department could run a small country. Same with the Butler family, clean as a whistle. Apart from Lizzie Butler's father serving time, there's nothing. And why would there be a connection between her and Frank Watts?"

"I can feel something, Danny. I just can't quite see it."

"So what now?"

Tyler's phone was flashing.

"What now? We could bring in Watts and Butler, try to squeeze something out of them. Otherwise all we've got is to wait for a break, something to come in. Rogers taking us off the case ... hang on."

Tyler took the call. When the call ended he said, "Looks like something's kicking off."

There was no anticipation in Tyler's expression. No look of the hunter smelling blood and preparing to move in for the kill. Instead something sorrowful; a foreshadowing of tragedy.

"Hanford," said Tyler. "The Richards' house. Move it!"

Mills drove down past the canal, close to the place where Adam Lane had been killed. From there he cut into Stoke and headed out for Hanford. Tyler called for backup, and then he told Mills what he knew.

"When Steele left Finch he went over to Lizzie Butler's. He was hammering on the door, but nobody was answering, so he sat in his car and waited. When Butler returned home he got out of his car. He was agitated, angry, really steaming. Butler was making it obvious that she didn't wish to conduct private business out on the street and they went inside—look, won't this thing go any faster? Put on the blues and twos and for God's sake step on it, will you."

Mills did as he was told, and Tyler wiped at his dry mouth, chewing on the back of his fist. They were barely a mile away from the Richards' house, but the traffic was playing its usual school run antics.

"Anyway, Steele left Butler's house soon after, leaving alone. He was still extremely agitated and he appeared to be highly distressed. The front door of the house had been left wide open, but no-one else came out. He got into his car and sped away. The tail called it in and followed him. Another patrol is on the way to Butler's address as we speak—Christ!" said Tyler, his fists clenched, and something like fear and despair etching into his face. He appeared to groan; a dark, foreboding sound echoing from a deep place inside him.

Mills did his best to sideswipe the traffic. They were less than half a mile from the Richards' house when Tyler took another call.

Mills glanced over as the DCI listened and then confirmed his position. It looked as though Steele was ahead of them, but not by much. Another call came in quickly, and this time Mills heard grief in Jim Tyler's voice. Then Mills took a call confirming that back up was two minutes away. As he turned the car into the road on which Richards and his mother lived, he saw Steele leap out of his car and run to the front door of the house, his fists pounding on the frame, shouting for Richards to come outside.

The DCI ended his call, and Mills heard him say, "He's killed her. He's bloody-well killed her."

Tyler scrambled out of the car before it had even stopped moving. The door of the house had opened and Steele was disappearing inside, swinging a fist at whoever had answered the door, Tyler shouting Steele's name as he ran down the drive towards the open door.

Mills was out of the car, following Tyler; the officer who had tailed Steele from Butler's house pulling up outside, radioing for urgent assistance. Steele was ranting, shouting about Lizzie Butler, his voice distorted, roughened almost beyond recognition while Richards' desperate attempts to respond were lost beneath the searing tone of Steele's savage indictments. The sound of blows was followed quickly by screaming.

Tyler had reached the door and he moved through it to witness Steele lunging at Richards, whose face was already bleeding, Steele holding something in his right hand; a vase taken from the fireplace, the discarded flowers strewn over the floor around Steele's feet; as Tyler ran at him he saw the arm pull back and descend towards the cowering target, the impact of the blow sending Richards rocking backwards, down onto the floor, shards of glass from the shattered vase glittering around him.

Richards was clutching at his face and Steele was on top of him, his arm already pulled back to strike again, the remains of the vase still gripped tightly in his fist as Tyler grabbed him, his forearm around his throat, pulling him backwards. But Steele's skinny frame belied a furious strength, and he broke the stranglehold, making once again for the prone figure of Richards, whose face was bleeding profusely now, Richards clearly incapable of defending himself.

Tyler grabbed again for Steele, pulling him away from Richards, Steele lashing out, catching the detective across the side of the head with the base of the vase, issuing a sickening crack; but Tyler wouldn't let go of him. The DCI was leaking blood from the gash on the side of his head, Mills joining in the fray, the two of them taking Steele to the ground; Tyler battling to hold him down as he cursed and spat, promising to kill Richards, while Mills fought to prise the remains of the smashed weapon from out of Steele's bleeding hand; and still he would not relinquish it, his grip like iron, and Tyler's face awash with blood as he struggled to keep Steele pinned to the ground until back-up arrived.

They took Billy Steele away in cuffs in the moments before the ambulance came for Johnny Richards. Tyler was looking groggy, and Mills, eyeing the cut on the side of the DCI's head, suggested that he get himself checked out.

"I'm okay," said Tyler, walking back through the house towards the open front door.

Falling through it.

CHAPTER FORTY

Jim Tyler woke up in hospital, dazed and not a little confused.

It had to be a dream. There was a man looking down on him, a man with a face remarkably similar to that of CS Graham Berkins. Except that it couldn't possibly be Berkins.

As long as anybody could recall Berkins had sported a moustache that belonged in comedy films from a bygone era. Tyler's mind was circling the idea that it might be the only one of its kind in captivity, and that it would undoubtedly accompany the man to his grave.

The cleanly shaved face smiled, and the voice followed. "Good morning, Jim."

It was Berkins, alright. *Life, Jim, but not as we know it.* Tyler took in his surroundings. *If this isn't a dream, why am I in hospital? And why is Berkins minus moustache?*

Then the face was gone, replaced by a large bunch of flowers. "Allow me to repay the compliment," said Berkins.

The recent memories flashed through Tyler's head. The race to the home of Johnny Richards; dragging Steele, kicking and screaming, off the bloodied Richards; Lizzie Butler also attacked by Steele ...

... dead?

He moved to a sitting position and felt the surge of pain engulf the side of his head.

"Nasty wound you've got there, Jim. But I reckon you'll live to fight another day. Touch of concussion, a few days' rest. It will take more than a bang on the head to keep you out of action for very—"

"Is she dead?" asked Tyler.

"If you're referring to Lizzie Butler," said Berkins. "I'm afraid so. She sustained serious head injuries and died at the scene. Steele has been charged with her murder. He has also admitted killing Adam Lane."

Jim Tyler lay quietly for a few minutes, taking it all in. "I'm calling it a day," he said at last.

"That blow on the head must have been worse than we realised."

"No, Graham, I'm thinking straight enough. But maybe I've finally seen the light."

"Let's hope not," said Berkins. "You're the best detective this city's got. If you ever see the light, we're doomed. But that's strictly off the record, of course. Look, it has been a difficult time for you, and this case—"

"I let my feelings cloud my judgement and that is unforgiveable."

"You're being hard on yourself, Jim. None of us are perfect, and I'm the living proof of that. You have my full support and the support of your team."

"Rogers a fan too, is he?"

"Only of himself. But there is some good news, at least I hope you will receive it as good news. I'm coming back to work in a few weeks, so by the time you've got over your concussion I will be your boss again."

When Tyler didn't respond Berkins said, "A smile might be customary, even if you don't mean it."

"I'm pleased, Graham, of course I am. I'm pleased for you, for the team, and for the city, for that matter. But what about Rogers?"

"Unfortunately, he will still be around, though at least not as your line manager. You've done nothing wrong. You have no case to answer. If anything, you've gone up even further in my estimation."

"I still let emotion get in the way."

Berkins shook his head. "You showed that you're human. And if that's a failing, then police work is no longer for me either. Rest up, and you will see things the right way up in a day or two, I promise you. We've all been there. What doesn't kill you, and all that.

"In a nutshell ..."

But Tyler was already drifting, and the words began to blur, along with the cleanly shaven face of Graham Berkins.

Mills visited the hospital later, and Tyler was waiting for him, demanding a full update. The DS had barely had chance to set down the chocolates and grapes when Tyler said, "So, Billy Steele has admitted killing Adam Lane."

Mills smiled. It was certainly good to see the DCI looking so bright and eager. "Wraps up the case nicely, I'd say."

"*The stupid ...*"

Mills was taken aback by the vehemence in the DCI's tone.

"There but for the grace of God," muttered Tyler.

"He killed Lizzie Butler. He attempted to kill Johnny Richards. You don't still believe he's covering for—who, Butler?"

When Tyler didn't answer, Mills said, "So, anyway, how are you feeling?"

"Angry."

"With anybody I know?"

"With a lot of people, actually, but mainly with myself. If we had nailed this case earlier ..."

"But we didn't. And that's nobody's fault and certainly not yours."

Tyler almost smiled. "I appreciate you coming. And I appreciate your kindness, too."

"All I'm doing is telling it like it is."

"I still have questions, Danny. I need answers. As soon as I get out of here—"

"Shouldn't you be resting?"

Tyler looked at the gifts that Mills had placed on the bedside table. "Tomorrow, filled to the gills with grapes and chocolate, I will be ready once again to take on the world. Perhaps you would care to accompany me. We'll be doing the rounds."

"The rounds?"

"Billy Steele, Daisy Finch and Johnny Richards. Though I haven't quite worked out the order yet."

Mills left the hospital with a rekindled sense of foreboding.

CHAPTER FORTY ONE

On Tyler's first day back on duty he took Mills out with him to visit Johnny Richards, another temporary resident at the City General hospital. The young man, tucked away in a side-ward, was barely recognisable. His face, which had so recently adorned countless magazine covers, newspapers and television screens, was now a mess of lacerations and bruising.

Mills asked how it was going and Richards surprised him, answering brightly. "I'm told I will make a full recovery. I won't be entering any beauty contests for a while, but still."

Mills asked about his plans for the band and Richards said that he was jacking it in. "Well," said Mills, "maybe now is not the time to be making big decisions. You're young and famous. There's no need to rush into anything. Take some time out and I've no doubt that things will work out for you."

"I don't think so," said Richards. "I don't want anything more to do with any of it."

"Early days," said Mills. "I'm sure you'll feel differently in a few weeks or so."

"Not a chance. I've had my fifteen minutes and it's enough to last a lifetime."

Mills looked unconvinced. "It's your life, Johnny. But a little birdie tells me I'll be looking out for you on *Top of the Pops* one of these days."

Richards cringed. Even Tyler cleared his throat. "The important thing," said Mills, "is that you make a good recovery. What you choose to do with the rest of your life is up to you."

Richards looked at Tyler, the marks of the fight with Steele still visible on the DCI. "Thank you, by the way," said Richards. "He would have killed me if you hadn't pulled him off."

"Don't mention it," said Tyler. "It's what we do."

"My best friend is dead," said Richards, suddenly looking close to tears. "Someone I thought was my friend killed Adam and tried to kill me. My one famous song - my one 'great song' - wasn't even mine. I'm a fake and a thief." He pointed at himself, at his bruised and lacerated face. "I deserve this. He should have killed me and done with."

He gazed into the distance. "I don't blame anyone else. I stole Adam's song and I tried to do the dirty on Billy. Adam should never have left the band. I wanted him back, but not because of the song. Not because I wanted him to keep quiet or anything like that. I missed him, I couldn't work with Billy; it wasn't the same. We tried hard to make it work, but it's just how it goes."

Richards went quiet, as though thinking deeply about something. "It's like I've been living in a fantasy for years and I've finally woken up. I needed Adam because I wasn't enough on my own. I thought I was really something, but now I know that I'm not. I'm just not all I thought I was."

"I think you're being a bit tough on yourself," said Mills.

"I'm being honest at last."

Tyler, looking unconvinced, said, "Watts put you up to it, didn't he?"

"No," said Richards. "He absolutely did not."

"Are you afraid of Watts?"

"I'm not afraid of him, why should I be? He gave me my big break, our big break."

"It was Watts' idea to get Adam back in the band, wasn't it? And when Adam refused, and threatened to expose the fact that he had written that song, Watts took care of things. That's the truth, isn't it, Johnny?"

"No."

Johnny Richards didn't say anything further for a few moments. Then: "Actually, Frank Watts is a piece of dirt."

"Go on," said Tyler.

"Not in the way you're thinking. He had nothing to do with Adam's death - that I know of, anyway. And I don't even blame him for ripping us off with that crap deal. We were young and naive and we thought we were going to rule the world."

"You're still young," said Mills.

"Not as young as I was." The words rang with hard-won wisdom. "Watts helped get things moving for us, and I knew that would come at a cost."

The words seemed to echo for a moment around the side-ward, and then Richards laughed. "They certainly came at a cost. But the music business is full of people like Watts. You hear all the stories, you hear about what's happened to other bands and artists and it's just how it's always been.

"The trouble is, you never think it's going to happen to you. You imagine that it'll be different, somehow, because you're special. You get blinded by the thought of success and it changes you."

"A few moments ago," said Tyler, "you referred to Watts as ... 'a piece of dirt.'"

"He was screwing Janine. Can you believe that?"

Neither detective commented.

"She's shacked up with him. It's been going on for a while. That's how we got the deal with Watts in the first place! Hilarious, isn't it?"

"I'm sorry to hear that," said Mills.

"I wish I had never met her or her sister. You know, it was her idea to change the name of the band, putting my name out front. I was never comfortable with that, not really, though I don't expect anyone will believe me. I might have been a bit of an egomaniac, I was from the start. But she didn't help."

Tyler, tiring of the self-pity, moved the conversation on. "You think all this - Adam's murder, Lizzie Butler's murder, was down to Billy's jealousy? Believing that you and Adam were seeing Lizzie?"

Richards looked uncomfortable. "I don't know if Adam was seeing her, maybe he was. He had a bit of a reputation. But I don't know. I didn't even know that Billy and Lizzie were together, to be honest. He never mentioned - Billy never mentioned her, not once."

"And you didn't have any ... *dealings* with her?" asked Tyler.

Richards shook his head again, failing to meet the eye of either detective. "That's what I don't get. I don't get why Billy thought I was seeing her."

It was time to go.

Wishing Johnny Richards a speedy recovery, they made their way out of the hospital, towards the carpark.

"So, do you think that's really the end of Johnny Richards' glittering career?"

"He certainly doesn't look so pretty these days," said Tyler. "But doubtless most of those scars will heal, eventually."

"The external ones at least," said Mills.

Tyler stopped walking and looked at Mills. "You think it really runs that deep? You think he has actually 'seen the light' and changed?"

Mills shrugged. "Who knows? You reckon he was telling the truth about not having anything to do with Lizzie Butler?"

They walked on towards the car. "Daisy Finch," said Tyler. "Let's get this over with."

CHAPTER FORTY TWO

She didn't look altogether surprised to see the detectives, and welcomed them inside. She was moving better, Mills noticed. The ribs that had taken a battering from her sister, were obviously healing.

Drinks were offered but Tyler declined and got straight down to business. "I imagine that you are aware that Billy Steele has been charged with the murders of Lizzie Butler and Adam Lane." Finch said that she was aware and Tyler asked if she had any thoughts on the matter.

"I'm glad that Adam's killer has been brought to justice, naturally I am," she said. Tyler waited to hear what might follow. When nothing did, he said, "You contacted Billy Steele on the day that Adam was killed."

"I've already—"

"You told him that Adam was meeting Lizzie Butler."

Finch barely blinked. "That's right," she said. "That's what I did."

"Can you explain why. And how you knew that a meeting had been arranged."

"I got the wrong end of the stick," she said. "Or at least I thought I did. I overheard Adam on the phone and I confronted him. He admitted that Lizzie Butler had called him. She'd got the number off Billy, after Billy had found out - after I'd told him about

Adam rejoining the band. He must have told her. She wanted to discuss the situation with Adam, face to face."

"At the back of the college?" said Tyler.

"Adam said that she wanted to be discreet. She had friends, or family, I'm not sure - but some nasty people, apparently. Not someone to mess with. She was bad news."

"You knew her?"

"I'd heard rumours."

"From who?"

"From people generally."

"You can't be more specific?"

"Not really."

"You knew that there was a relationship between Billy and Lizzie?"

"They kept it quiet, for whatever reason. But when I'd been at gigs, or just around - when they were there I could tell they were *together*."

"So, this meeting," said Tyler. "Did Adam feel threatened? Was he afraid that she would attempt to intimidate him, to frighten him off rejoining the band?"

"Adam had no intention of rejoining, so no reason to be fearful. That's what he said. He preferred to meet with her, if that's what it took, and lay any rumours to rest."

"And you believed him?"

"I wasn't sure. At first I didn't but then it seemed plausible. I was so in love with Adam, I didn't think that he would cheat on me. I didn't want to believe that it was possible. But on the other hand,

I was afraid of losing him. I wasn't sure what to think, to be honest."

"So you rang Billy?"

"I wanted to sound him out. I wanted to know if he was aware of the meeting. If he was, then I guessed there wouldn't be anything to worry about."

"You didn't ring Billy to tell him that you thought Adam and Lizzie were having an affair? You weren't laying a trap for Adam, for having an affair with Lizzie Butler?"

"That's ridiculous. I didn't know that there was any affair."

"But you suspected that there might be."

"Like I said, I didn't know."

"So why do you imagine Billy killed Adam?"

"I've thought about that."

"Have you now?"

"I mean, since I found out he admitted it, of course."

"Of course," said Tyler. "*And ...?*"

"I think Billy was insanely protective of Lizzie. I think, if she was trying to scare Adam off, given her contacts - I wonder if he killed him to prevent her getting further involved."

"Do you really think that's likely?" said Tyler.

"I don't know what happened. But something like that, I think. I don't know what else to make of it."

"I believe," said Tyler, "that your sister has left Johnny Richards and taken up with Frank Watts."

"Nothing would surprise me with that bitch. Money and glory, that's all she ever wanted. That's why she was with Johnny in the first place. But if I know her, she would have been hedging her bets. If she was screwing Watts at the same time then she was playing the percentages."

"Do you know of any connection between Lizzie Butler and Frank Watts? Or between Lizzie and your sister?"

Daisy Finch's eyes narrowed. "Conspiring to have Adam killed - to make sure he didn't spill the beans about the song? Protecting their asset, the great Johnny Richards - using Lizzie Butler and her *connections*."

"You've thought about it?"

"I've thought about a lot of things."

"But you don't think it likely?" asked Tyler.

She paused. Tyler caught the moment of hesitation, and in that instant, like a lightning flash across an interior sky, the truth came bursting through.

I want it to be Watts, at the back of all this. And now I've raised it, given it credibility, Finch sees it as a convenient smokescreen.

But it's simpler than that.

"You're a liar," he said.

"What?"

"If you believed that Watts and your sister were behind Adam's death, you would have said so. You would have called it in, you're not that stupid. And if you'd thought Billy had killed Adam, for the same reason - because of anything to do with the band - you would have acted likewise."

She was taking in a lot of air, trying to speak and at the same time scrambling to get her thoughts in order.

"There's only one scenario I can come up with, where you wouldn't have called it in and called us out. The scenario involving *you*. Your belief that Adam was having an affair. Setting Billy up to teach Adam a lesson for cheating on you."

She broke down; deep sobs yielding to a cascade of tears. The detectives sat back and watched; they had seen it before, and it didn't become any more convincing with the repetition.

"Okay," she said. "I had suspicions about Adam going to meet that loser Ian Taylor. Part of me wanted Billy to do something. But I rang him hoping that he would put my mind at rest - I did, it's true."

"Hard to separate out the truth," said Tyler. "Easy to leave it all nesting in confusion. And impossible to prove. *However*."

The room fell silent with anticipation.

"The same thing happened again, didn't it?"

"I don't know what you're talking about."

"You told Billy that Johnny had also been having an affair with Lizzie."

Finch appeared shell-shocked.

"I wonder what you said to convince him? Or was he so possessive, so lacking in confidence, in self-esteem - so damaged and lacking in self-belief that in the hands of someone like you ... he didn't stand a chance, did he? It was like arming a nuclear warhead. And you pointed him at Johnny Richards, didn't you?"

Her mouth was opening and closing but nothing was coming out.

"But first he went to Lizzie Butler. And he killed her.

"And you have the blood of them all on your hands. Because in the end this had nothing to do with music, with bands, with songs, with corrupt managers, with fame and fortune. In the end it all came down to punishing the two men you loved and who you thought were cheating on you."

She appeared to implode. As though the light had finally died, the instinct to deny reduced to ashes. The fire in Daisy Finch had been replaced by a strange calm.

"I didn't imagine," she said, "not for one single moment that Billy would hurt Lizzie."

"But the rest?"

"I knew what he was capable of."

Tyler was adding it all up inside his head. "How did you know that Richards and Butler were seeing each other?"

Finch started to laugh. "Poetic justice."

"Meaning?"

"*Janine.*"

"Your sister told you?"

"Not in so many words. She rang up, out of the blue, wanting to know where Butler lived. That's when I knew. That's when it all fell into place."

"What do you mean by that?"

"I knew there was someone else. All the time I was with Johnny, I knew something was going on. Lizzie Butler was screwing both of them. That's why Adam and Johnny fell out—it was over *her!* She kept it going all that time, I'll give her that. I always said that Johnny and Janine deserved each other."

A look of victory, beginning in the eyes, spread over her until she was radiant with it.

"And so I won't be spilling any tears for any of them. Cosy little fuck-pad in Shelton, by the college. That's where Adam was heading that night. The only one of the whole damned lot worth crying over is Billy Steele. Now, isn't that *ironic?*"

CHAPTER FORTY THREE

They visited Steele in the cells, and Mills thought how childlike he looked. A skinny waif, let down early in life, desperate to be loved and to belong. He seemed incapable of anger, let alone violence, and yet this pale thing, sitting alone in his cell, waiting for the machinery of justice to process him in accordance with the law of the land, had killed at least one person, possibly two, and had tried to kill a third.

Tyler did the talking. He wanted to know why Steele had done what he had done. Why he had killed Lane, killed Butler, attacked and attempted to kill Richards.

Steele looked at Tyler questioningly and then he closed his eyes. The fight had gone out of him, observed Mills, an almost deathly serenity replacing all that had gone before it.

"I'm not here to do any deals," said Tyler. "There's nothing on the table, and nothing under it either. You don't have to say anything."

Steele's eyes opened, without warning, startling the detectives.

"I killed them, that's all there is to it."

"Something's bugging me," said Tyler. "Lizzie had her head bashed in, a frenzied assault—and you tried to do the same to Johnny. And yet for Adam a single blow to the head sufficed. Not really your style, Billy. Not so much rage-fuelled frenzy as a professional job."

"It was a lucky blow, it must have been. He fell into the water."

"It isn't Lizzie's reputation that you're protecting, Billy. It's the likes of her father, or Frank Watts. People who get others to do their dirty work. Maybe she did have an affair with Lane, and with Richards too, and wanted to make amends. Give you the chance she felt you deserved."

"I killed him. It had nothing to do with Lizzie or anyone else. I did it."

"Daisy Finch convinced you that Adam and Johnny were both having an affair with Lizzie?"

"Yes."

"And you believed her, just like that?"

"I already knew."

"You already knew that she was having affairs?"

"With Lane, yes, I suspected it, anyway. And when Daisy told me, I had to do something. Lizzie was making a fool of me."

"But you carried on seeing her?"

Steele looked away. "She was sorry, that's what she told me. She begged for my forgiveness and I wanted to believe her. I did believe her. She wanted me to succeed, she convinced me."

"And yet Finch later convinced you that Lizzie had also been seeing Johnny Richards?"

Again the hesitation. "Billy?"

"No, Daisy didn't convince me. I knew she hated Richards."

"You thought she might have been using you—to hurt Richards?"

"I didn't think that at the time. I was angry because of what Lizzie had done with Lane. She was an easy target, people could make up anything about her, taking me for a fool.

"I drove to Lizzie's place. I wanted to tell her what people were saying. I wanted to hear her tell me that it was all lies."

His eyes were misting.

"But I could see, as soon as I saw her, that it was all true. That she had been with Richards. She told me that there had been others too, that she couldn't help herself, and that I was better off without her. I wanted to kill Richards, but I still didn't want to lose her, even after what she had told me."

The tears were falling. "I loved her and she loved me. She's the only person who ever loved me. I didn't want to hurt her, but I couldn't leave, knowing that was the end."

The grief came thick and fast. "I don't even remember what happened. I don't remember attacking her. I was standing over her ... blood ... I was covered in it ... I saw what I'd done and I blamed Lane and Richards and I went after him to kill him and then I would have killed myself."

He looked up at the detectives. "I don't regret killing Lane and I would gladly do it again. He fell into the water and I watched him drown and I enjoyed every second of it. My only regret ... I wish I had killed Richards."

Tyler waited a few moments. "Okay, Billy. For whatever reason, you had to get that out of your system. Now I would like you to tell me what really happened ..."

CHAPTER FORTY FOUR

Billy Steele sat in silence. Then the silence broke.

" ... When Daisy rang me, I didn't know what to do. Everything went through my head. In the end I got in my car and I drove over to Lizzie's."

"In Shelton?"

Steele shook his head.

"Go on," said Tyler.

"At first she denied it. She said that she had no plans to see Adam. She said she had arranged to visit her father and that I could follow her if I didn't believe her. But then ... she changed her mind ... she told me."

"What did she tell you, Billy?"

"That she had been seeing Adam, but it was over, it had been a *mistake*. I said that I didn't believe her. She asked if I loved her and I told her that of course I did. She said that something was going to happen, and that if I loved her I was going to have to keep my mouth shut about what she was going to tell me.

"I agreed. She said that she would have to tell me now because I would find out anyway on the news.

"I asked her what she meant and she said that Adam had been trying to blackmail her family over something that he'd found out. She said it was something serious that would cause a lot of trouble for a lot of people. That it would hurt her too. She wouldn't tell me what it was; she said that it was better if I didn't know - in case anyone came after me for information.

"She told me that someone was going to meet Adam, and that Adam thought he was meeting her. I asked what was going to happen and she said they were planning to pay him off, to end the blackmailing.

"I didn't think they were going to kill him.

"It was the gig the following night, and I was trying to stay focused on that. I was trying to put all this other stuff to the back of my mind. Then Johnny went missing and I got scared. I didn't know what was happening. I didn't see how any of that could be related, but I was thinking all kinds of things. I didn't know what to think.

"Then it came on the news about Adam. About him being found dead. I got back in touch with Lizzie and I met up with her. She told me that I had to keep my mouth shut or else I was putting my own life in danger. I asked if Johnny had got caught up in it but she said that she didn't know anything about that. Then they found Johnny and it seemed like he wasn't hiding anything. He was cool. I had no reason to think that he was involved with Lizzie or any of that shit."

"And so you went to see Daisy Finch."

"You kept asking me about Adam. I wanted to know if she had told you something, told you that she had called me about Adam meeting Lizzie, setting me up. I don't know, I was confused. I needed to know what was going on. And so I went to see her, and she told me. She said I ought to know about Lizzie seeing

Johnny too, and I flipped. It all made sense. That this secret life of hers was all—that it was just *convenient*. Lizzie was using people, using me. I left Daisy's flat and I went to see Lizzie. I wanted her to tell me I was wrong, but she didn't deny it, any of it. She turned on me."

"Turned on you, Billy?"

"Said she was sick of having to spare the feelings of someone who ought to grow up. She would see who she wanted to see. She said she'd been seeing Johnny even longer than Adam, that she had fancied them since school.

"I never saw her act like that before. It was like she was taunting me, trying to hurt me, as though she *hated* me. I asked her what she was doing, why she was doing it, but she just kept on, mocking me, like she was trying to provoke me to do something."

"Are you saying that she wanted you to attack her, Billy?"

"I think she wanted me to end it, one way or another. She wanted to be out of the situation she was in, but I don't know and I never will know. But I lost it. I went for her ... and then I couldn't stop."

It was coming out of him in torrents; anger, sorrow, grief. Tyler and Mills sat impotently, witnessing silently until it was over.

On the drive back Tyler asked Mills to take a detour. They pulled up outside the home in Penkhull. The Meadows, on Chamberlain Drive. The two detectives sat in the car looking at the place that had been home to Billy Steele and Lizzie Butler. At last Tyler said, "I'm inclined to agree with Daisy Finch."

"Sir?"

"Maybe Billy Steele *was* the only one worth a damn. Though you wouldn't know it by the way he was treated. Finch was happy to use him to settle her own scores." Tyler laughed. "Who would have thought it: hard-nosed detective turns softie ... turns the stomach, doesn't it?

"I wanted there to be gangsters, and in the end all we have behind bars is a pitiful young man. Whatever Adam Lane knew that cost him his life, there's no proof, no evidence. From the information Billy's given, we may still nail the enforcer, though frankly I doubt it. At least we've got the property chain. Trevor Butler channelled the funds through the rentals around Shelton and Hanley, and maybe that's what Adam Lane knew and what cost him his life. At least when they let Butler out in another year or so he'll be struggling to pay the bills on what's left."

"If Lizzie Butler's father was behind Lane's death, sir, I think he's paid the price."

"And Frank Watts ..."

"Whatever role Watts played, he won't benefit from any of this. And his reputation has taken a hammering."

"Are you trying to console me?"

"I certainly am, sir."

"Billy's relationship with Lizzie Butler sealed his fate, one way or another; and yet in many ways she was the best thing that ever happened to him. As for Watts ... he didn't kill anybody. He doesn't need to. He skins them alive and he leaves a trail of broken dreams behind him. Number thirteen, Trinty Street."

"Used to be the old casino, apparently," said Mills. "And when Watts bought it out he kept the gimmick."

"*Lucky For Some*. It certainly is, but mainly for Frank Watts." Tyler shook his head. "But he operates within the law, just about. This world is full of the likes of Frank Watts and doubtless it always will be."

"Should we head back, sir?"

Tyler continued to look out at the building in front of him. "Billy Steele will never leave prison, you know that? They'll get to him or he'll choose to end it; either way it's over. And for us ... this case is over."

Mills started the engine. He looked at Tyler, but the DCI was still staring out through the car window, his gaze fixed on the care home, remembering one like it, or a thousand times worse. Pain came in many shapes and sizes.

"There was something raw inside Billy Steele, and in the end it destroyed him. A lesson to be learned. I've decided to summon reinforcements."

"Sir?"

"Do I have to spell it out?"

"You mean ..?"

"Precisely. I'm going under the knife." He turned to Mills. "Well, aren't you going to say something?"

"Congratulations?" said Mills.

"*Drive.*"

CHAPTER FORTY FIVE

At the end of the school day, on his day off, Tyler waited on the car park at River Trent High. The coast appeared to be clear, the kids having left for the day. But at least one member of staff would be sitting in her office for a while yet, tackling the eternal mountain of paperwork.

He made his way into the building.

Outside the headteacher's office he hesitated, looking at the name on the door: Miss A. Hayburn. Not so long ago he had established what 'A' stood for. Not so long ago he had indulged the fantasy that with the likes of Alison Hayburn running the school, no child would ever go short of a listening ear. An ally when things were getting tough, here and in the outside world. There was still only so much that a listening ear could achieve, but it could make a start. It could certainly do that.

He knocked on the door, and entered.

Miss Hayburn was busy and looking a little stressed herself. He hadn't imagined that someone as strong and wise as her could possibly suffer from the condition. He didn't wish to add to her burden. Without sitting down, Tyler said, "I want to thank you."

She waved a hand as though to dismiss the very idea. "No problem," she said. "Always glad to help the police, any time."

"That's all I wanted to say." He started to leave when she said, "A tragic case, by all accounts. Please, take a seat. I'm going to be here all evening. Five minutes distraction from my duties is neither here nor there."

Tyler took a seat. Alison Hayburn was looking straight at him, giving him her full attention. Her look of understanding engulfed him.

"Forgive me if I'm talking out of turn here," she said. "But I can see that you're taking it hard. I would have thought your job was to uncover the facts as they are, not the facts as you might hope them to be."

Is she reading my mind? thought Tyler.

"I'm sorry, I should stick to minding my own—"

"No, you're right," said Tyler. "And I want to thank you for opening my eyes. I've decided to ... seek help."

"You don't need to thank me for anything. I hope that you benefit. I believe that you might."

The awkwardness descended, breaking the spell. Tyler felt a sudden sense of loneliness rise up inside, hollow and cold.

Can I ever love? Be loved?

He swallowed hard at the lump in his throat, though he couldn't seem to shift it.

"Was there something else?" she asked him.

A thousand words and phrases flashed through his mind but remained unspoken. He stood up, and stretched out a hand. "No, that's all. Goodbye, Alison."

That night, restless, unable to settle, fearing sleep for the nightmares and longings that it might bring with it, Jim Tyler put on his running clothes and set out into the darkness. Without conscious intention he followed the streets of Penkhull down the hill into Stoke and up into Shelton, entering Hanley Park. Standing on the canal side, he stared deeply into the unforgiving water where the life of Adam Lane had ended - the life that Billy Steele had falsely claimed to have taken - and thought of lives snuffed out before they had begun, and others ruined beyond repair. Closing his eyes he reflected, in an attitude of prayer that the vale of tears that was this life on Earth had merely opened and closed on another brutal chapter.

Looking at the dark sky, feeling the coolness of the breeze that was whipping up off the water, he sensed a storm coming, or else one dying down. Sometimes it was impossible to tell.

The End

A Note from the Author

Many thanks for reading *Blue Murder*. I hope you enjoyed reading it as much as I enjoyed writing it. *Blue Murder* is the second in the series featuring DCI Tyler and DS Mills.

Red Is The Colour, the first book to feature the detectives, was shortlisted for the 2018 Arnold Bennett Book Prize.

I would like to thank Kath Middleton, Joe Fowler, Jacky Dahlhaus, Julian Middleton and Fiona for reading earlier drafts of Blue Murder, and providing invaluable feedback and encouragement. And thank you Caroline Vincent for your support and technical expertise over the past two years, and for suggesting the cover image.

Finally, thank you to everyone who kept asking me when the next book was coming out!

Blue Murder

Printed in Poland
by Amazon Fulfillment
Poland Sp. z o.o., Wrocław